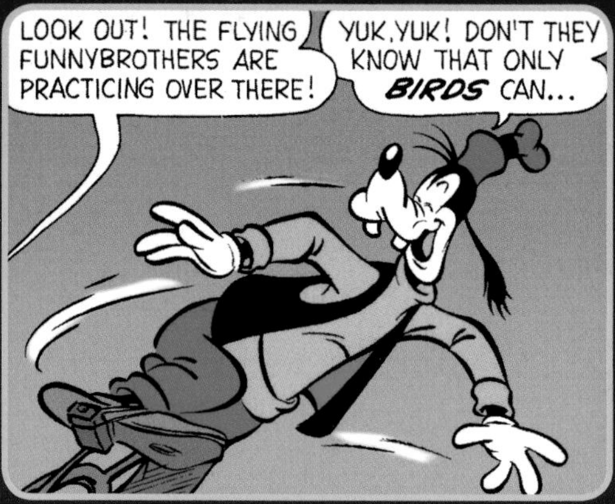
LOOK OUT! THE FLYING FUNNYBROTHERS ARE PRACTICING OVER THERE!
YUK, YUK! DON'T THEY KNOW THAT ONLY *BIRDS* CAN...

Riding High
From *Donald Duck* #64, 1959
Artist: Jack Bradbury
Colorist: Digikore Studios
Letterer: Rome Simeon

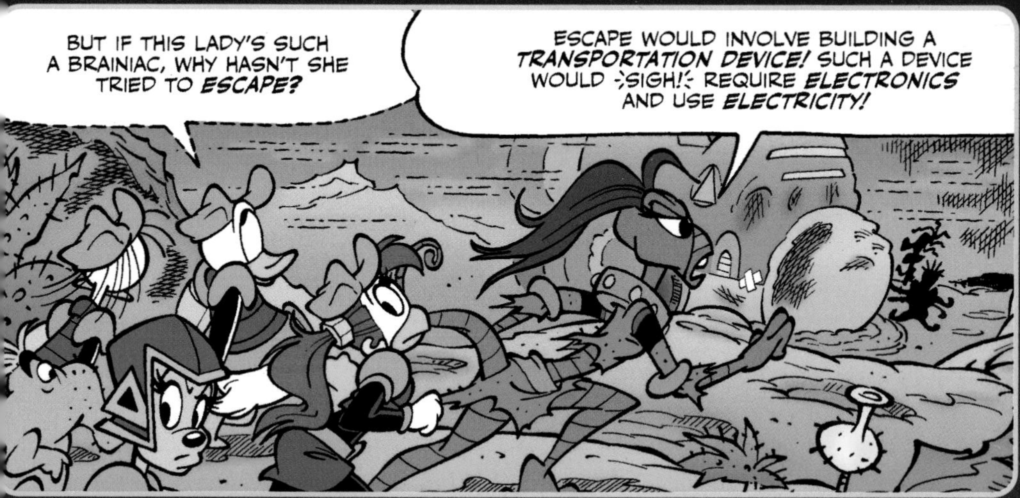
BUT IF THIS LADY'S SUCH A BRAINIAC, WHY HASN'T SHE TRIED TO *ESCAPE?*
ESCAPE WOULD INVOLVE BUILDING A *TRANSPORTATION DEVICE!* SUCH A DEVICE WOULD -SIGH!- REQUIRE *ELECTRONICS* AND USE *ELECTRICITY!*

Prisoners of Zartac 2
From German *Lustiges Taschenbuch* #372, 2008
Writers: Lars Jensen and David Gerstein
Artist: Flemming Andersen
Colorists: Egmont and Digikore Studios
Letterers: Tràvis and Nicole Seitler

Series Editor: Chris Cerasi
Archival Editor: David Gerstein

Cover Artists: Massimo Fecchi and Fernando Güell
Cover Colorists: Egmont and Ronda Pattison
Collection Editors: Justin Eisinger
& Alonzo Simon
Collection Designer: Clyde Grapa
Publisher: Greg Goldstein

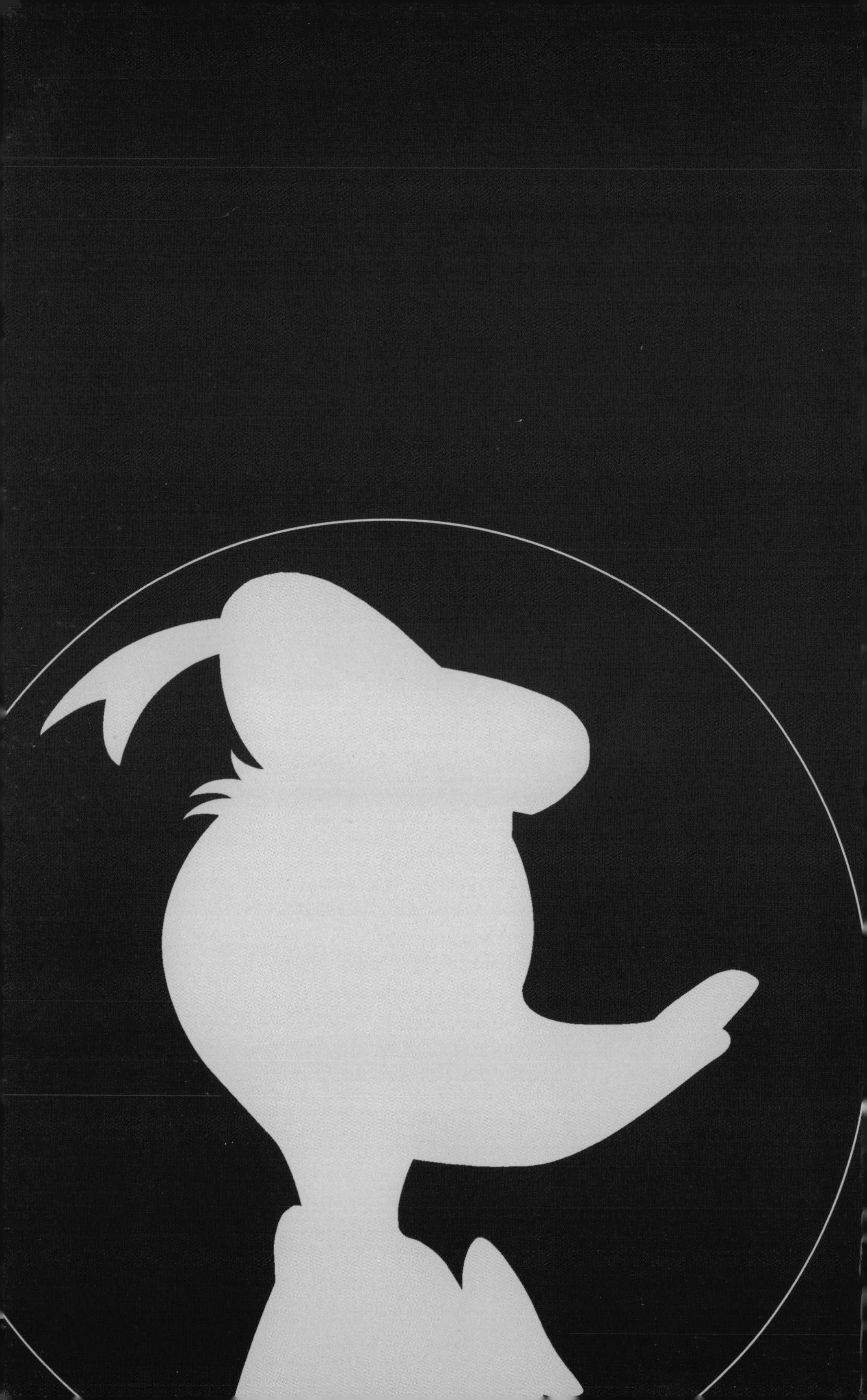

WALT DISNEY's
Donald Duck

Nest of the Demonbirds

SORRY— MEALTIME JUST *ENDED!*

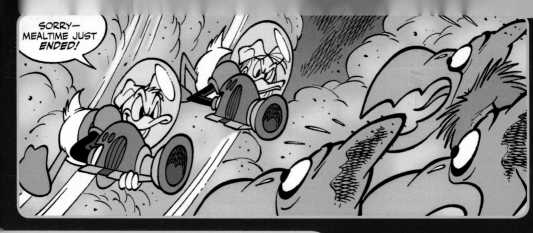

Nest of the Demonbirds
From German *Lustiges Taschenbusch* #362, 2007
Writer: Lars Jensen
Artist: Flemming Andersen
Colorists: Egmont and Digikore Studios
Letterers: Travis and Nicole Seitler
Dialogue: Lars Jensen and David Gerstein

Assaulting Battery
From Polish *Kaczor Donald* #7/2012
Writer: Francois Corteggiani
Artists: Daan Jippes and Ulrich Schroeder
Colorist: Digikore Studios
Letterers: Travis and Nicole Seitler

Pigphobia
From Dutch *Donald Duck* #18/1976
Writer: Dick Matena
Artists: Dick Matena with Daan Jippes
Colorist: Digikore Studios
Letterers: Nicole and Travis Seitler
Translation and Dialogue: Thad Komorowski

Special thanks to Eugene Paraszczuk, Julie Dorris, Carlotta Quattricolo, Manny Mederos, Chris Troise, Roberto Santillo, Camille Vedove, and Stefano Ambrosio. | For international rights, contact **licensing@idwpublishing.com**

ISBN: 978-1-68405-133-5

21 20 19 18 1 2 3 4

IDW®
www.IDWPUBLISHING.com

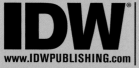

Greg Goldstein, President & Publisher • **Robbie Robbins,** EVP & Sr. Art Director • **Chris Ryall,** Chief Creative Officer & Editor-in-Chief • **Matthew Ruzicka,** CPA, Chief Financial Officer • **David Hedgecock,** Associate Publisher • **Laurie Windrow,** Senior Vice President of Sales & Marketing • **Lorelei Bunjes,** VP of Digital Services • **Eric Moss,** Sr. Director, Licensing & Business Development
Ted Adams, Founder & CEO of IDW Media Holdings

Facebook: facebook.com/idwpublishing • Twitter: @idwpublishing • YouTube: youtube.com/idwpublishing
Tumblr: tumblr.idwpublishing.com • Instagram: instagram.com/idwpublishing

Originally published as WALT DISNEY'S COMICS AND STORIES issues #739–740.

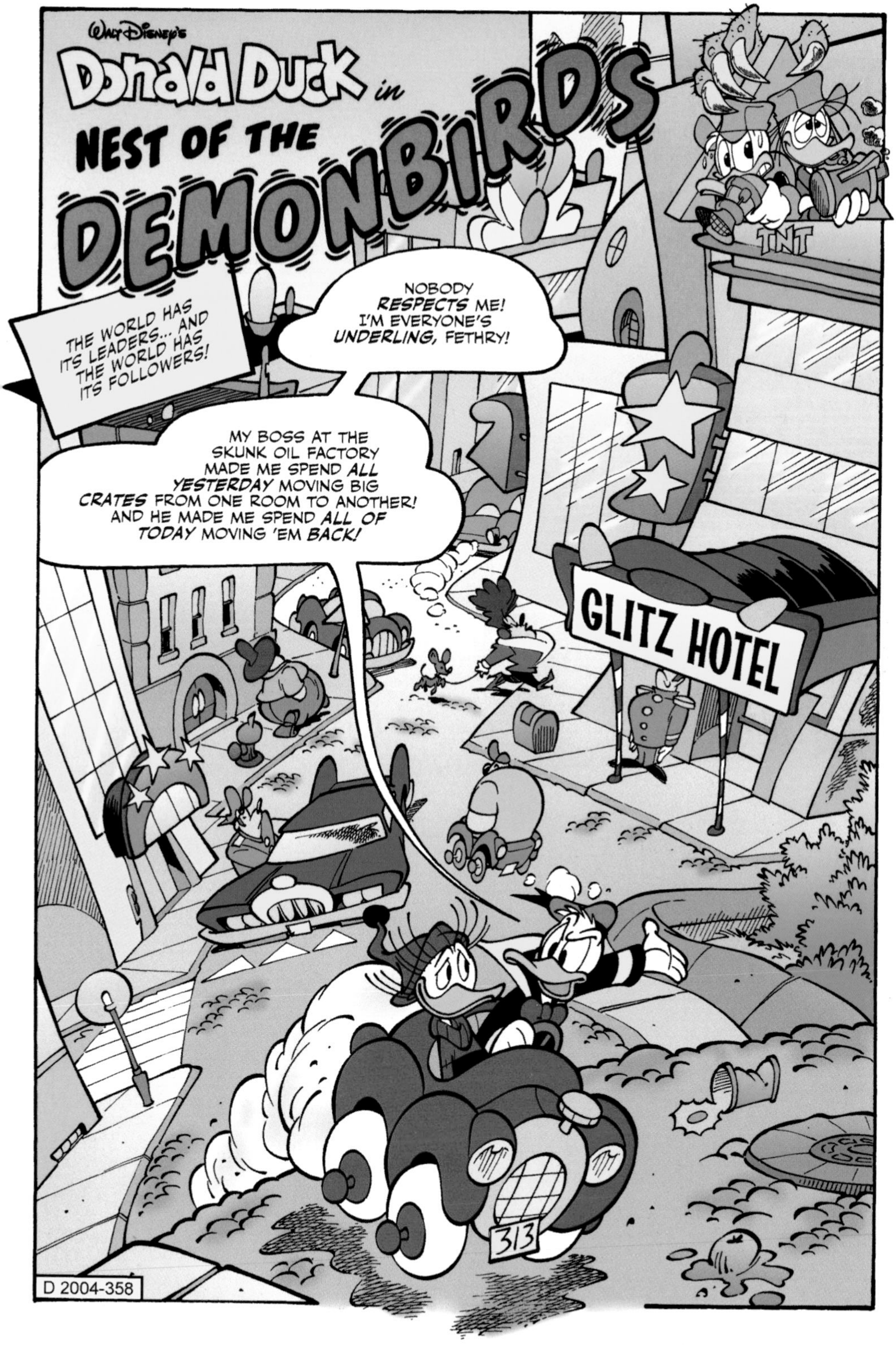
WALT DISNEY'S
DONALD DUCK in
NEST OF THE DEMONBIRDS
THE WORLD HAS ITS LEADERS... AND THE WORLD HAS ITS FOLLOWERS!
NOBODY *RESPECTS* ME! I'M EVERYONE'S *UNDERLING*, FETHRY!
MY BOSS AT THE SKUNK OIL FACTORY MADE ME SPEND *ALL YESTERDAY* MOVING BIG *CRATES* FROM ONE ROOM TO ANOTHER! AND HE MADE ME SPEND *ALL OF TODAY* MOVING 'EM *BACK!*
TNT
GLITZ HOTEL
313
D 2004-358

Originally published in *Lustiges Taschenbusch* #362 (Germany, 2007)

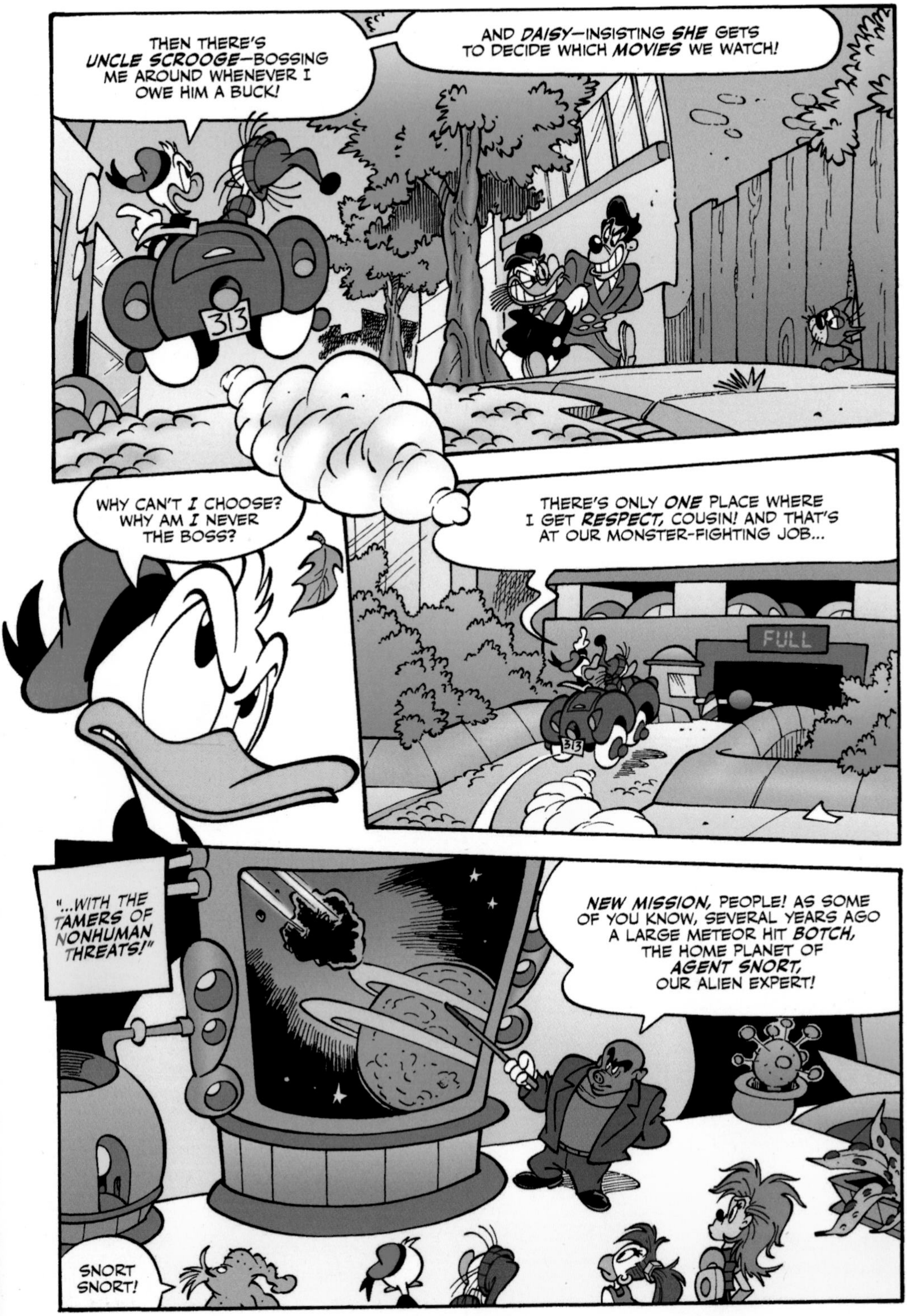
THEN THERE'S UNCLE SCROOGE—BOSSING ME AROUND WHENEVER I OWE HIM A BUCK!
AND DAISY—INSISTING SHE GETS TO DECIDE WHICH MOVIES WE WATCH!
313
WHY CAN'T I CHOOSE? WHY AM I NEVER THE BOSS?
THERE'S ONLY ONE PLACE WHERE I GET RESPECT, COUSIN! AND THAT'S AT OUR MONSTER-FIGHTING JOB...
FULL
313
"...WITH THE TAMERS OF NONHUMAN THREATS!"
NEW MISSION, PEOPLE! AS SOME OF YOU KNOW, SEVERAL YEARS AGO A LARGE METEOR HIT BOTCH, THE HOME PLANET OF AGENT SNORT, OUR ALIEN EXPERT!
SNORT SNORT!

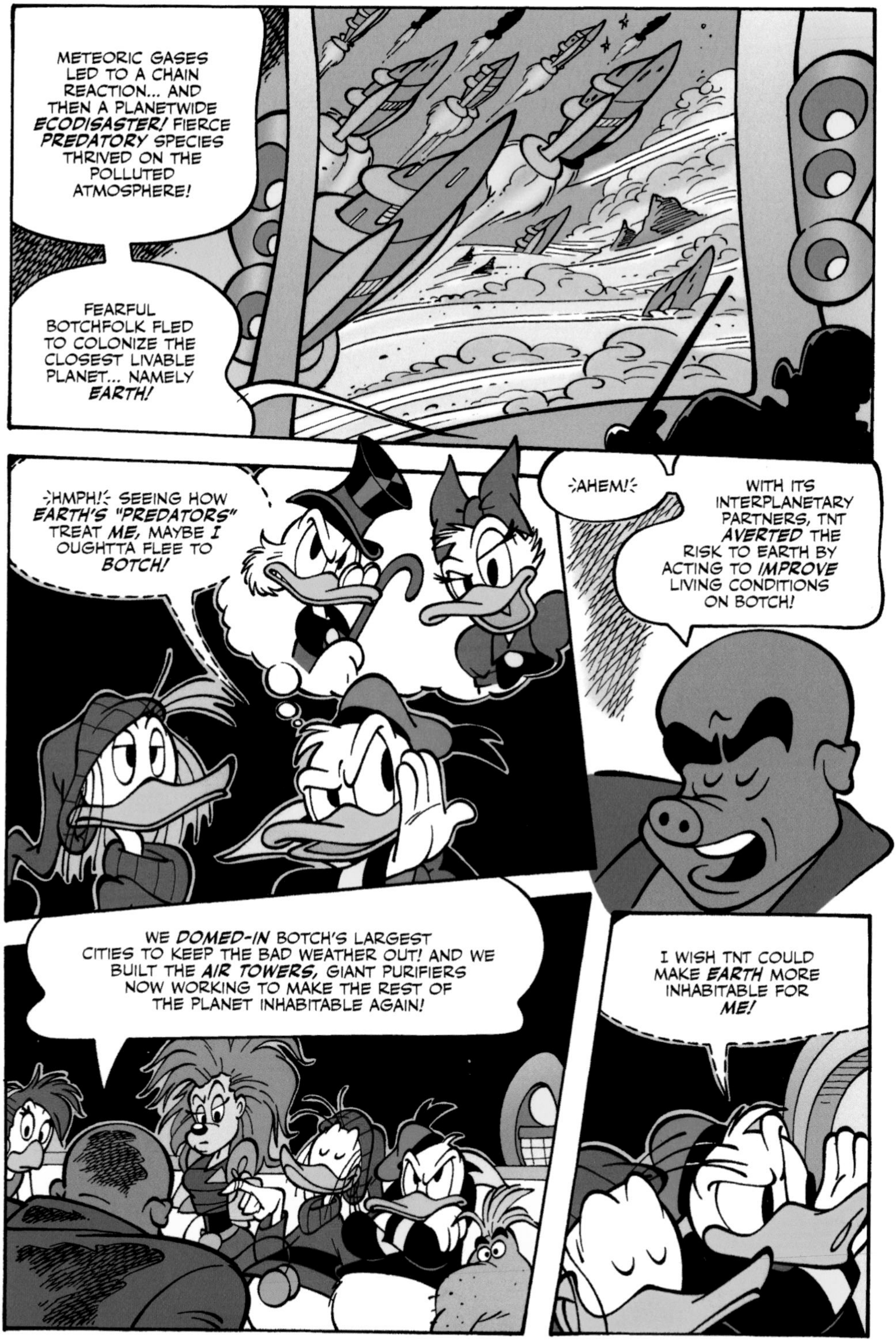
METEORIC GASES LED TO A CHAIN REACTION... AND THEN A PLANETWIDE ECODISASTER! FIERCE PREDATORY SPECIES THRIVED ON THE POLLUTED ATMOSPHERE!
FEARFUL BOTCHFOLK FLED TO COLONIZE THE CLOSEST LIVABLE PLANET... NAMELY EARTH!
HMPH! SEEING HOW EARTH'S "PREDATORS" TREAT ME, MAYBE I OUGHTTA FLEE TO BOTCH!
AHEM!
WITH ITS INTERPLANETARY PARTNERS, TNT AVERTED THE RISK TO EARTH BY ACTING TO IMPROVE LIVING CONDITIONS ON BOTCH!
WE DOMED-IN BOTCH'S LARGEST CITIES TO KEEP THE BAD WEATHER OUT! AND WE BUILT THE AIR TOWERS, GIANT PURIFIERS NOW WORKING TO MAKE THE REST OF THE PLANET INHABITABLE AGAIN!
I WISH TNT COULD MAKE EARTH MORE INHABITABLE FOR ME!

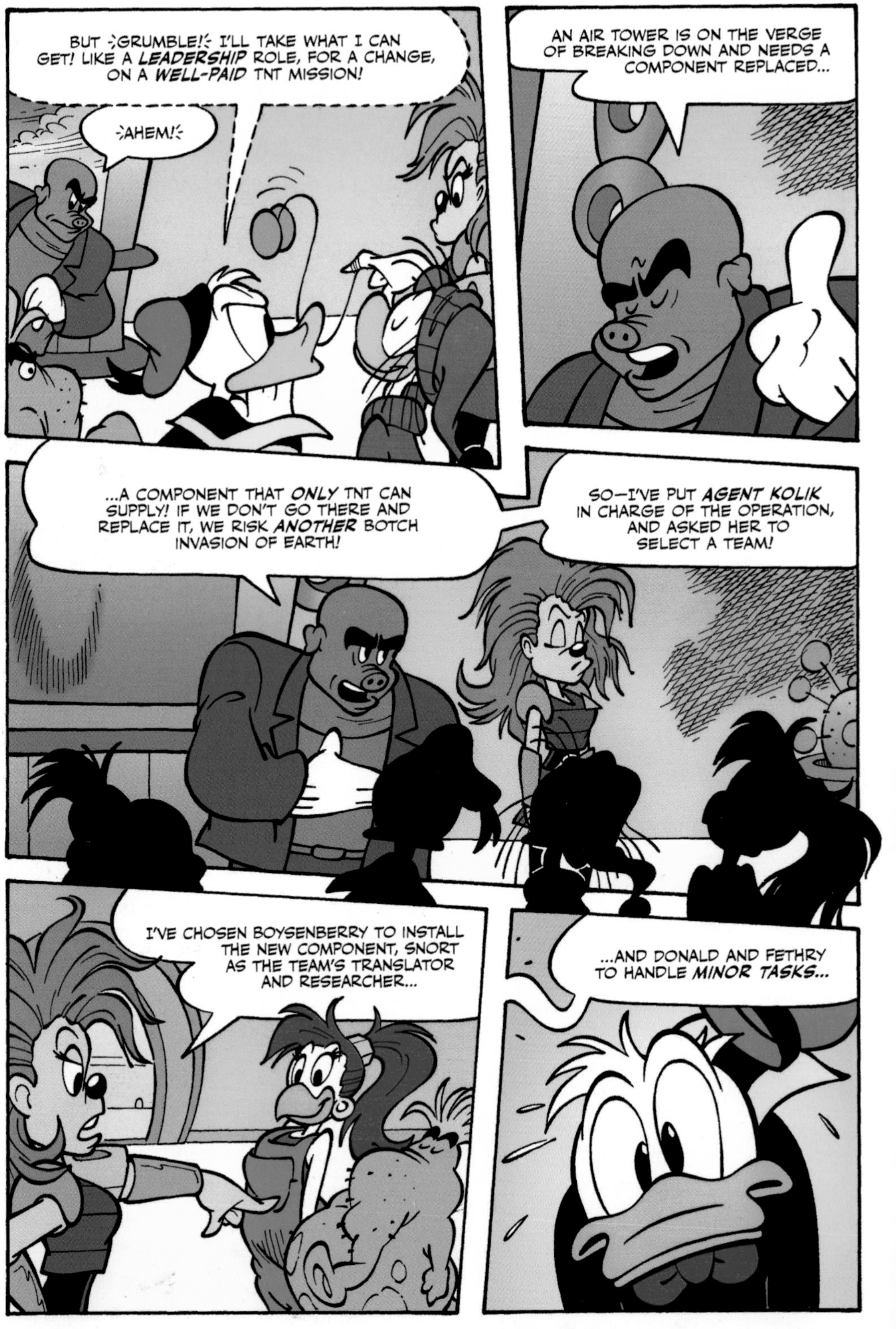
BUT -GRUMBLE!- I'LL TAKE WHAT I CAN GET! LIKE A *LEADERSHIP* ROLE, FOR A CHANGE, ON A *WELL-PAID* TNT MISSION!
-AHEM!-
AN AIR TOWER IS ON THE VERGE OF BREAKING DOWN AND NEEDS A COMPONENT REPLACED...
...A COMPONENT THAT *ONLY* TNT CAN SUPPLY! IF WE DON'T GO THERE AND REPLACE IT, WE RISK *ANOTHER* BOTCH INVASION OF EARTH!
SO—I'VE PUT *AGENT KOLIK* IN CHARGE OF THE OPERATION, AND ASKED HER TO SELECT A TEAM!
I'VE CHOSEN BOYSENBERRY TO INSTALL THE NEW COMPONENT, SNORT AS THE TEAM'S TRANSLATOR AND RESEARCHER...
...AND DONALD AND FETHRY TO HANDLE *MINOR TASKS*...

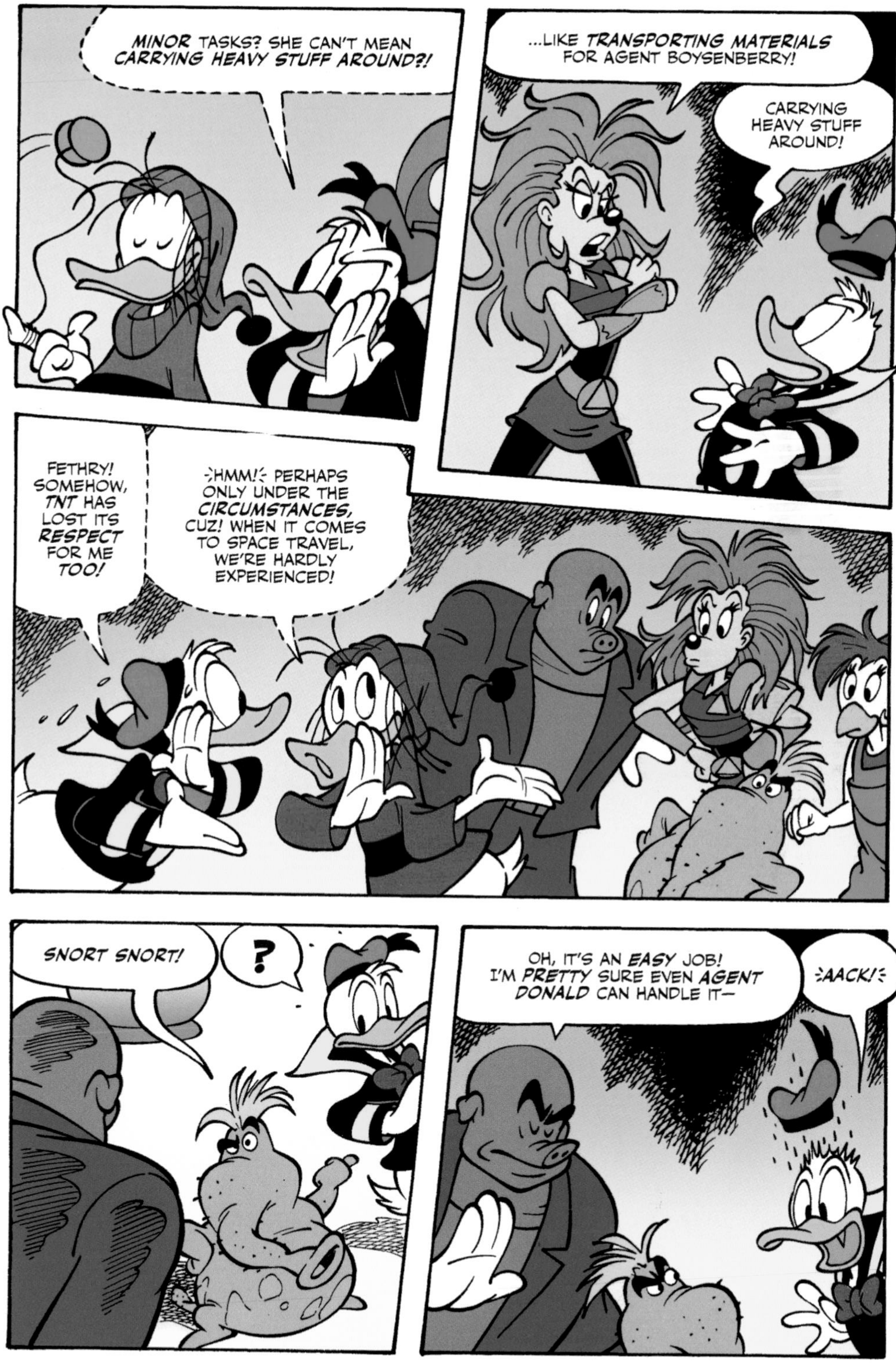
MINOR TASKS? SHE CAN'T MEAN CARRYING HEAVY STUFF AROUND?!
...LIKE TRANSPORTING MATERIALS FOR AGENT BOYSENBERRY!
CARRYING HEAVY STUFF AROUND!
FETHRY! SOMEHOW, TNT HAS LOST ITS RESPECT FOR ME TOO!
HMM! PERHAPS ONLY UNDER THE CIRCUMSTANCES, CUZ! WHEN IT COMES TO SPACE TRAVEL, WE'RE HARDLY EXPERIENCED!
SNORT SNORT!
?
OH, IT'S AN EASY JOB! I'M PRETTY SURE EVEN AGENT DONALD CAN HANDLE IT—
AACK!

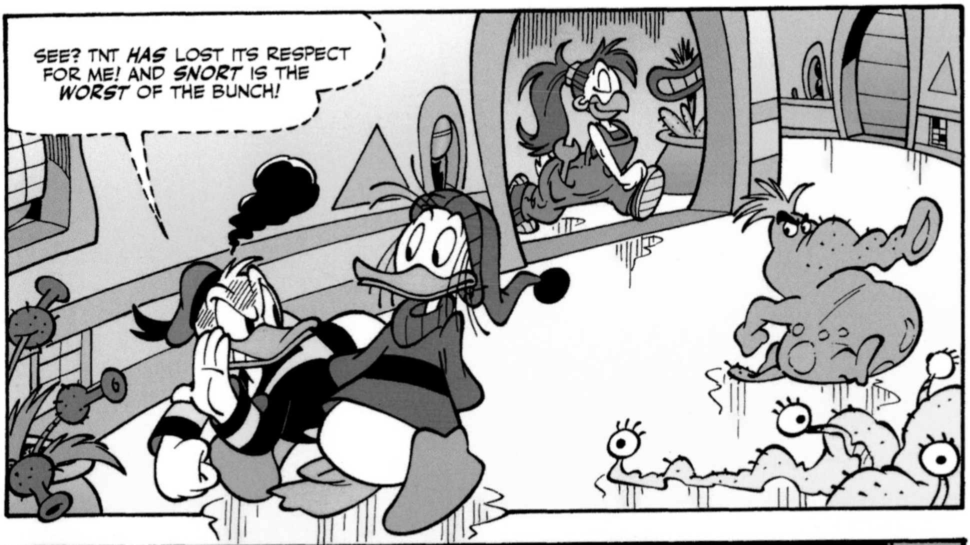
SEE? TNT HAS LOST ITS RESPECT FOR ME! AND SNORT IS THE WORST OF THE BUNCH!

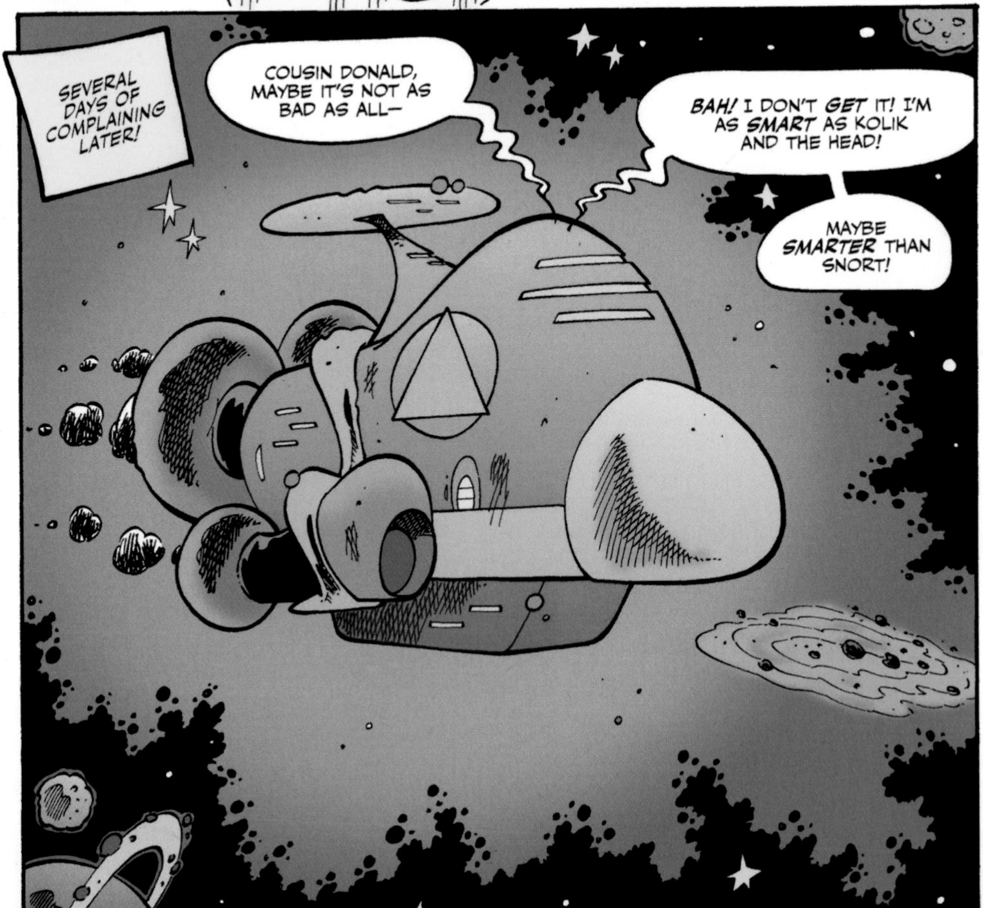
SEVERAL DAYS OF COMPLAINING LATER!
COUSIN DONALD, MAYBE IT'S NOT AS BAD AS ALL—
BAH! I DON'T GET IT! I'M AS SMART AS KOLIK AND THE HEAD!
MAYBE SMARTER THAN SNORT!

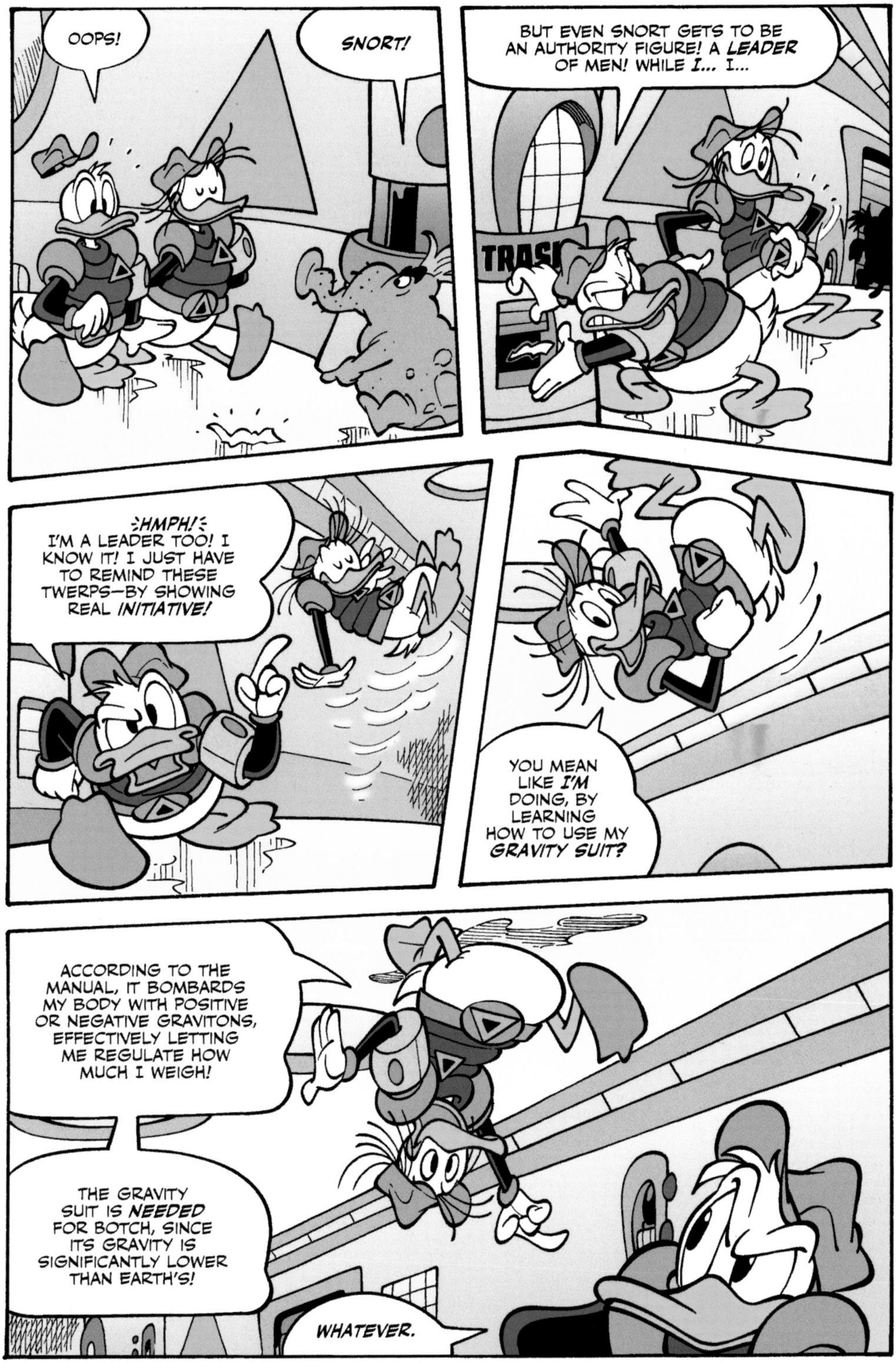
OOPS!
SNORT!
BUT EVEN SNORT GETS TO BE AN AUTHORITY FIGURE! A LEADER OF MEN! WHILE I... I...
TRASH
HMPH! I'M A LEADER TOO! I KNOW IT! I JUST HAVE TO REMIND THESE TWERPS—BY SHOWING REAL INITIATIVE!
YOU MEAN LIKE I'M DOING, BY LEARNING HOW TO USE MY GRAVITY SUIT?
ACCORDING TO THE MANUAL, IT BOMBARDS MY BODY WITH POSITIVE OR NEGATIVE GRAVITONS, EFFECTIVELY LETTING ME REGULATE HOW MUCH I WEIGH!
THE GRAVITY SUIT IS NEEDED FOR BOTCH, SINCE ITS GRAVITY IS SIGNIFICANTLY LOWER THAN EARTH'S!
WHATEVER.

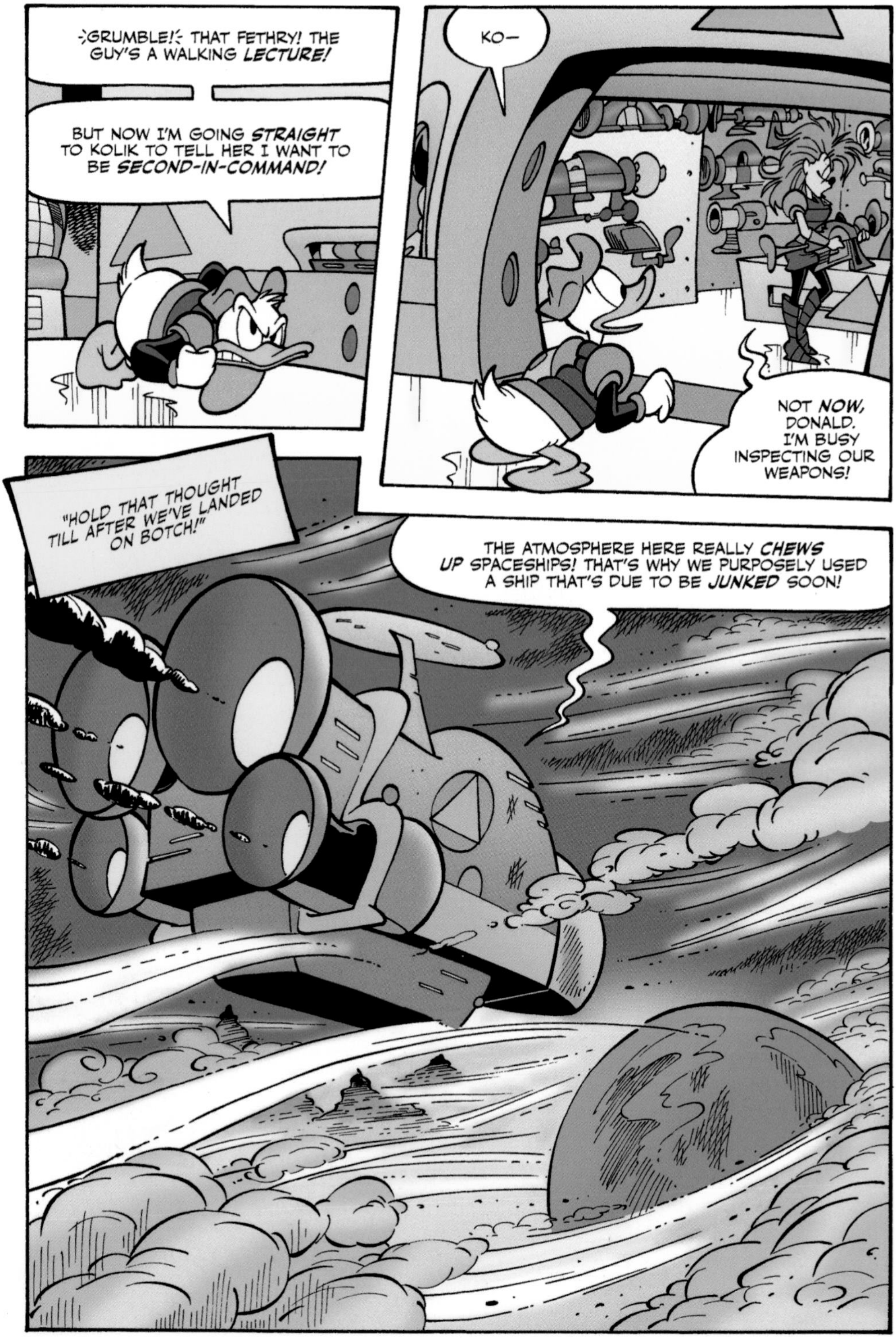

¡GRUMBLE!¡ THAT FETHRY! THE GUY'S A WALKING LECTURE!
BUT NOW I'M GOING STRAIGHT TO KOLIK TO TELL HER I WANT TO BE SECOND-IN-COMMAND!
KO—
NOT NOW, DONALD. I'M BUSY INSPECTING OUR WEAPONS!
"HOLD THAT THOUGHT TILL AFTER WE'VE LANDED ON BOTCH!"
THE ATMOSPHERE HERE REALLY CHEWS UP SPACESHIPS! THAT'S WHY WE PURPOSELY USED A SHIP THAT'S DUE TO BE JUNKED SOON!

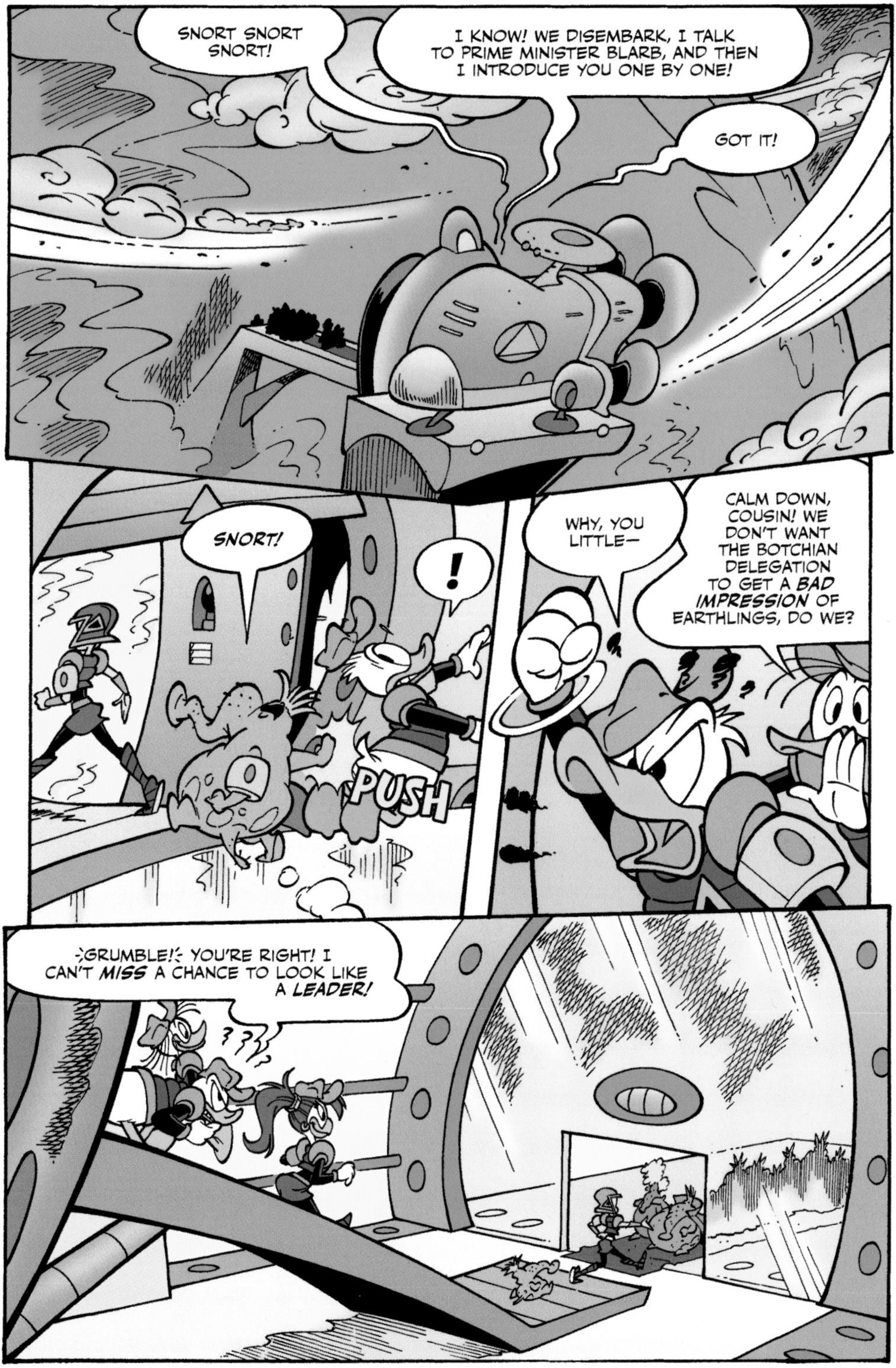
SNORT SNORT SNORT!
I KNOW! WE DISEMBARK, I TALK TO PRIME MINISTER BLARB, AND THEN I INTRODUCE YOU ONE BY ONE!
GOT IT!
SNORT!
!
PUSH
WHY, YOU LITTLE—
CALM DOWN, COUSIN! WE DON'T WANT THE BOTCHIAN DELEGATION TO GET A BAD IMPRESSION OF EARTHLINGS, DO WE?
GRUMBLE! YOU'RE RIGHT! I CAN'T MISS A CHANCE TO LOOK LIKE A LEADER!
???

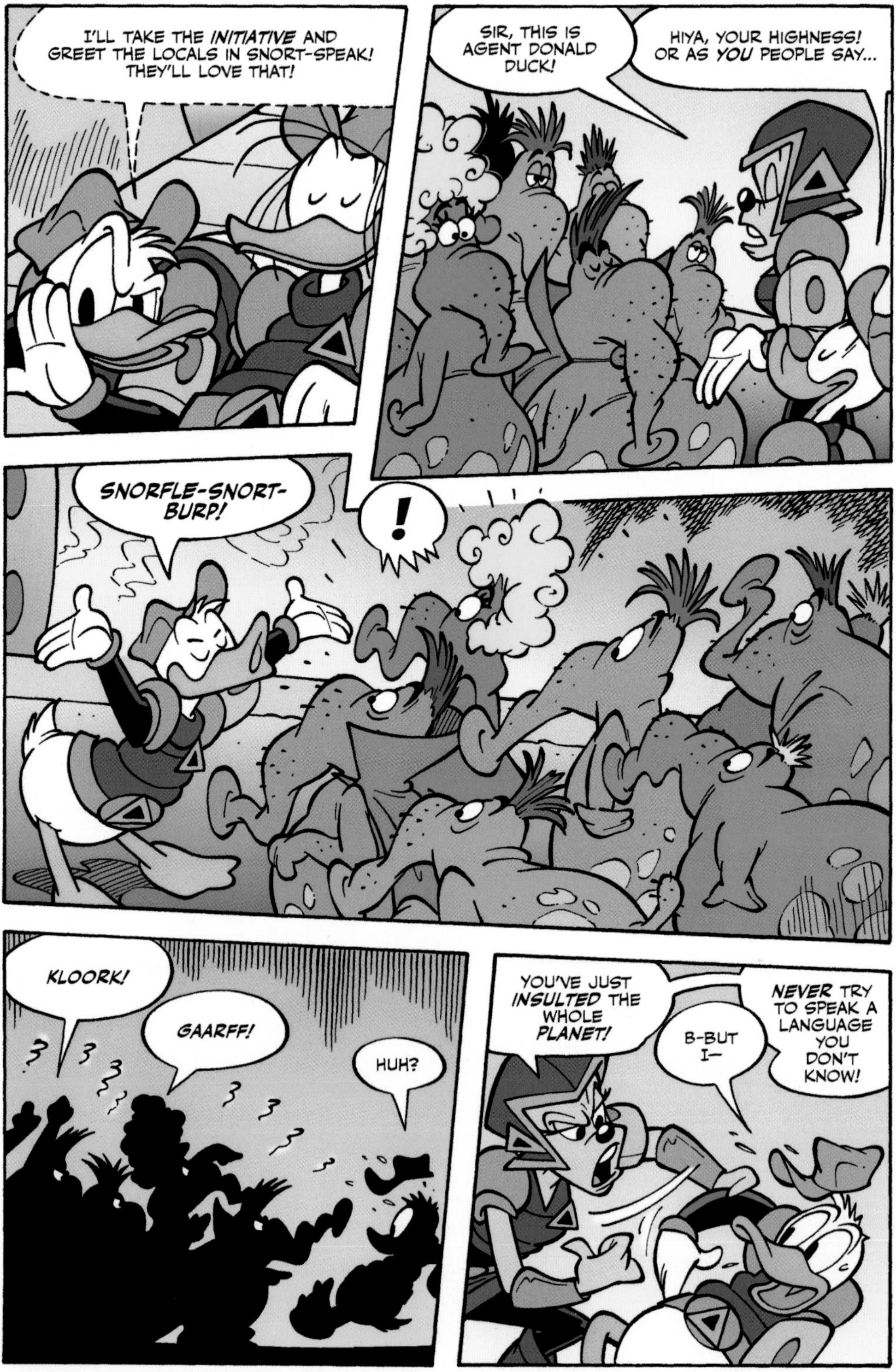
I'LL TAKE THE *INITIATIVE* AND GREET THE LOCALS IN SNORT-SPEAK! THEY'LL LOVE THAT!
SIR, THIS IS AGENT DONALD DUCK!
HIYA, YOUR HIGHNESS! OR AS *YOU* PEOPLE SAY...
SNORFLE-SNORT-BURP!
!
KLOORK!
GAARFF!
HUH?
YOU'VE JUST *INSULTED* THE WHOLE *PLANET!*
B-BUT I—
NEVER TRY TO SPEAK A LANGUAGE YOU DON'T KNOW!

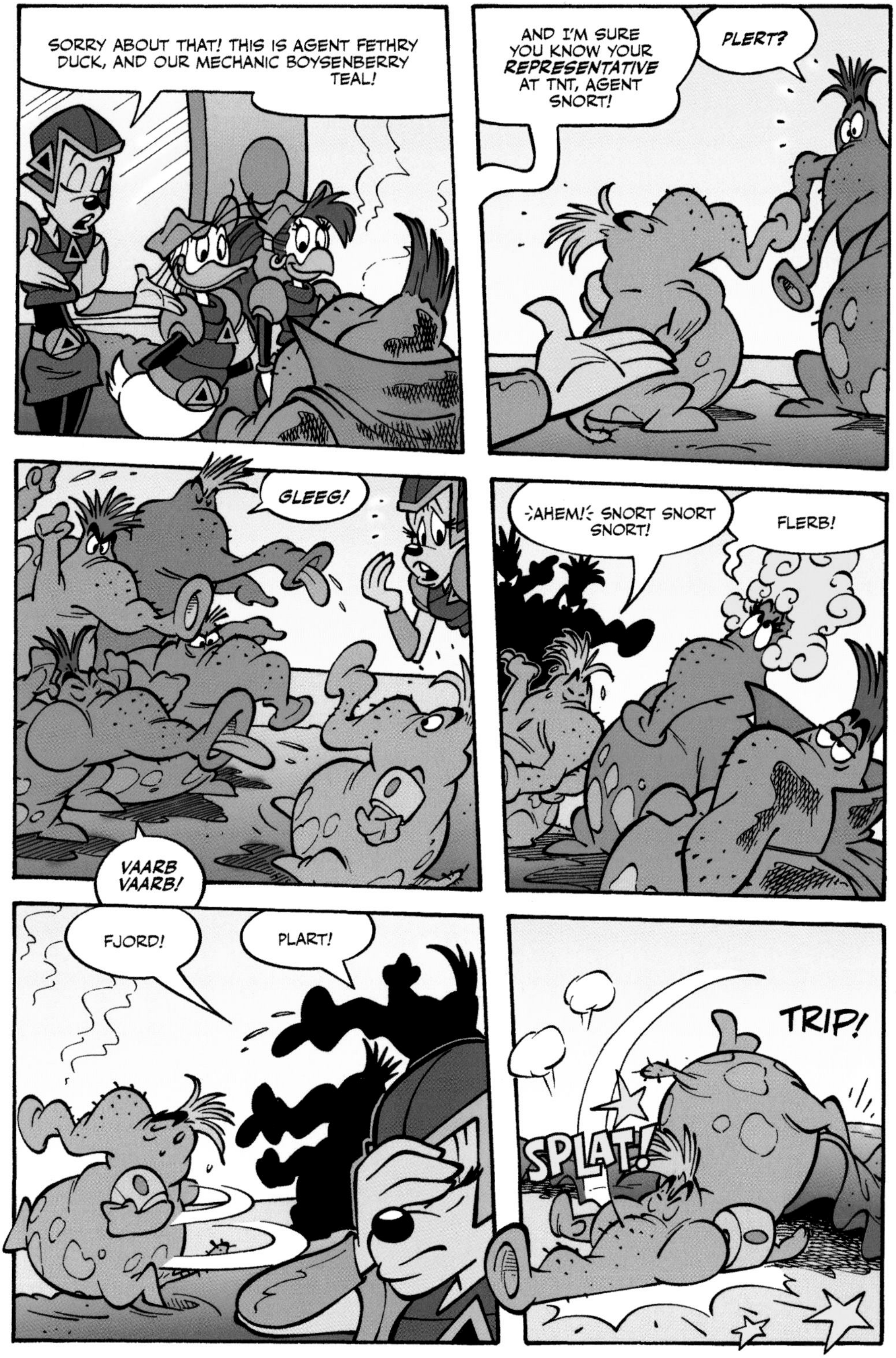
SORRY ABOUT THAT! THIS IS AGENT FETHRY DUCK, AND OUR MECHANIC BOYSENBERRY TEAL!
AND I'M SURE YOU KNOW YOUR *REPRESENTATIVE* AT TNT, AGENT SNORT!
PLERT?
GLEEG!
VAARB VAARB!
AHEM! SNORT SNORT SNORT!
FLERB!
FJORD!
PLART!
TRIP!
SPLAT!

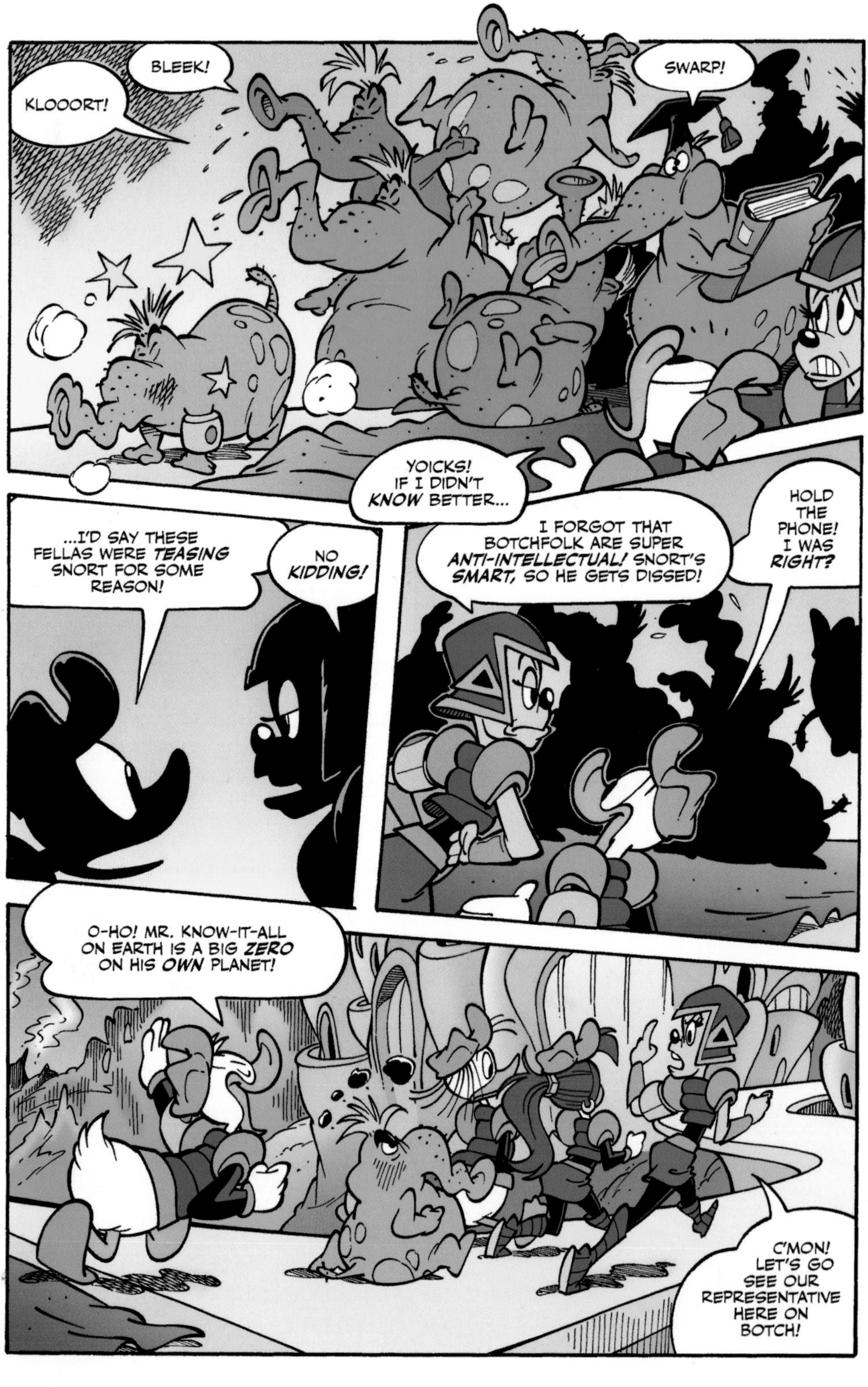
KLOOORT!
BLEEK!
SWARP!
YOICKS! IF I DIDN'T KNOW BETTER...
...I'D SAY THESE FELLAS WERE TEASING SNORT FOR SOME REASON!
NO KIDDING!
I FORGOT THAT BOTCHFOLK ARE SUPER ANTI-INTELLECTUAL! SNORT'S SMART, SO HE GETS DISSED!
HOLD THE PHONE! I WAS RIGHT?
O-HO! MR. KNOW-IT-ALL ON EARTH IS A BIG ZERO ON HIS OWN PLANET!
C'MON! LET'S GO SEE OUR REPRESENTATIVE HERE ON BOTCH!

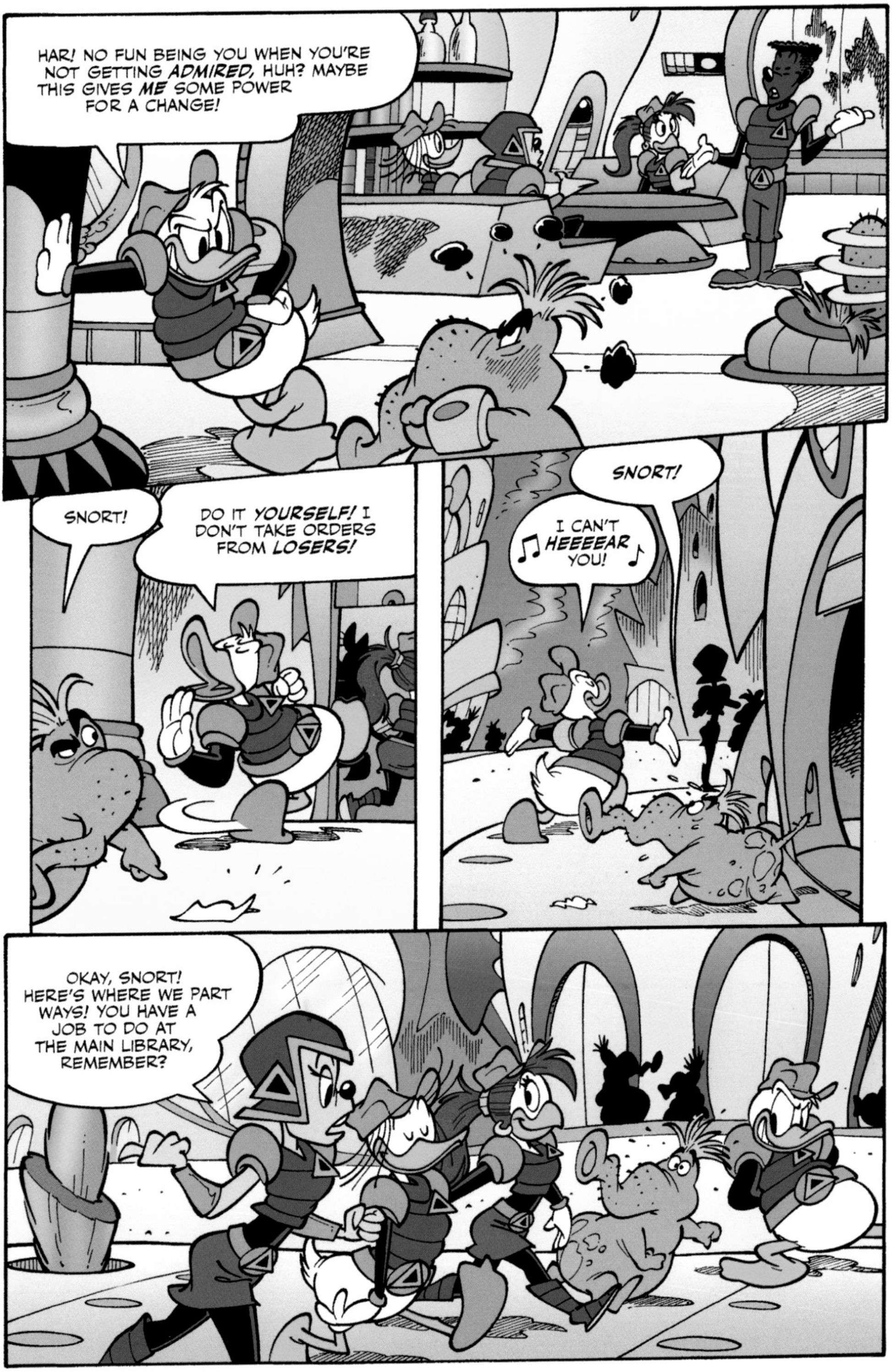

HAR! NO FUN BEING YOU WHEN YOU'RE NOT GETTING *ADMIRED*, HUH? MAYBE THIS GIVES *ME* SOME POWER FOR A CHANGE!
SNORT!
DO IT *YOURSELF!* I DON'T TAKE ORDERS FROM *LOSERS!*
SNORT!
♫ I CAN'T *HEEEEAR* YOU! ♪
OKAY, SNORT! HERE'S WHERE WE PART WAYS! YOU HAVE A JOB TO DO AT THE MAIN LIBRARY, REMEMBER?

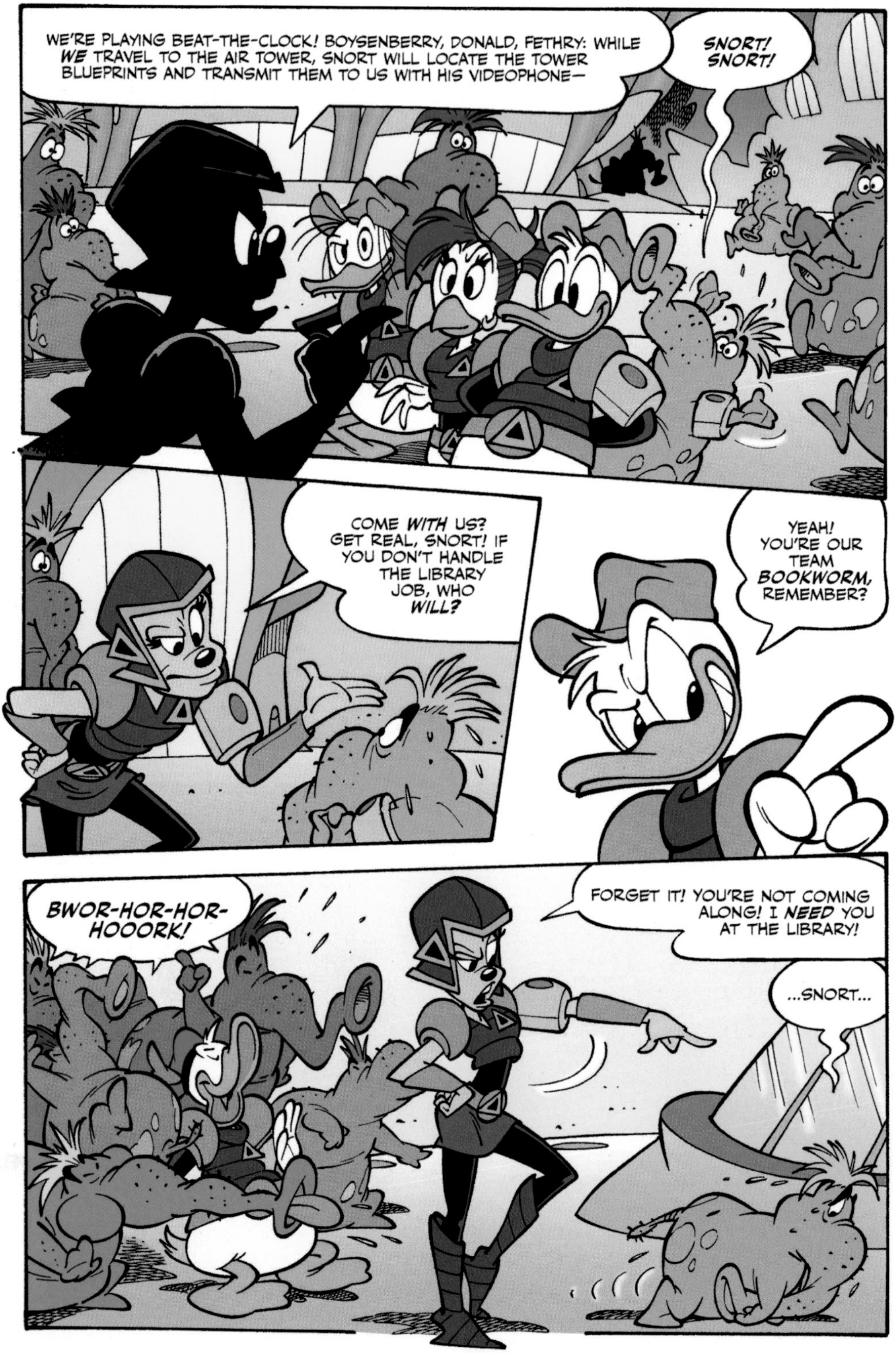
WE'RE PLAYING BEAT-THE-CLOCK! BOYSENBERRY, DONALD, FETHRY: WHILE WE TRAVEL TO THE AIR TOWER, SNORT WILL LOCATE THE TOWER BLUEPRINTS AND TRANSMIT THEM TO US WITH HIS VIDEOPHONE—
SNORT! SNORT!
COME WITH US? GET REAL, SNORT! IF YOU DON'T HANDLE THE LIBRARY JOB, WHO WILL?
YEAH! YOU'RE OUR TEAM BOOKWORM, REMEMBER?
BWOR-HOR-HOR-HOOORK!
FORGET IT! YOU'RE NOT COMING ALONG! I NEED YOU AT THE LIBRARY!
...SNORT...

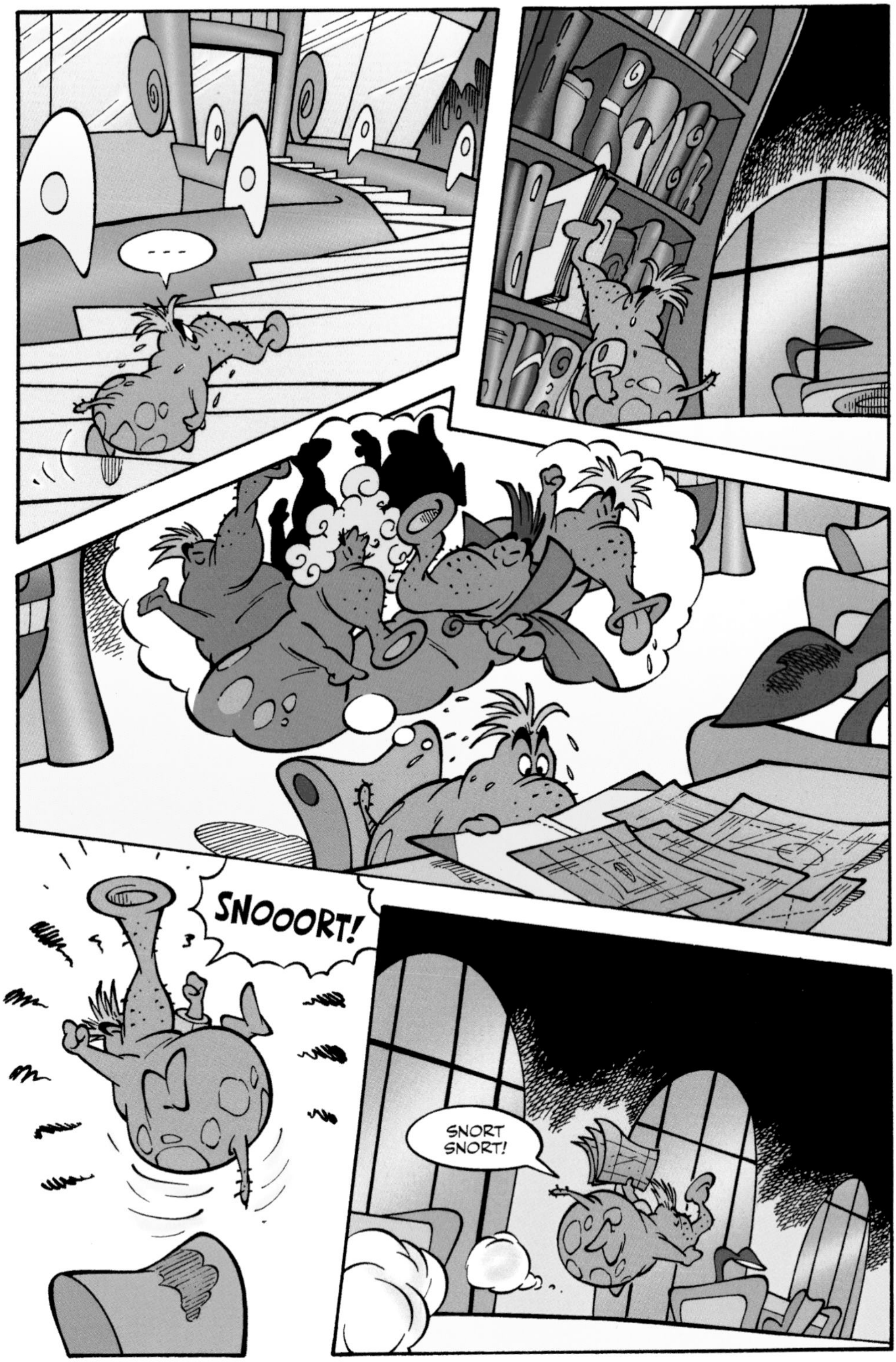

SNOOORT!
SNORT SNORT!

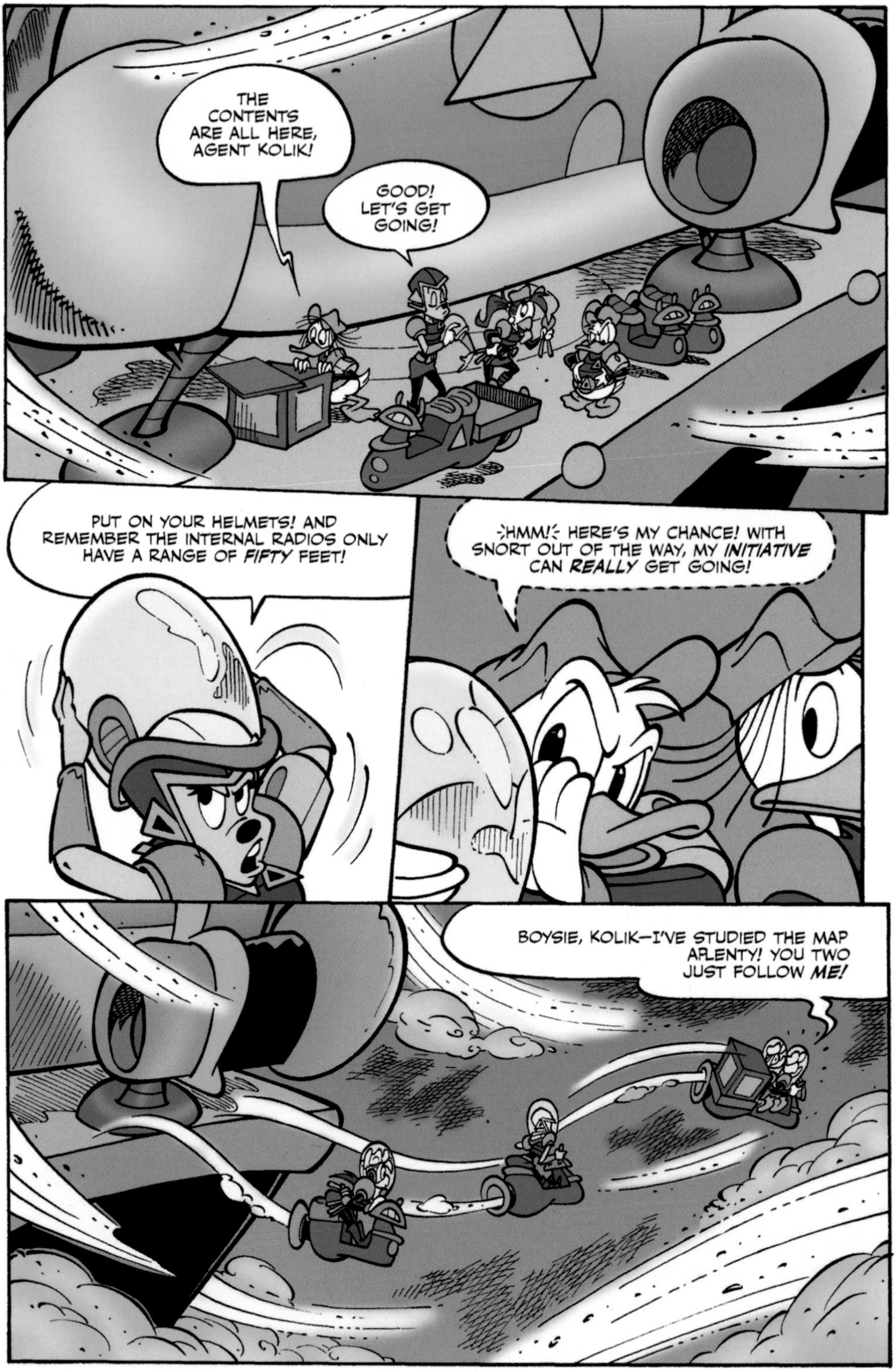
THE CONTENTS ARE ALL HERE, AGENT KOLIK!
GOOD! LET'S GET GOING!
PUT ON YOUR HELMETS! AND REMEMBER THE INTERNAL RADIOS ONLY HAVE A RANGE OF FIFTY FEET!
HMM! HERE'S MY CHANCE! WITH SNORT OUT OF THE WAY, MY INITIATIVE CAN REALLY GET GOING!
BOYSIE, KOLIK—I'VE STUDIED THE MAP APLENTY! YOU TWO JUST FOLLOW ME!

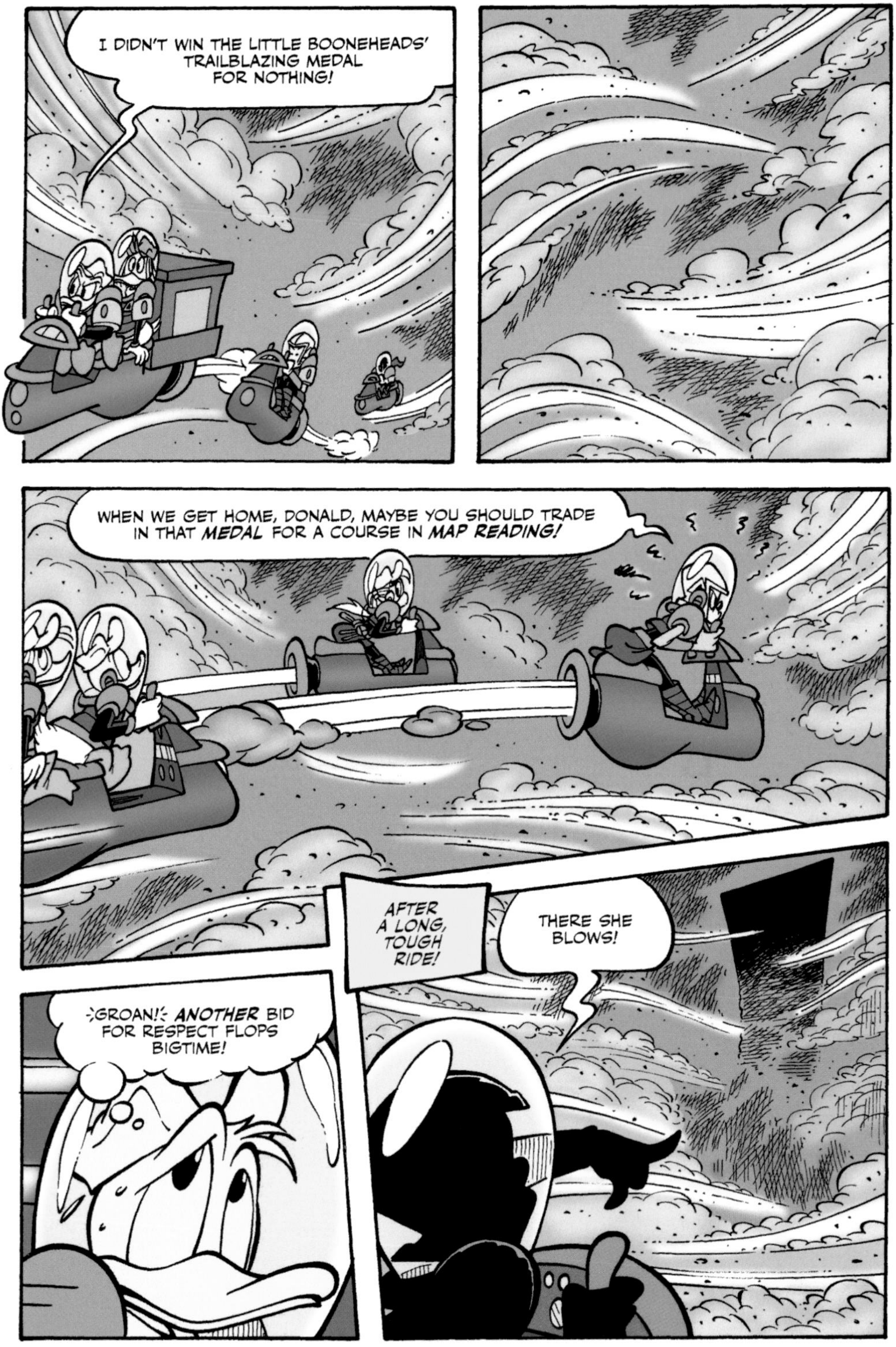
I DIDN'T WIN THE LITTLE BOONEHEADS' TRAILBLAZING MEDAL FOR NOTHING!
WHEN WE GET HOME, DONALD, MAYBE YOU SHOULD TRADE IN THAT MEDAL FOR A COURSE IN MAP READING!
AFTER A LONG, TOUGH RIDE!
THERE SHE BLOWS!
GROAN! ANOTHER BID FOR RESPECT FLOPS BIGTIME!

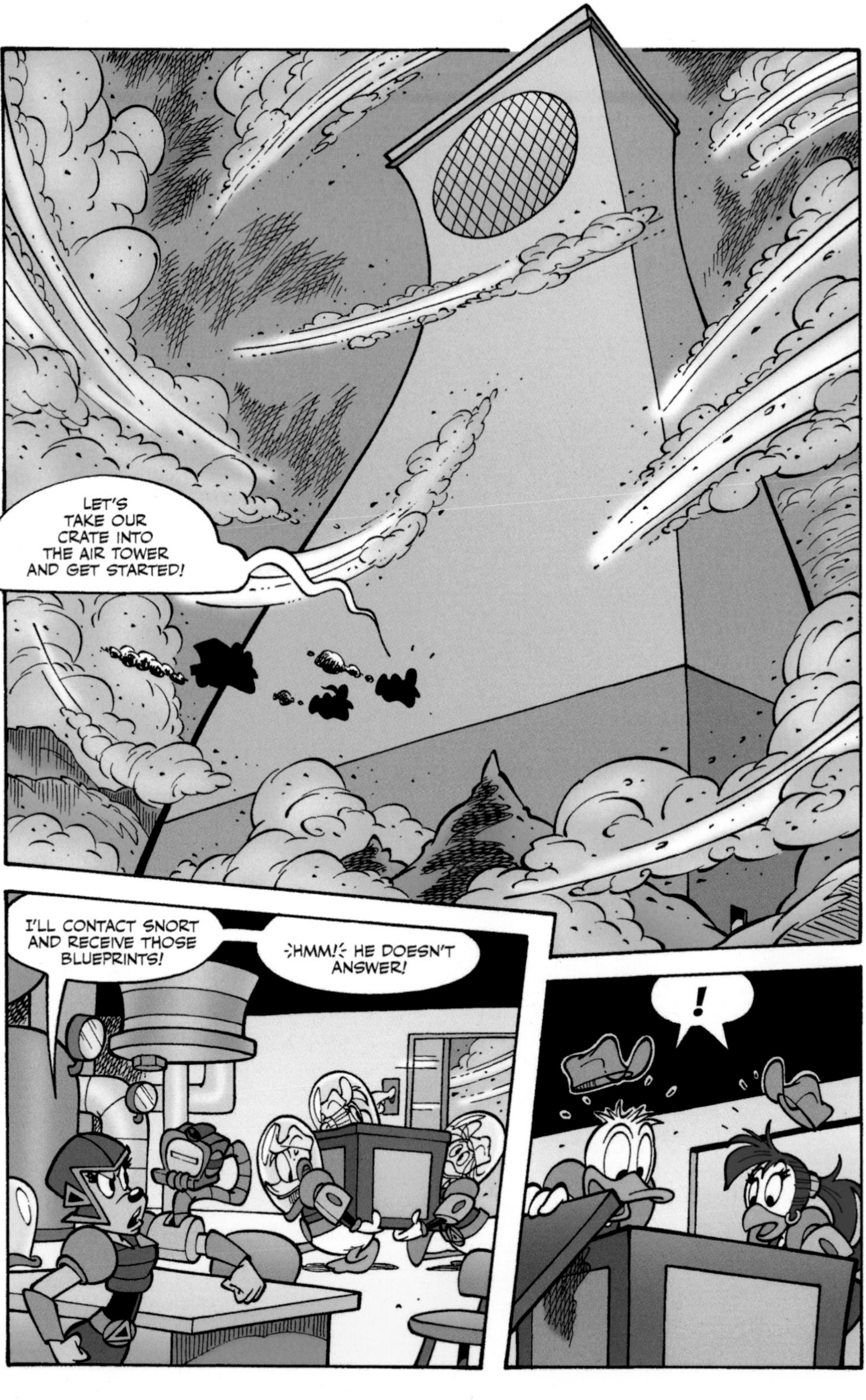
LET'S TAKE OUR CRATE INTO THE AIR TOWER AND GET STARTED!
I'LL CONTACT SNORT AND RECEIVE THOSE BLUEPRINTS!
HMM! HE DOESN'T ANSWER!
!

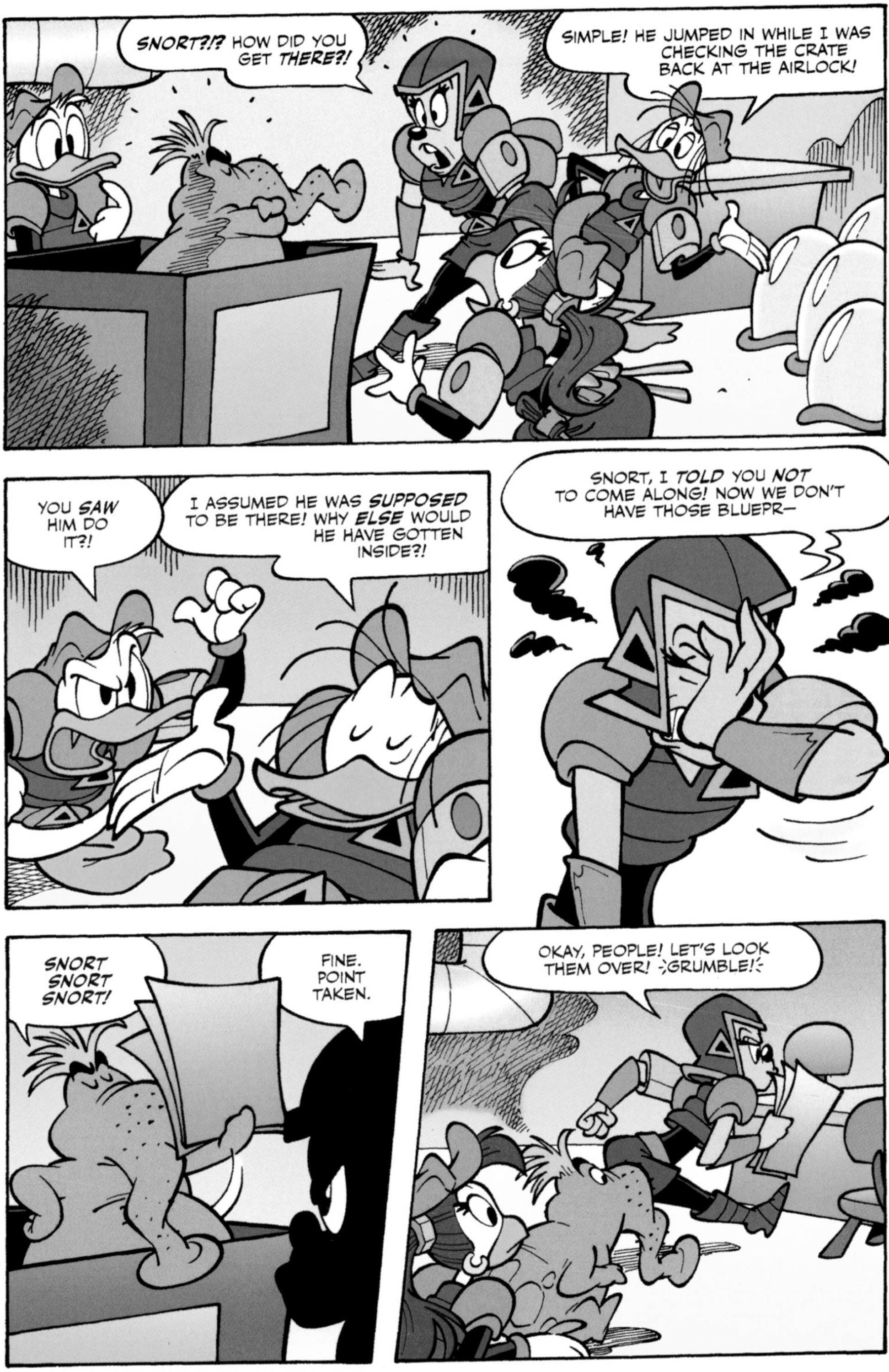
SNORT?!? HOW DID YOU GET THERE?!
SIMPLE! HE JUMPED IN WHILE I WAS CHECKING THE CRATE BACK AT THE AIRLOCK!
YOU SAW HIM DO IT?!
I ASSUMED HE WAS SUPPOSED TO BE THERE! WHY ELSE WOULD HE HAVE GOTTEN INSIDE?!
SNORT, I TOLD YOU NOT TO COME ALONG! NOW WE DON'T HAVE THOSE BLUEPR—
SNORT SNORT SNORT!
FINE. POINT TAKEN.
OKAY, PEOPLE! LET'S LOOK THEM OVER! -GRUMBLE!-

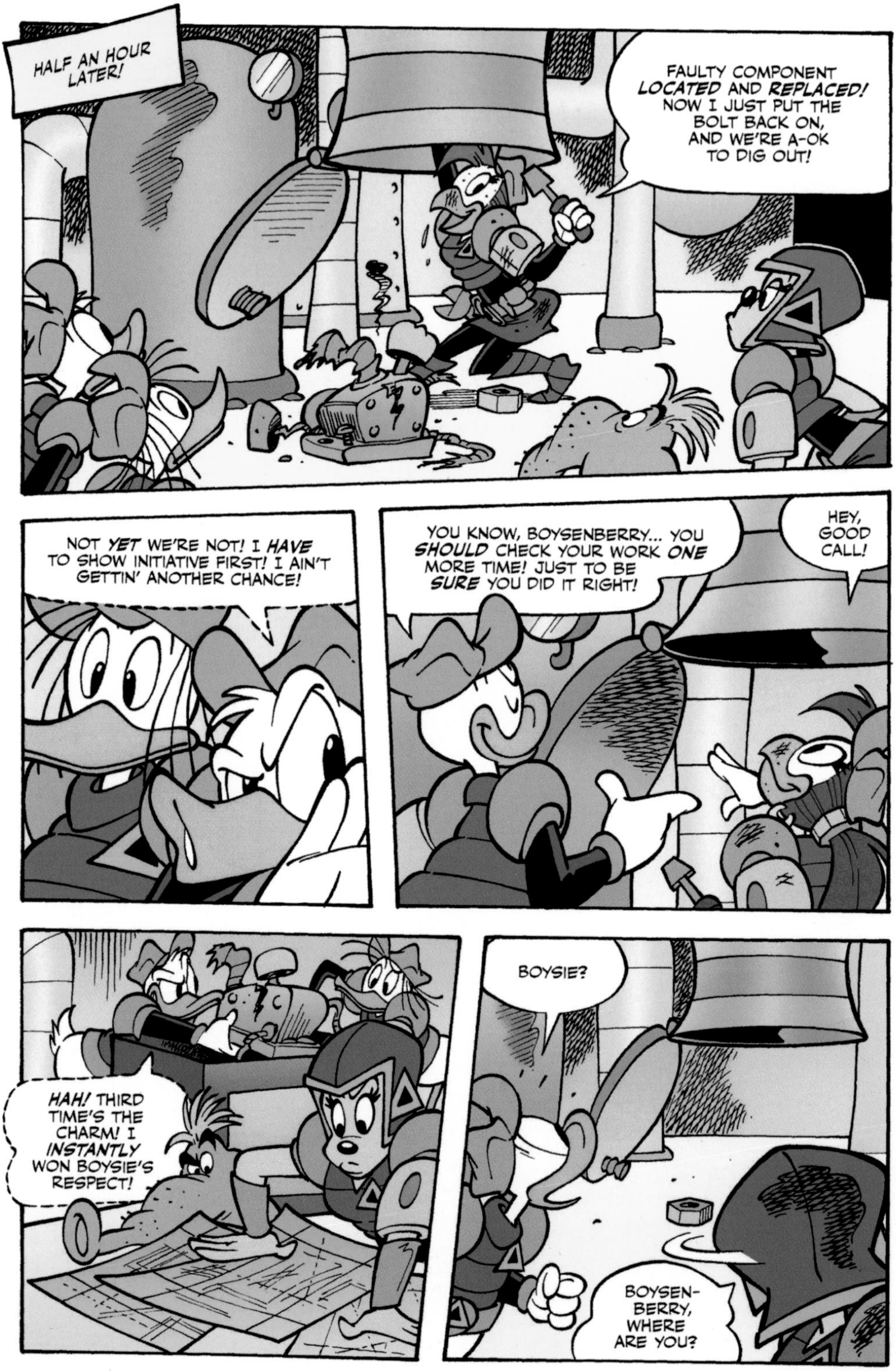
HALF AN HOUR LATER!
FAULTY COMPONENT LOCATED AND REPLACED! NOW I JUST PUT THE BOLT BACK ON, AND WE'RE A-OK TO DIG OUT!
NOT YET WE'RE NOT! I HAVE TO SHOW INITIATIVE FIRST! I AIN'T GETTIN' ANOTHER CHANCE!
YOU KNOW, BOYSENBERRY... YOU SHOULD CHECK YOUR WORK ONE MORE TIME! JUST TO BE SURE YOU DID IT RIGHT!
HEY, GOOD CALL!
HAH! THIRD TIME'S THE CHARM! I INSTANTLY WON BOYSIE'S RESPECT!
BOYSIE?
BOYSEN-BERRY, WHERE ARE YOU?

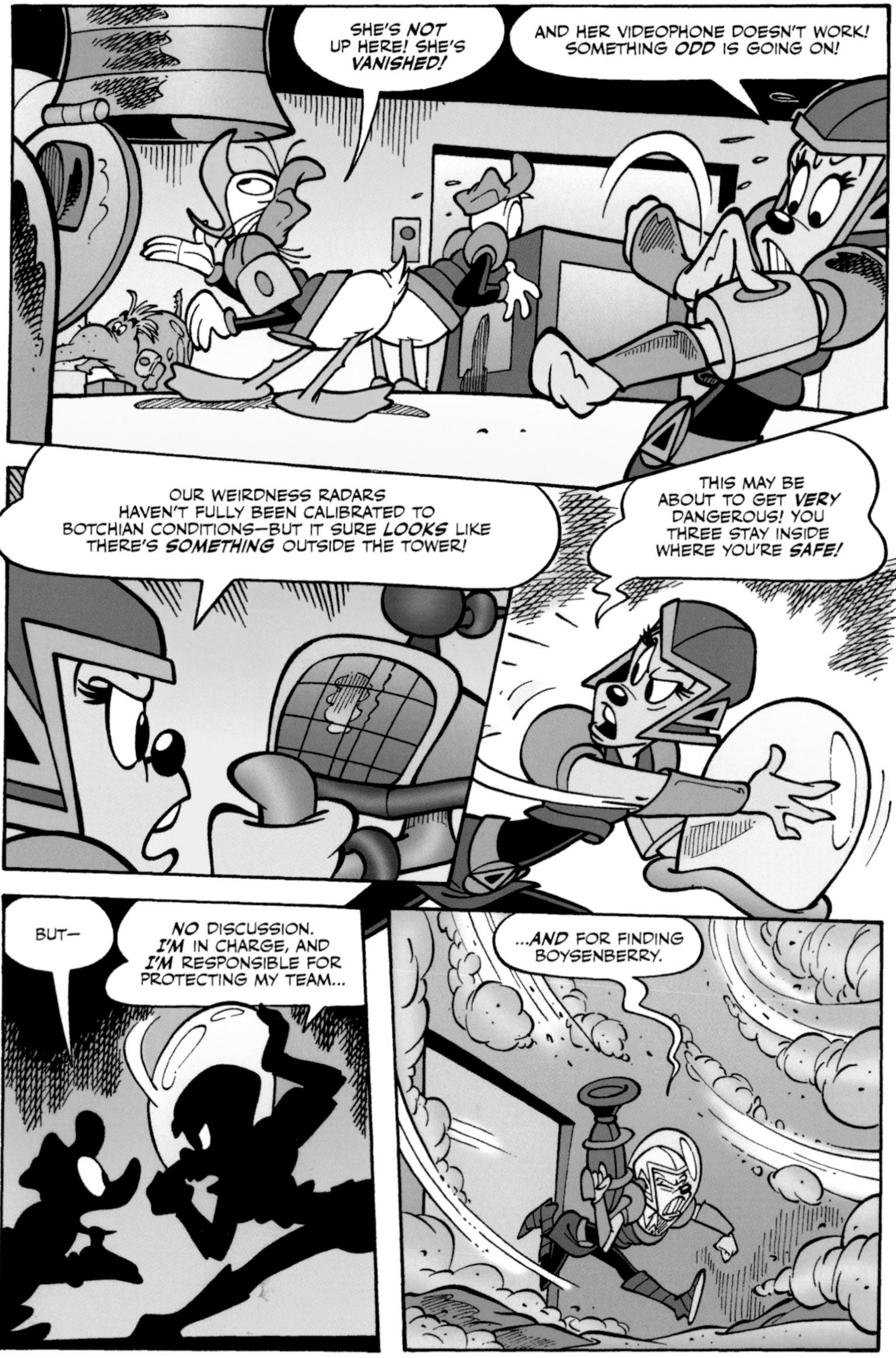
SHE'S NOT UP HERE! SHE'S VANISHED!
AND HER VIDEOPHONE DOESN'T WORK! SOMETHING ODD IS GOING ON!
OUR WEIRDNESS RADARS HAVEN'T FULLY BEEN CALIBRATED TO BOTCHIAN CONDITIONS—BUT IT SURE LOOKS LIKE THERE'S SOMETHING OUTSIDE THE TOWER!
THIS MAY BE ABOUT TO GET VERY DANGEROUS! YOU THREE STAY INSIDE WHERE YOU'RE SAFE!
BUT—
NO DISCUSSION. I'M IN CHARGE, AND I'M RESPONSIBLE FOR PROTECTING MY TEAM...
...AND FOR FINDING BOYSENBERRY.

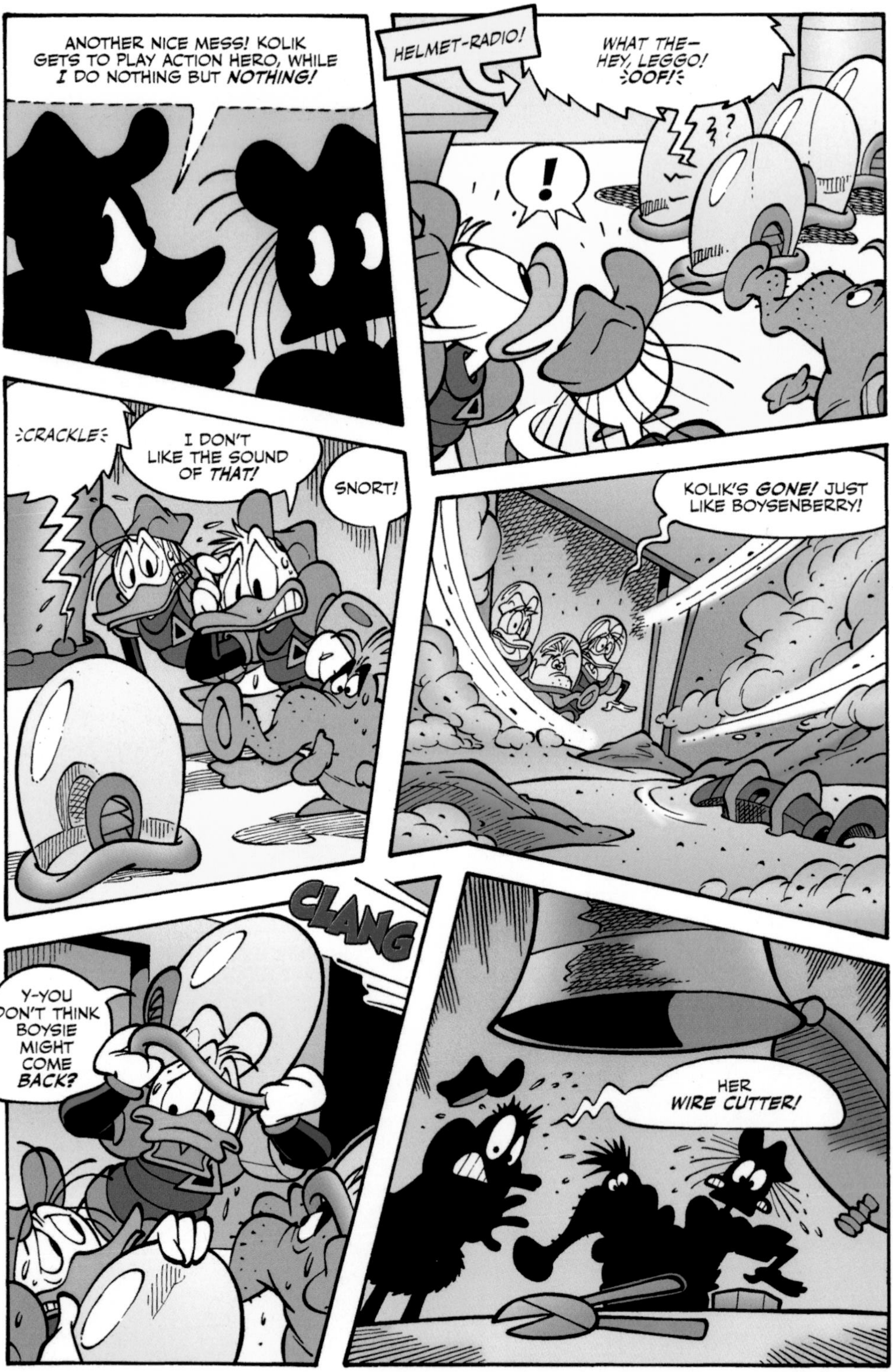
ANOTHER NICE MESS! KOLIK GETS TO PLAY ACTION HERO, WHILE I DO NOTHING BUT NOTHING!
HELMET-RADIO!
WHAT THE— HEY, LEGGO! OOF!
!
CRACKLE
I DON'T LIKE THE SOUND OF THAT!
SNORT!
KOLIK'S GONE! JUST LIKE BOYSENBERRY!
CLANG
Y-YOU DON'T THINK BOYSIE MIGHT COME BACK?
HER WIRE CUTTER!

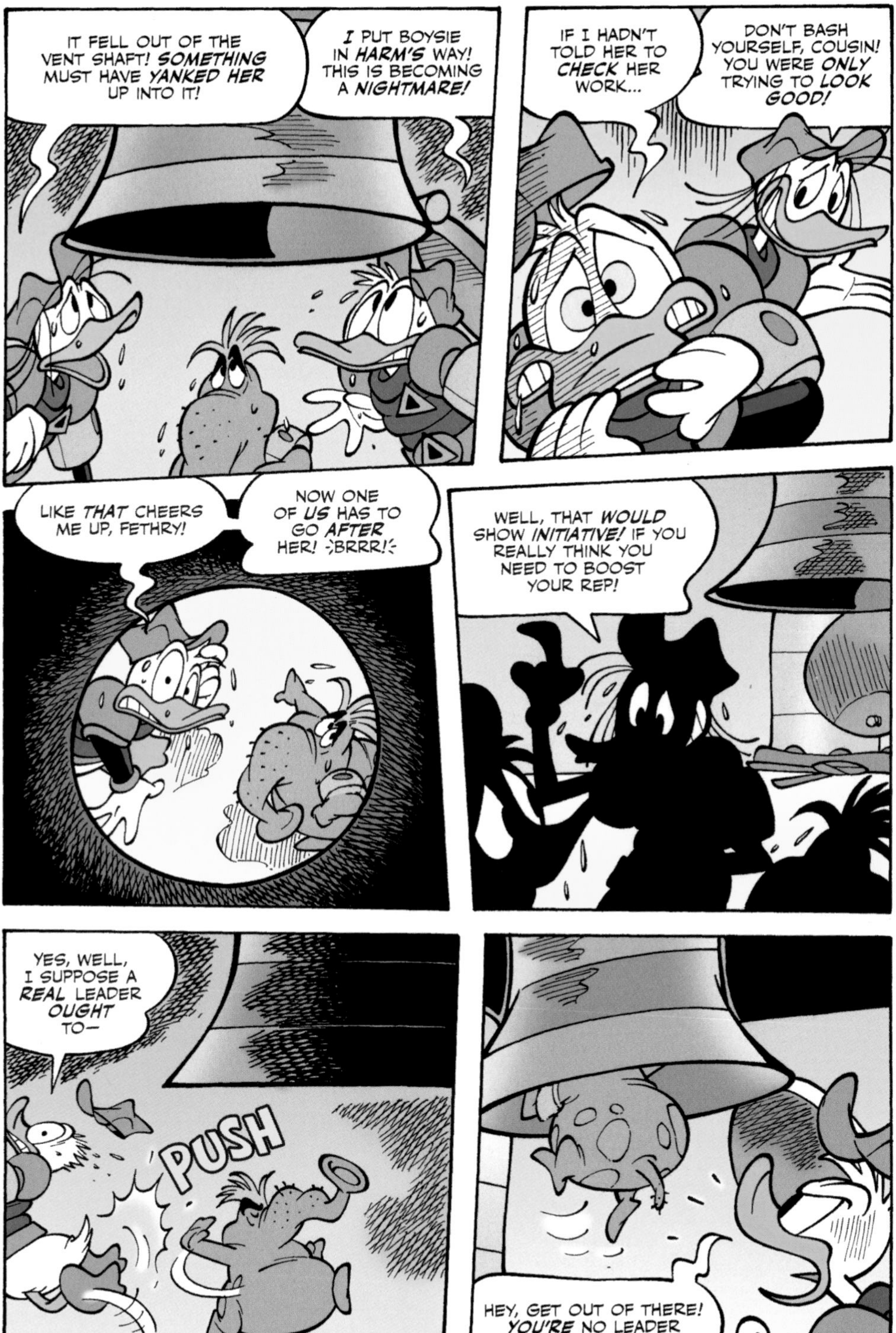

IT FELL OUT OF THE VENT SHAFT! SOMETHING MUST HAVE YANKED HER UP INTO IT!
I PUT BOYSIE IN HARM'S WAY! THIS IS BECOMING A NIGHTMARE!
IF I HADN'T TOLD HER TO CHECK HER WORK...
DON'T BASH YOURSELF, COUSIN! YOU WERE ONLY TRYING TO LOOK GOOD!
LIKE THAT CHEERS ME UP, FETHRY!
NOW ONE OF US HAS TO GO AFTER HER! BRRR!
WELL, THAT WOULD SHOW INITIATIVE! IF YOU REALLY THINK YOU NEED TO BOOST YOUR REP!
YES, WELL, I SUPPOSE A REAL LEADER OUGHT TO—
PUSH
HEY, GET OUT OF THERE! YOU'RE NO LEADER ANYMORE! I AM! ME!

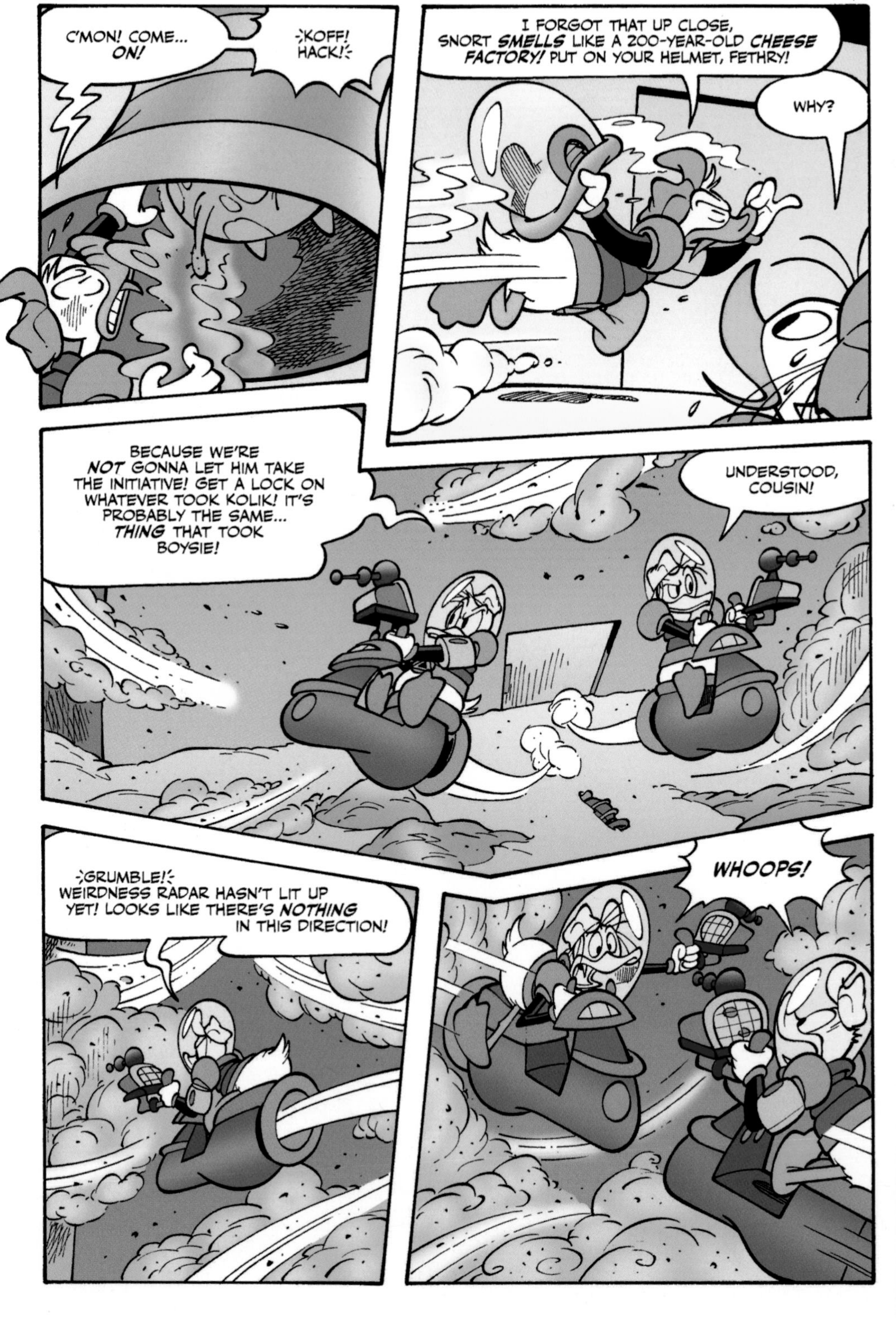
C'MON! COME... ON!
-KOFF! HACK!-
I FORGOT THAT UP CLOSE, SNORT SMELLS LIKE A 200-YEAR-OLD CHEESE FACTORY! PUT ON YOUR HELMET, FETHRY!
WHY?
BECAUSE WE'RE NOT GONNA LET HIM TAKE THE INITIATIVE! GET A LOCK ON WHATEVER TOOK KOLIK! IT'S PROBABLY THE SAME... THING THAT TOOK BOYSIE!
UNDERSTOOD, COUSIN!
-GRUMBLE!- WEIRDNESS RADAR HASN'T LIT UP YET! LOOKS LIKE THERE'S NOTHING IN THIS DIRECTION!
WHOOPS!

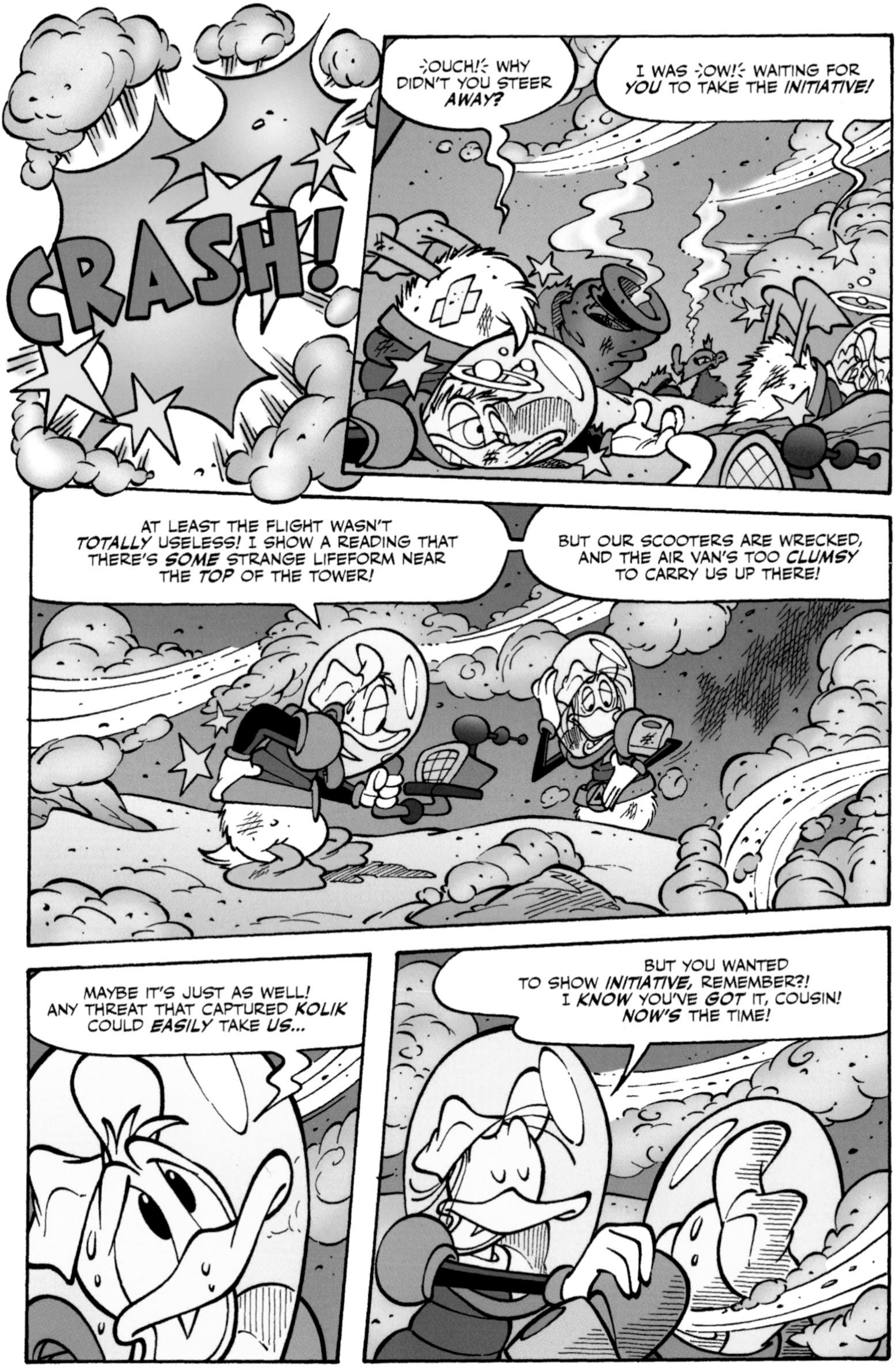
CRASH!
-OUCH!- WHY DIDN'T YOU STEER *AWAY?*
I WAS -OW!- WAITING FOR *YOU* TO TAKE THE *INITIATIVE!*
AT LEAST THE FLIGHT WASN'T *TOTALLY* USELESS! I SHOW A READING THAT THERE'S *SOME* STRANGE LIFEFORM NEAR THE *TOP* OF THE TOWER!
BUT OUR SCOOTERS ARE WRECKED, AND THE AIR VAN'S TOO *CLUMSY* TO CARRY US UP THERE!
MAYBE IT'S JUST AS WELL! ANY THREAT THAT CAPTURED *KOLIK* COULD *EASILY* TAKE *US...*
BUT YOU WANTED TO SHOW *INITIATIVE,* REMEMBER?! I *KNOW* YOU'VE *GOT* IT, COUSIN! *NOW'S* THE TIME!

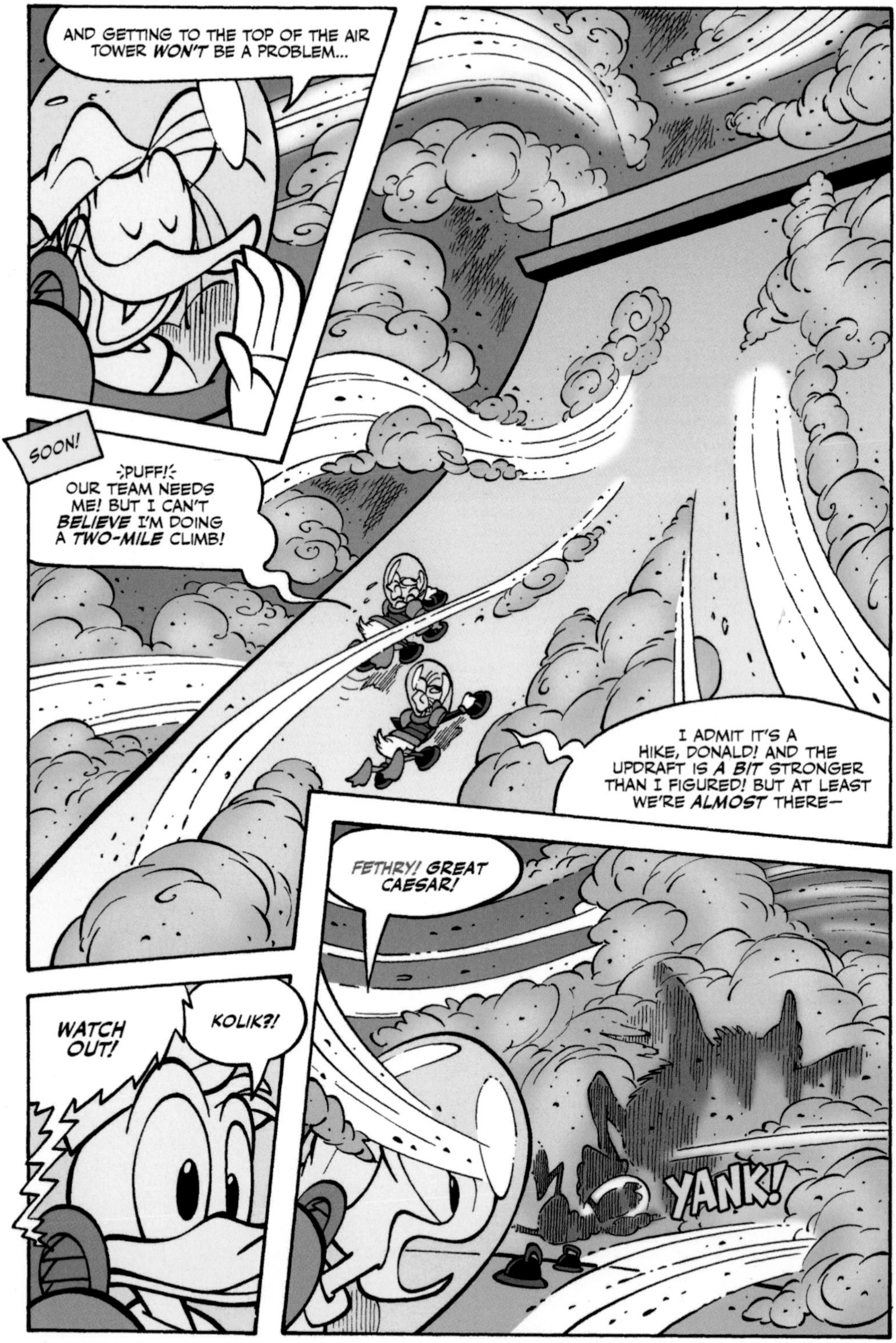
AND GETTING TO THE TOP OF THE AIR TOWER WON'T BE A PROBLEM...
SOON!
-PUFF!- OUR TEAM NEEDS ME! BUT I CAN'T BELIEVE I'M DOING A TWO-MILE CLIMB!
I ADMIT IT'S A HIKE, DONALD! AND THE UPDRAFT IS A BIT STRONGER THAN I FIGURED! BUT AT LEAST WE'RE ALMOST THERE—
FETHRY! GREAT CAESAR!
WATCH OUT!
KOLIK?!
YANK!

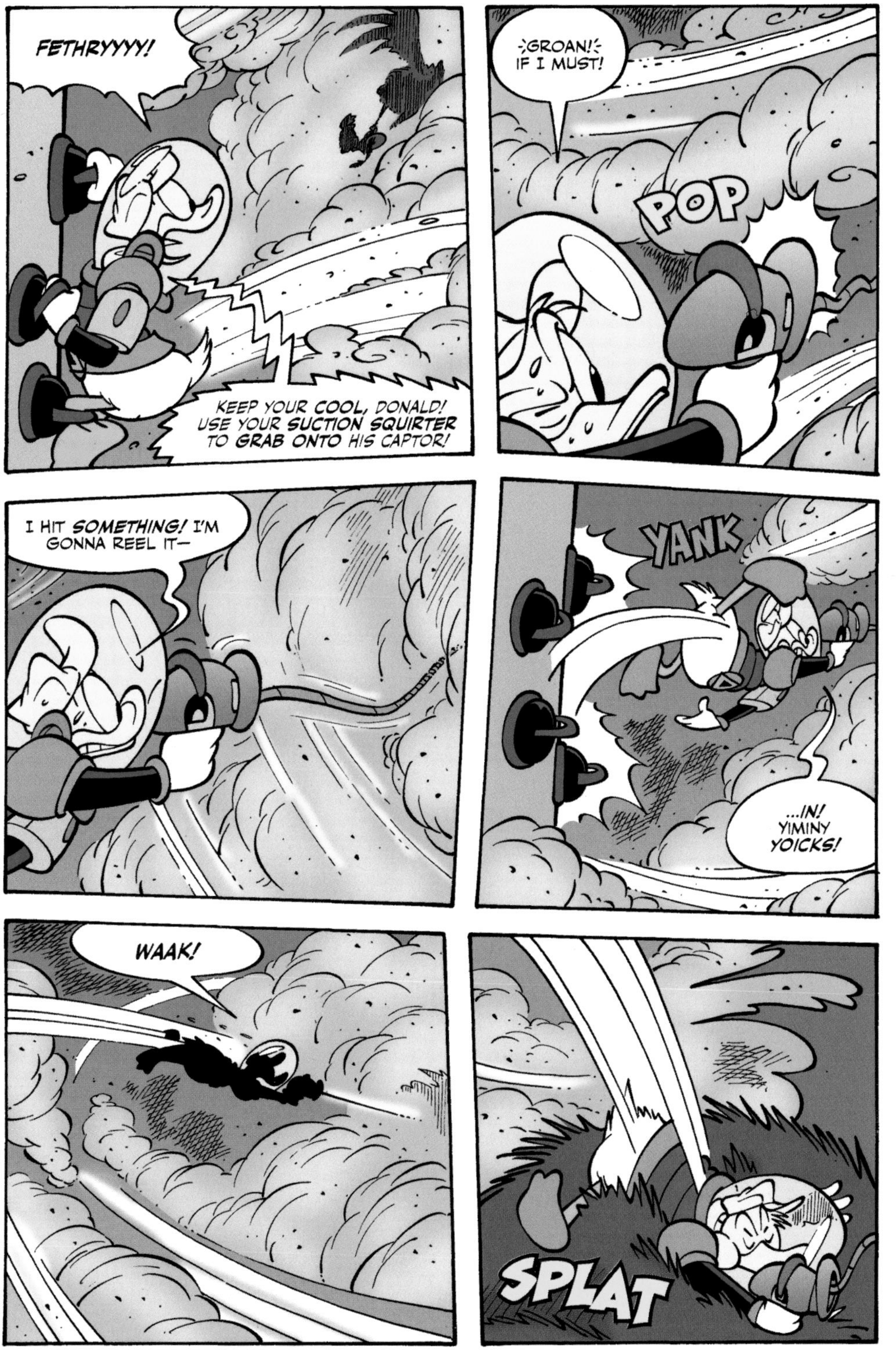
FETHRYYYY!
KEEP YOUR COOL, DONALD! USE YOUR SUCTION SQUIRTER TO GRAB ONTO HIS CAPTOR!
GROAN! IF I MUST!
POP
I HIT SOMETHING! I'M GONNA REEL IT—
YANK
...IN! YIMINY YOICKS!
WAAK!
SPLAT

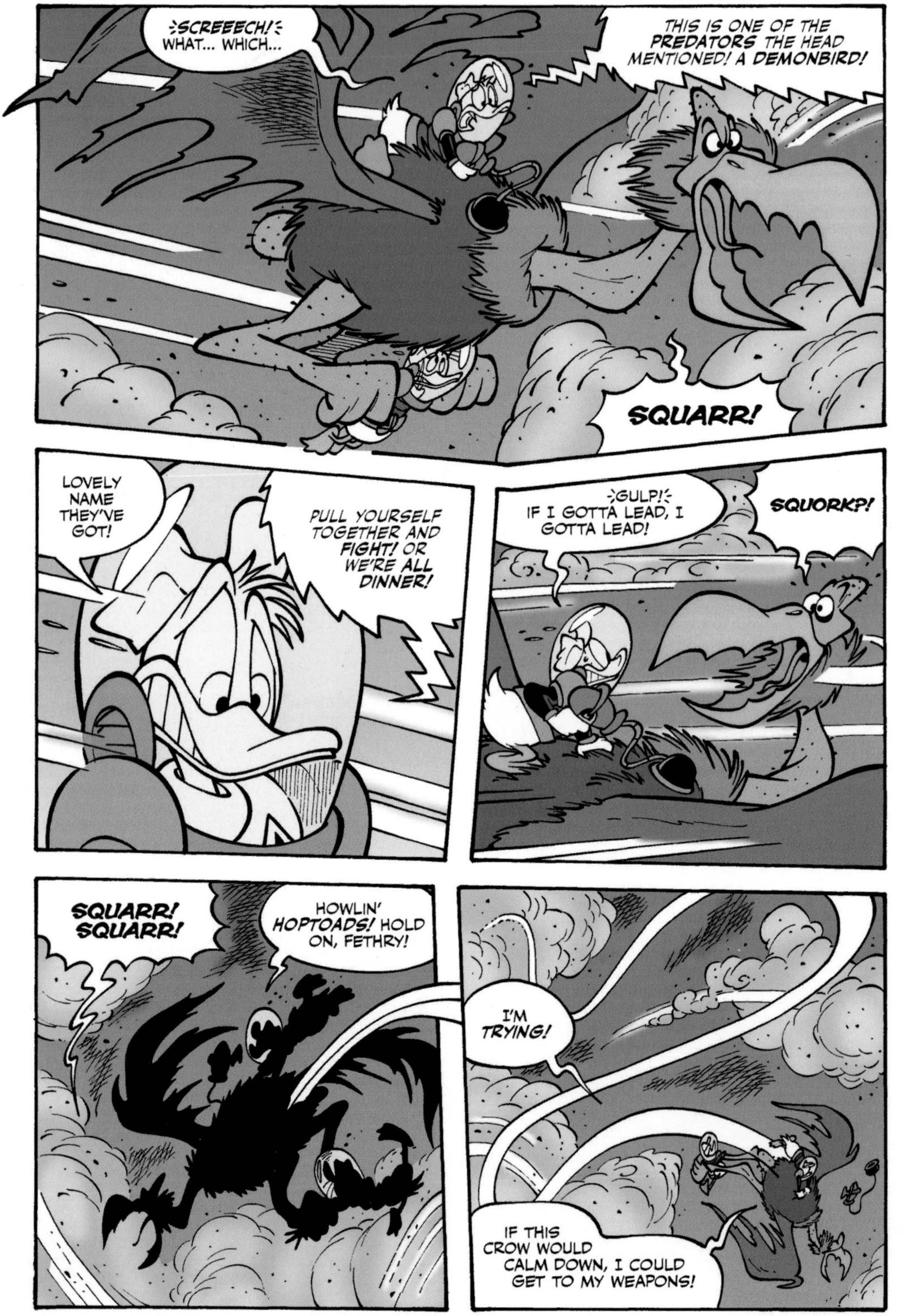

SCREEECH! WHAT... WHICH...
THIS IS ONE OF THE PREDATORS THE HEAD MENTIONED! A DEMONBIRD!
SQUARR!
LOVELY NAME THEY'VE GOT!
PULL YOURSELF TOGETHER AND FIGHT! OR WE'RE ALL DINNER!
GULP! IF I GOTTA LEAD, I GOTTA LEAD!
SQUORK?!
SQUARR! SQUARR!
HOWLIN' HOPTOADS! HOLD ON, FETHRY!
I'M TRYING!
IF THIS CROW WOULD CALM DOWN, I COULD GET TO MY WEAPONS!

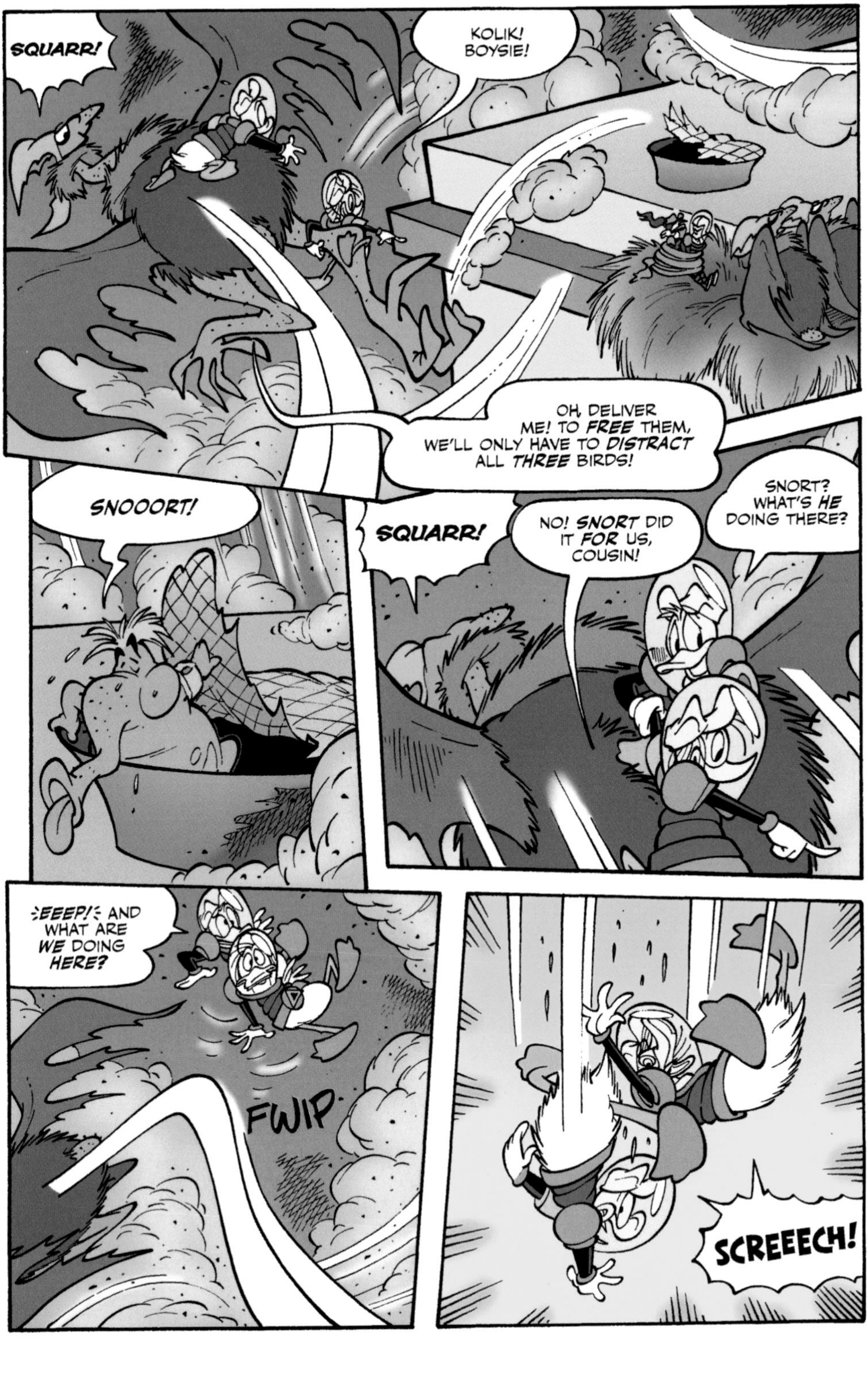
SQUARR!
KOLIK! BOYSIE!
OH, DELIVER ME! TO FREE THEM, WE'LL ONLY HAVE TO DISTRACT ALL THREE BIRDS!
SNOOORT!
SQUARR!
SNORT? WHAT'S HE DOING THERE?
NO! SNORT DID IT FOR US, COUSIN!
EEEP! AND WHAT ARE WE DOING HERE?
FWIP
SCREEECH!

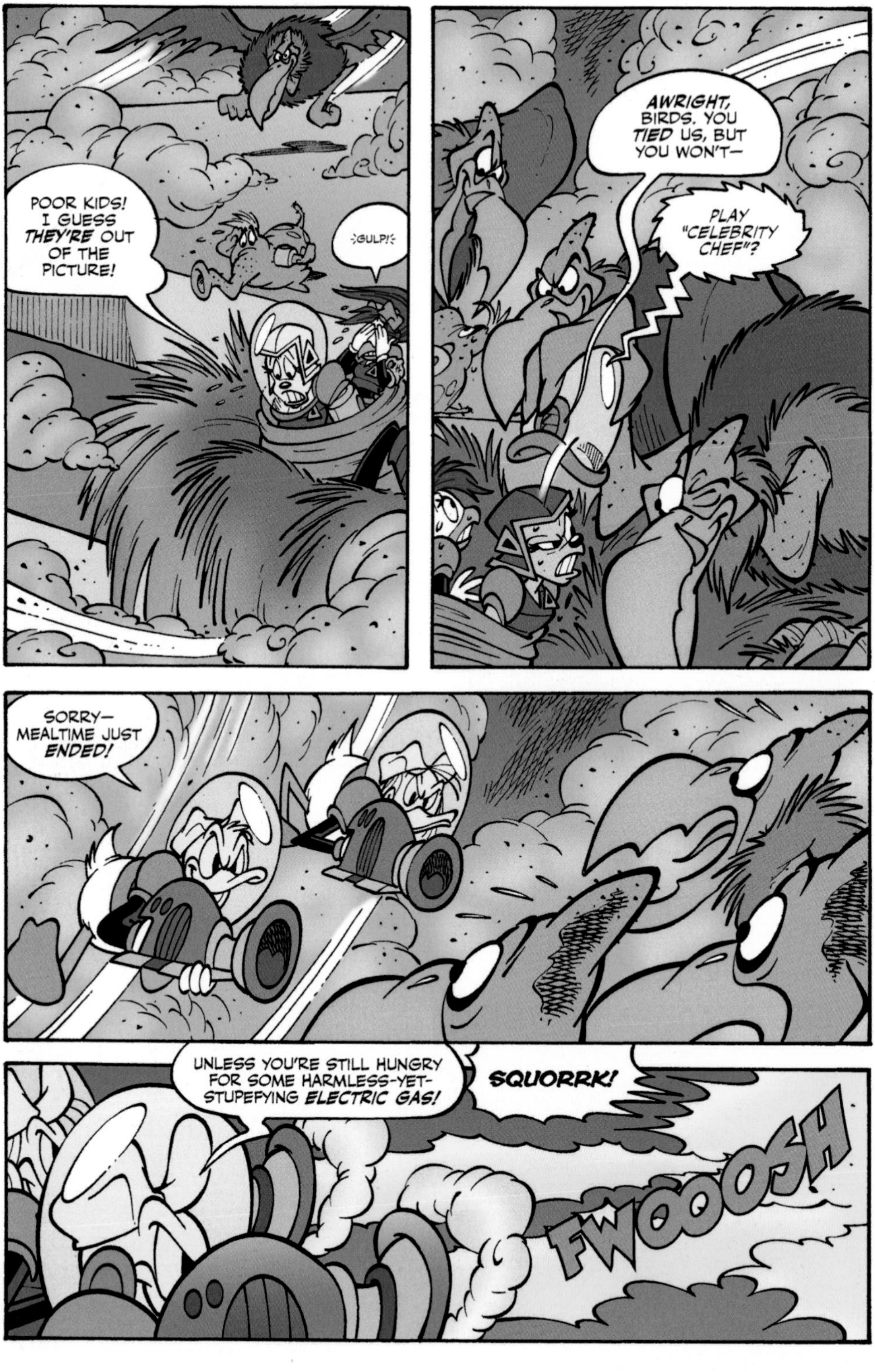
POOR KIDS! I GUESS THEY'RE OUT OF THE PICTURE!
GULP!
AWRIGHT, BIRDS. YOU TIED US, BUT YOU WON'T—
PLAY "CELEBRITY CHEF"?
SORRY— MEALTIME JUST ENDED!
UNLESS YOU'RE STILL HUNGRY FOR SOME HARMLESS-YET-STUPEFYING ELECTRIC GAS!
SQUORRK!
FWOOOSH

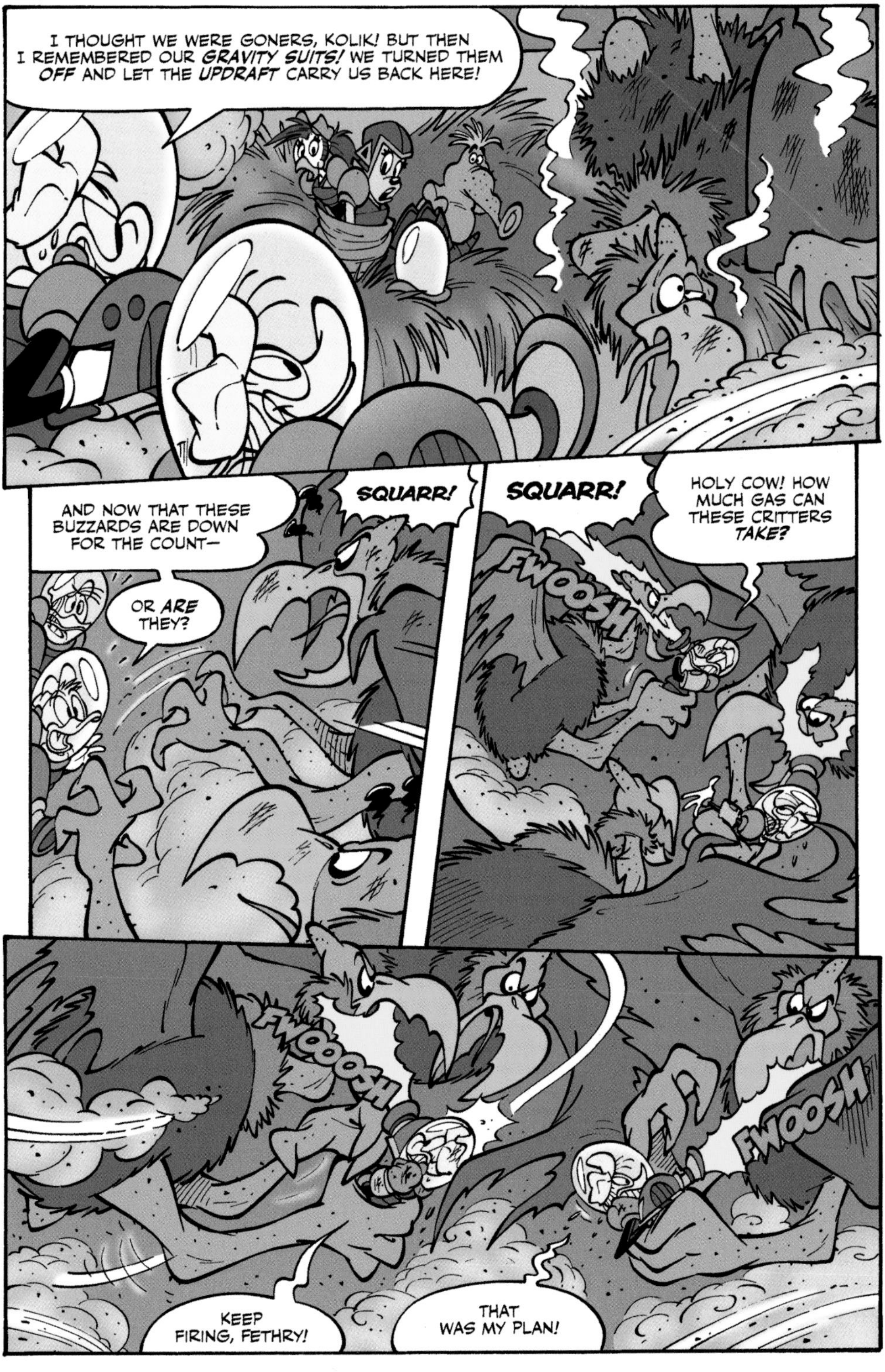
I THOUGHT WE WERE GONERS, KOLIK! BUT THEN I REMEMBERED OUR *GRAVITY SUITS!* WE TURNED THEM *OFF* AND LET THE *UPDRAFT* CARRY US BACK HERE!
AND NOW THAT THESE BUZZARDS ARE DOWN FOR THE COUNT—
OR *ARE* THEY?
SQUARR!
SQUARR!
HOLY COW! HOW MUCH GAS CAN THESE CRITTERS *TAKE?*
FWOOSH
FWOOOSH
FWOOSH
KEEP FIRING, FETHRY!
THAT WAS MY PLAN!

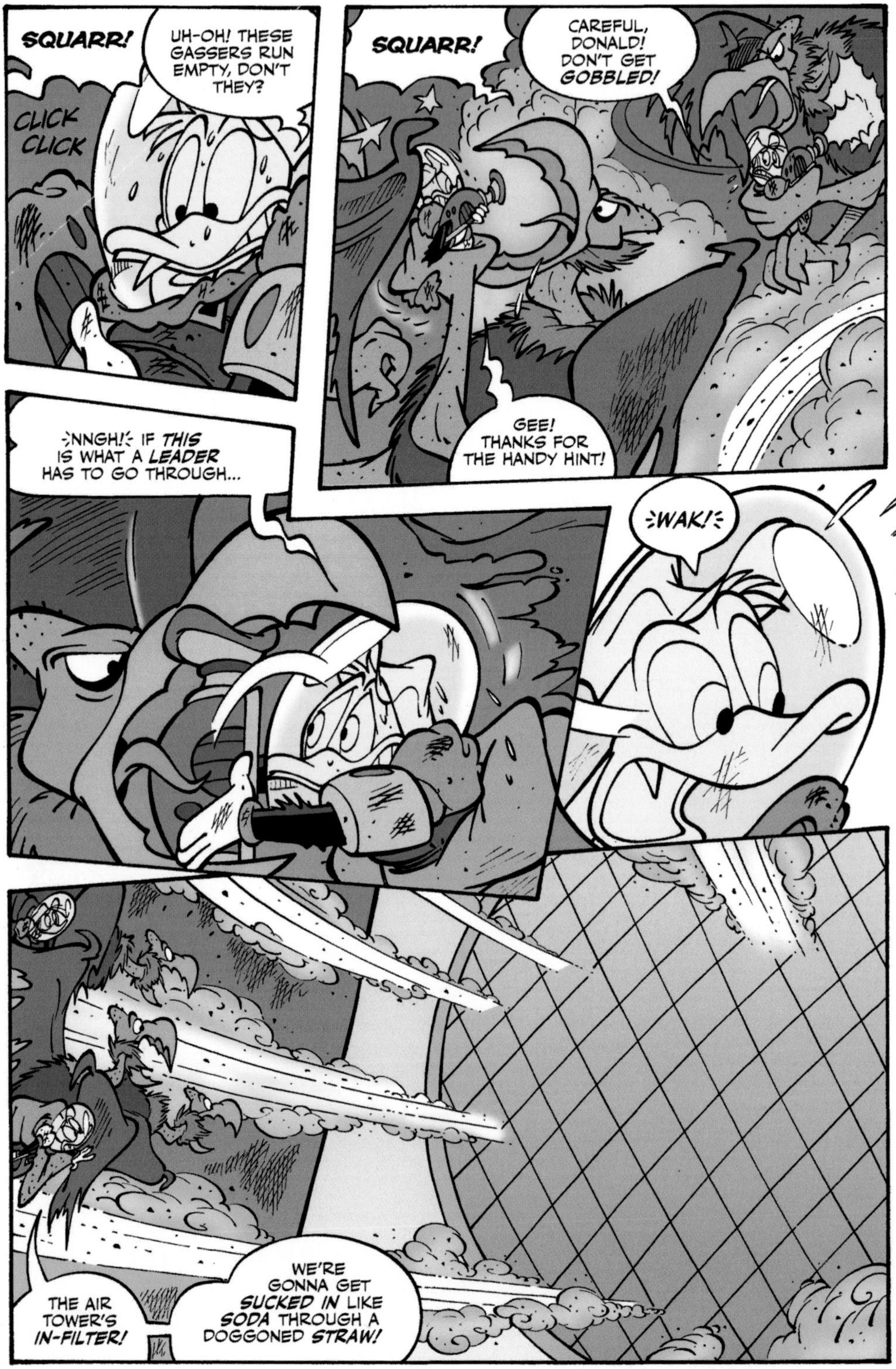
SQUARR!
UH-OH! THESE GASSERS RUN EMPTY, DON'T THEY?
CLICK CLICK
SQUARR!
CAREFUL, DONALD! DON'T GET GOBBLED!
GEE! THANKS FOR THE HANDY HINT!
NNGH! IF THIS IS WHAT A LEADER HAS TO GO THROUGH...
WAK!
THE AIR TOWER'S IN-FILTER!
WE'RE GONNA GET SUCKED IN LIKE SODA THROUGH A DOGGONED STRAW!

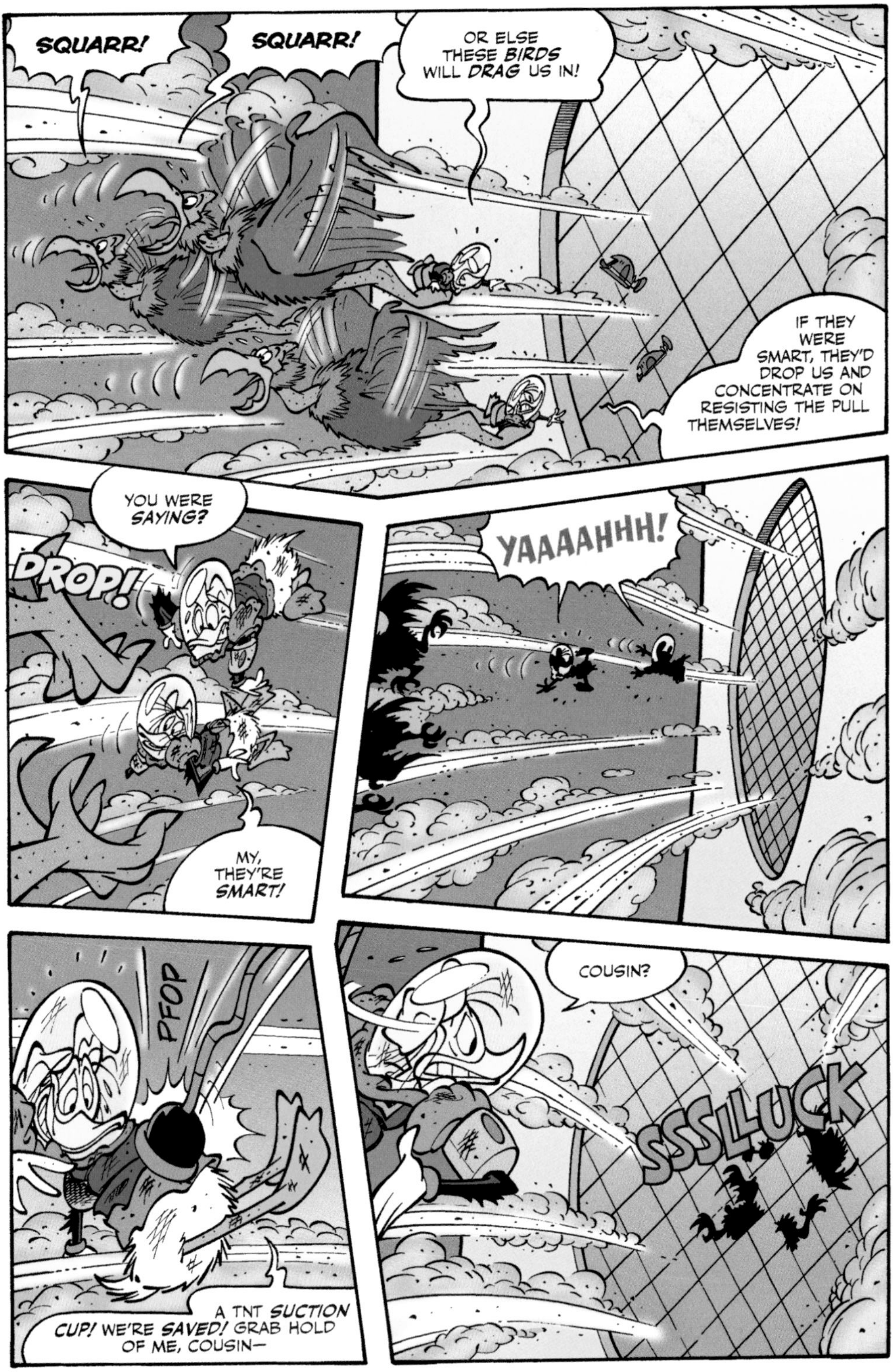
SQUARR!
SQUARR!
OR ELSE THESE BIRDS WILL DRAG US IN!
IF THEY WERE SMART, THEY'D DROP US AND CONCENTRATE ON RESISTING THE PULL THEMSELVES!
YOU WERE SAYING?
DROP!
MY, THEY'RE SMART!
YAAAAHHH!
PFOP
A TNT SUCTION CUP! WE'RE SAVED! GRAB HOLD OF ME, COUSIN—
COUSIN?
SSSLUCK

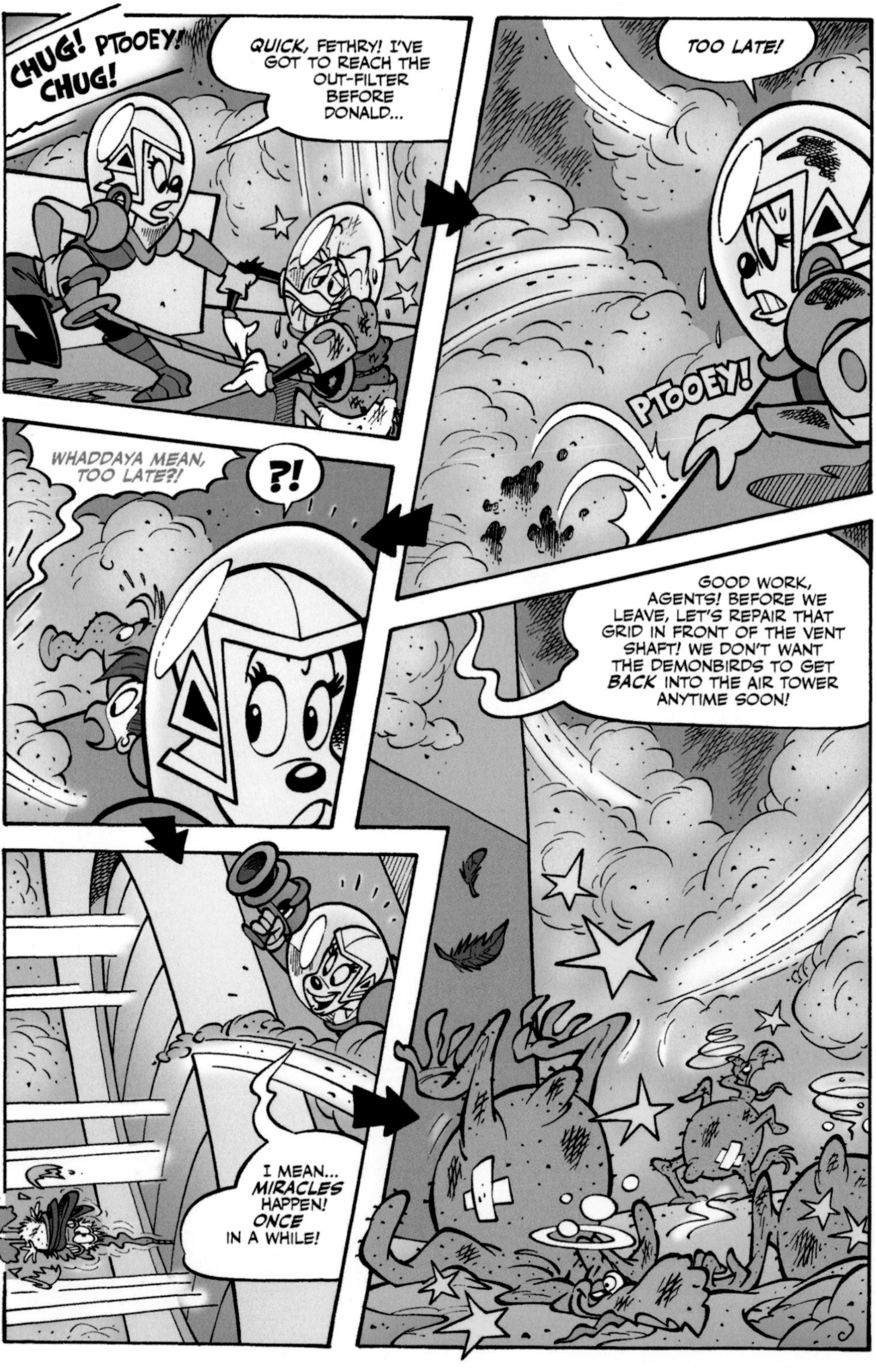
CHUG! CHUG!
PTOOEY!
QUICK, FETHRY! I'VE GOT TO REACH THE OUT-FILTER BEFORE DONALD...
TOO LATE!
PTOOEY!
WHADDAYA MEAN, TOO LATE?!
?!
GOOD WORK, AGENTS! BEFORE WE LEAVE, LET'S REPAIR THAT GRID IN FRONT OF THE VENT SHAFT! WE DON'T WANT THE DEMONBIRDS TO GET BACK INTO THE AIR TOWER ANYTIME SOON!
I MEAN... MIRACLES HAPPEN! ONCE IN A WHILE!

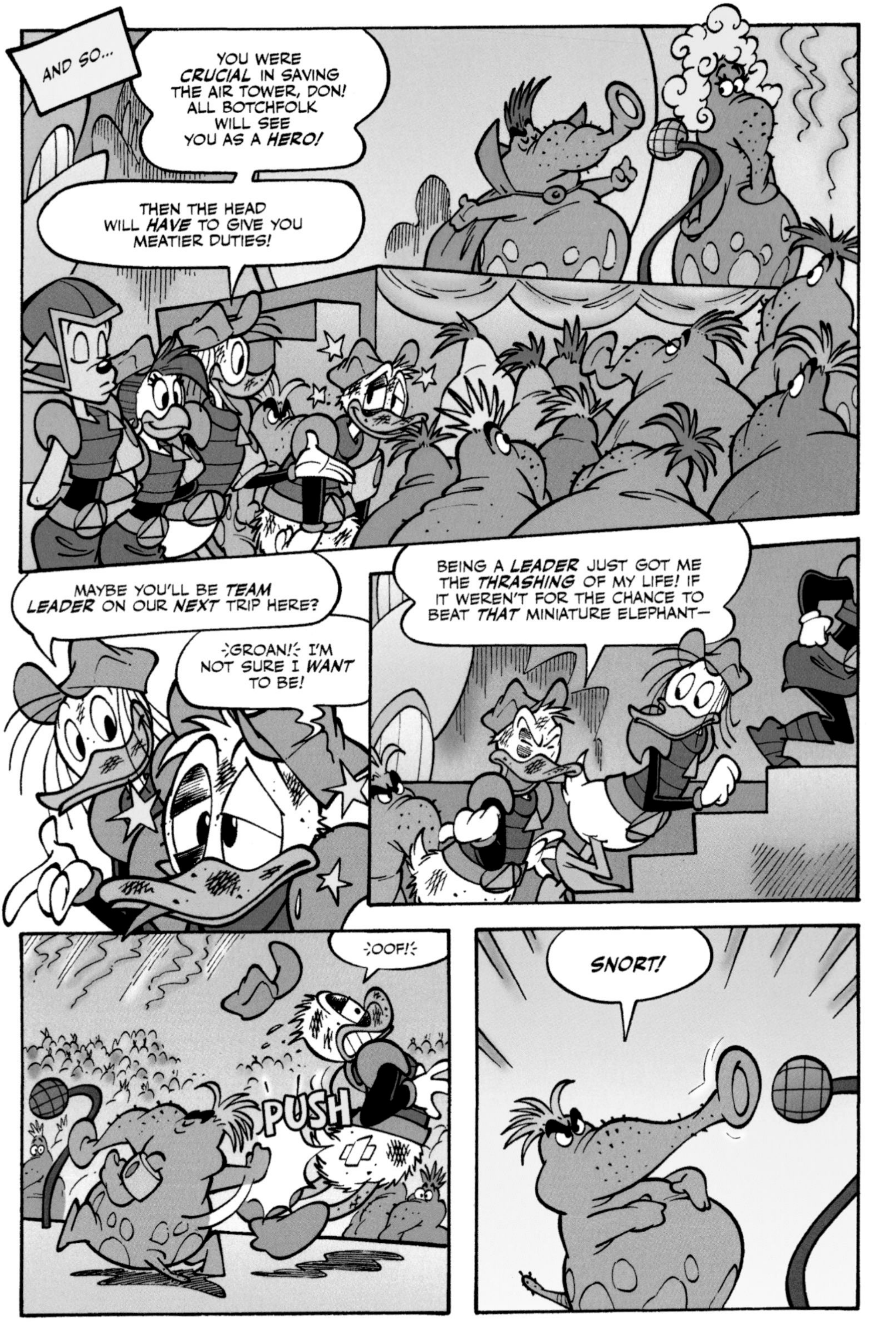
AND SO...
YOU WERE CRUCIAL IN SAVING THE AIR TOWER, DON! ALL BOTCHFOLK WILL SEE YOU AS A HERO!
THEN THE HEAD WILL HAVE TO GIVE YOU MEATIER DUTIES!
MAYBE YOU'LL BE TEAM LEADER ON OUR NEXT TRIP HERE?
GROAN! I'M NOT SURE I WANT TO BE!
BEING A LEADER JUST GOT ME THE THRASHING OF MY LIFE! IF IT WEREN'T FOR THE CHANCE TO BEAT THAT MINIATURE ELEPHANT—
OOF!
PUSH
SNORT!

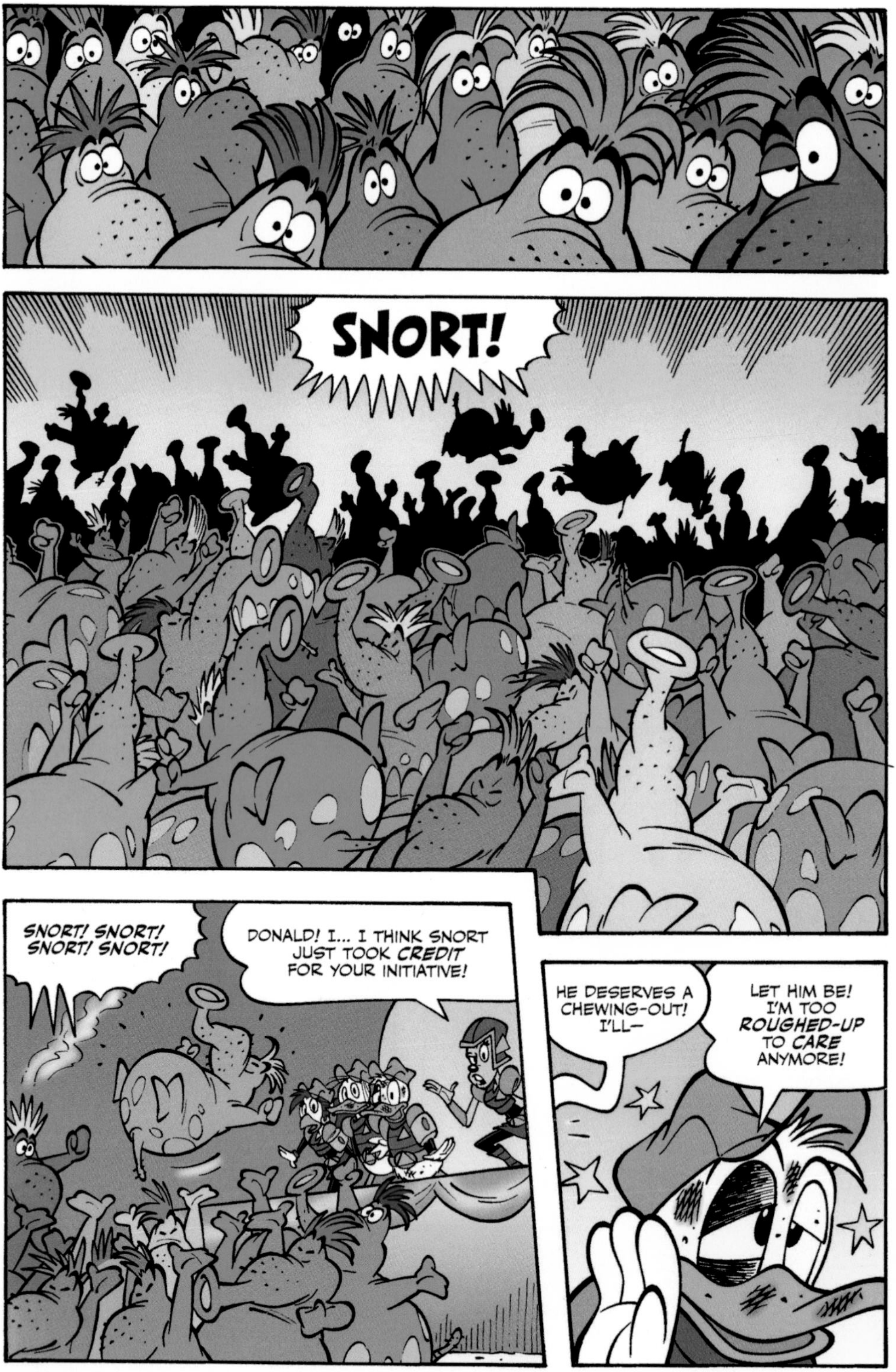
SNORT!
SNORT! SNORT! SNORT! SNORT!
DONALD! I... I THINK SNORT JUST TOOK CREDIT FOR YOUR INITIATIVE!
HE DESERVES A CHEWING-OUT! I'LL—
LET HIM BE! I'M TOO ROUGHED-UP TO CARE ANYMORE!

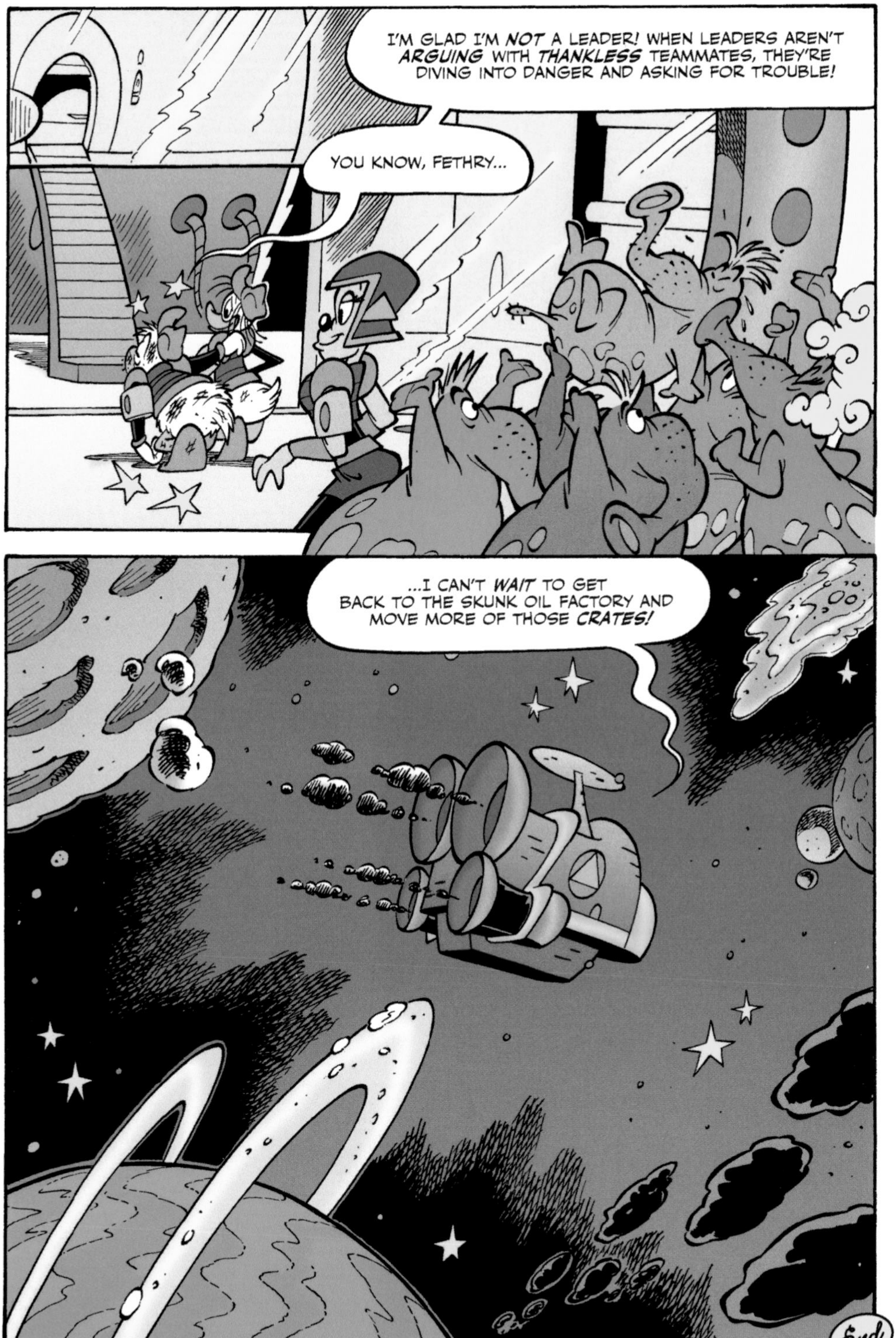
YOU KNOW, FETHRY...
I'M GLAD I'M *NOT* A LEADER! WHEN LEADERS AREN'T *ARGUING* WITH *THANKLESS* TEAMMATES, THEY'RE DIVING INTO DANGER AND ASKING FOR TROUBLE!
...I CAN'T *WAIT* TO GET BACK TO THE SKUNK OIL FACTORY AND MOVE MORE OF THOSE *CRATES!*
End

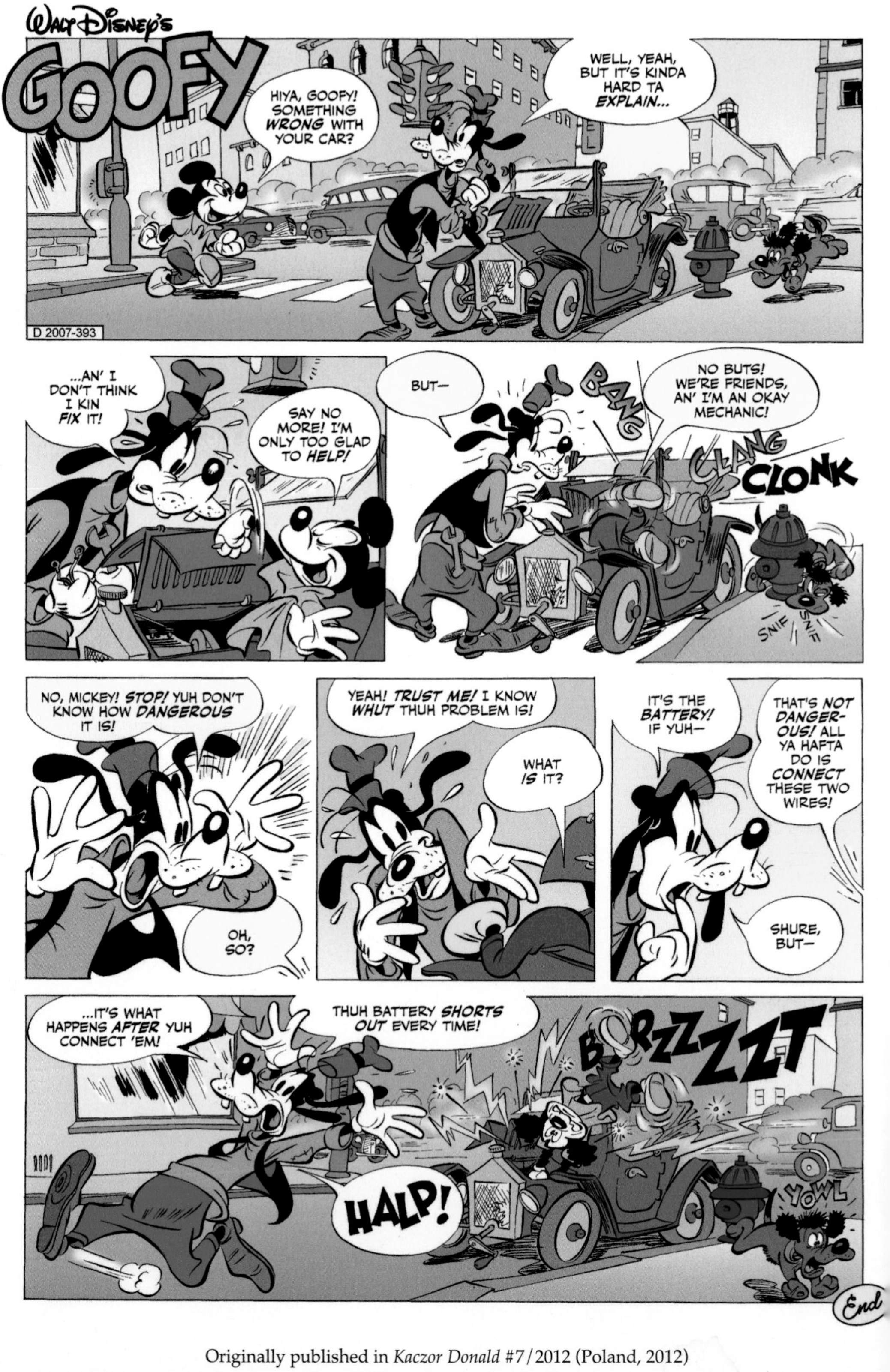

WALT DISNEY'S
GOOFY
HIYA, GOOFY! SOMETHING WRONG WITH YOUR CAR?
WELL, YEAH, BUT IT'S KINDA HARD TA EXPLAIN...
D 2007-393
...AN' I DON'T THINK I KIN FIX IT!
SAY NO MORE! I'M ONLY TOO GLAD TO HELP!
BUT—
BANG
NO BUTS! WE'RE FRIENDS, AN' I'M AN OKAY MECHANIC!
CLANG
CLONK
SNIF SNIF
NO, MICKEY! STOP! YUH DON'T KNOW HOW DANGEROUS IT IS!
OH, SO?
YEAH! TRUST ME! I KNOW WHUT THUH PROBLEM IS!
WHAT IS IT?
IT'S THE BATTERY! IF YUH—
THAT'S NOT DANGEROUS! ALL YA HAFTA DO IS CONNECT THESE TWO WIRES!
SHURE, BUT—
...IT'S WHAT HAPPENS AFTER YUH CONNECT 'EM!
THUH BATTERY SHORTS OUT EVERY TIME!
BRZZZZZT
HALP!
YOWL
End

Originally published in *Kaczor Donald* #7/2012 (Poland, 2012)

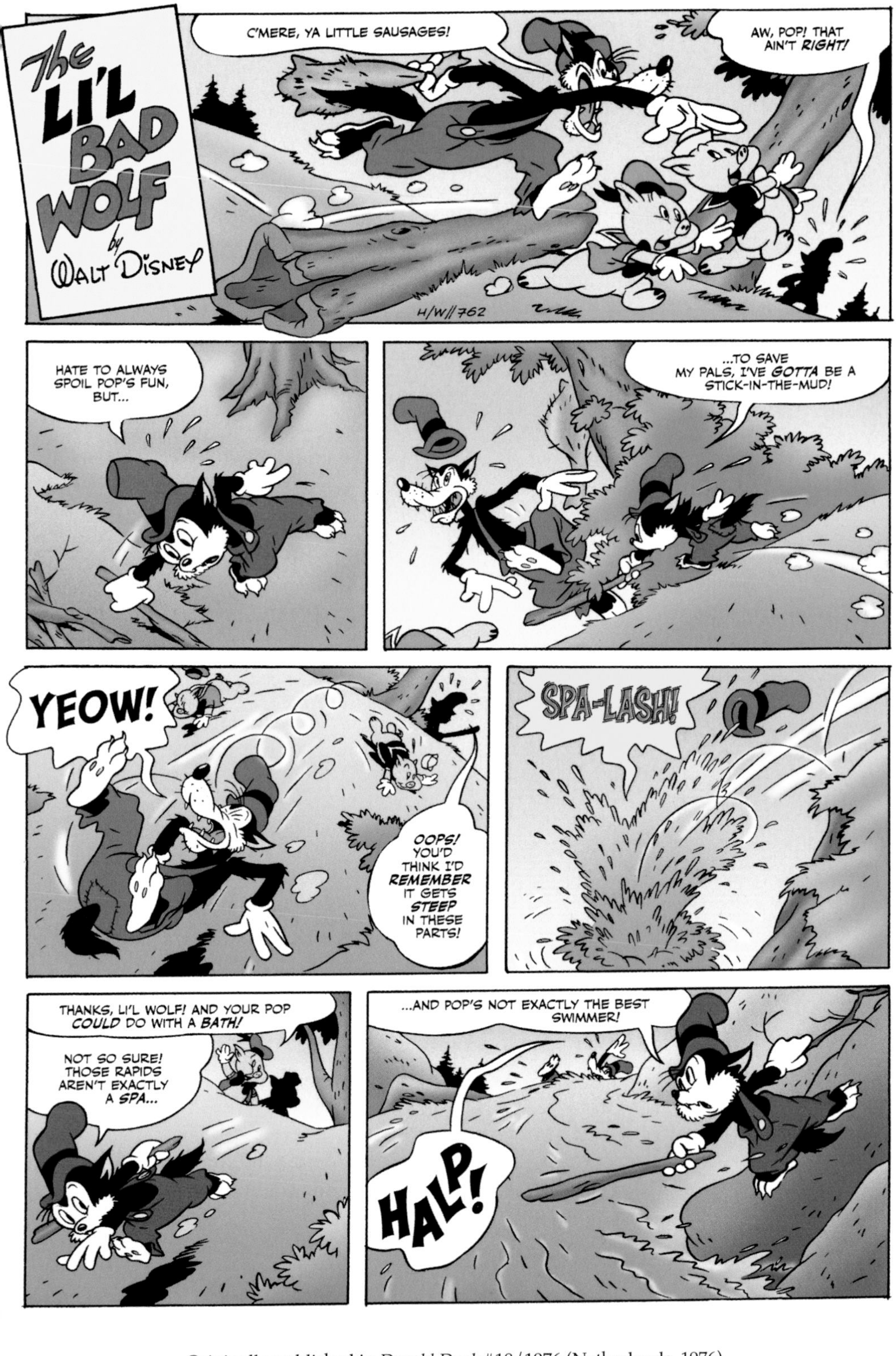
The LI'L BAD WOLF
by Walt Disney
C'MERE, YA LITTLE SAUSAGES!
AW, POP! THAT AIN'T RIGHT!
H/W//762
HATE TO ALWAYS SPOIL POP'S FUN, BUT...
...TO SAVE MY PALS, I'VE GOTTA BE A STICK-IN-THE-MUD!
YEOW!
OOPS! YOU'D THINK I'D REMEMBER IT GETS STEEP IN THESE PARTS!
SPA-LASH!
THANKS, LI'L WOLF! AND YOUR POP COULD DO WITH A BATH!
NOT SO SURE! THOSE RAPIDS AREN'T EXACTLY A SPA...
...AND POP'S NOT EXACTLY THE BEST SWIMMER!
HALP!

Originally published in *Donald Duck* #18/1976 (Netherlands, 1976)

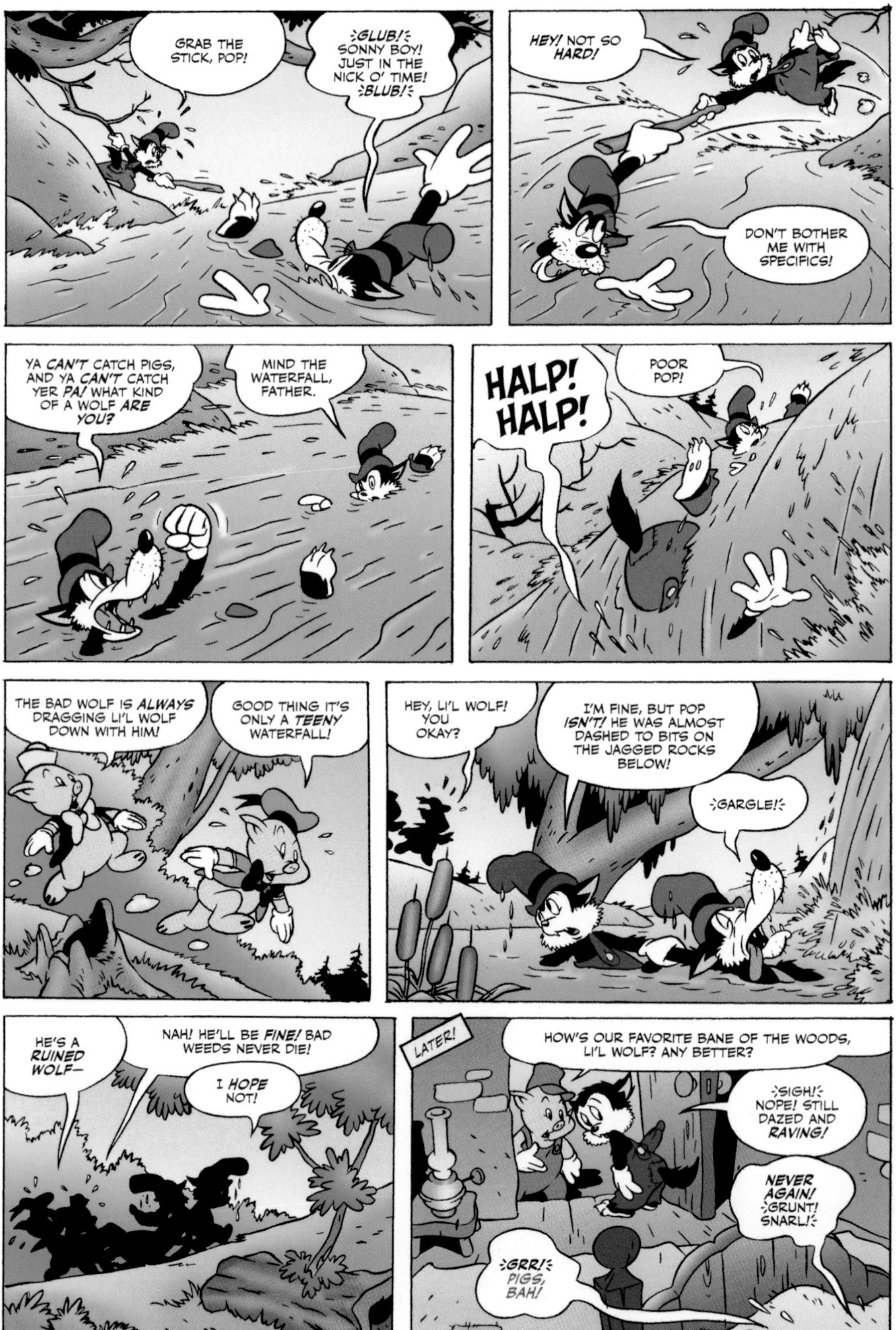
GRAB THE STICK, POP!
¡GLUB!¡ SONNY BOY! JUST IN THE NICK O' TIME! ¡BLUB!¡
HEY! NOT SO HARD!
DON'T BOTHER ME WITH SPECIFICS!
YA CAN'T CATCH PIGS, AND YA CAN'T CATCH YER PA! WHAT KIND OF A WOLF ARE YOU?
MIND THE WATERFALL, FATHER.
HALP! HALP!
POOR POP!
THE BAD WOLF IS ALWAYS DRAGGING LI'L WOLF DOWN WITH HIM!
GOOD THING IT'S ONLY A TEENY WATERFALL!
HEY, LI'L WOLF! YOU OKAY?
I'M FINE, BUT POP ISN'T! HE WAS ALMOST DASHED TO BITS ON THE JAGGED ROCKS BELOW!
¡GARGLE!¡
HE'S A RUINED WOLF—
NAH! HE'LL BE FINE! BAD WEEDS NEVER DIE!
I HOPE NOT!
LATER!
HOW'S OUR FAVORITE BANE OF THE WOODS, LI'L WOLF? ANY BETTER?
¡SIGH!¡ NOPE! STILL DAZED AND RAVING!
NEVER AGAIN! ¡GRUNT! SNARL!¡
¡GRR!¡ PIGS, BAH!

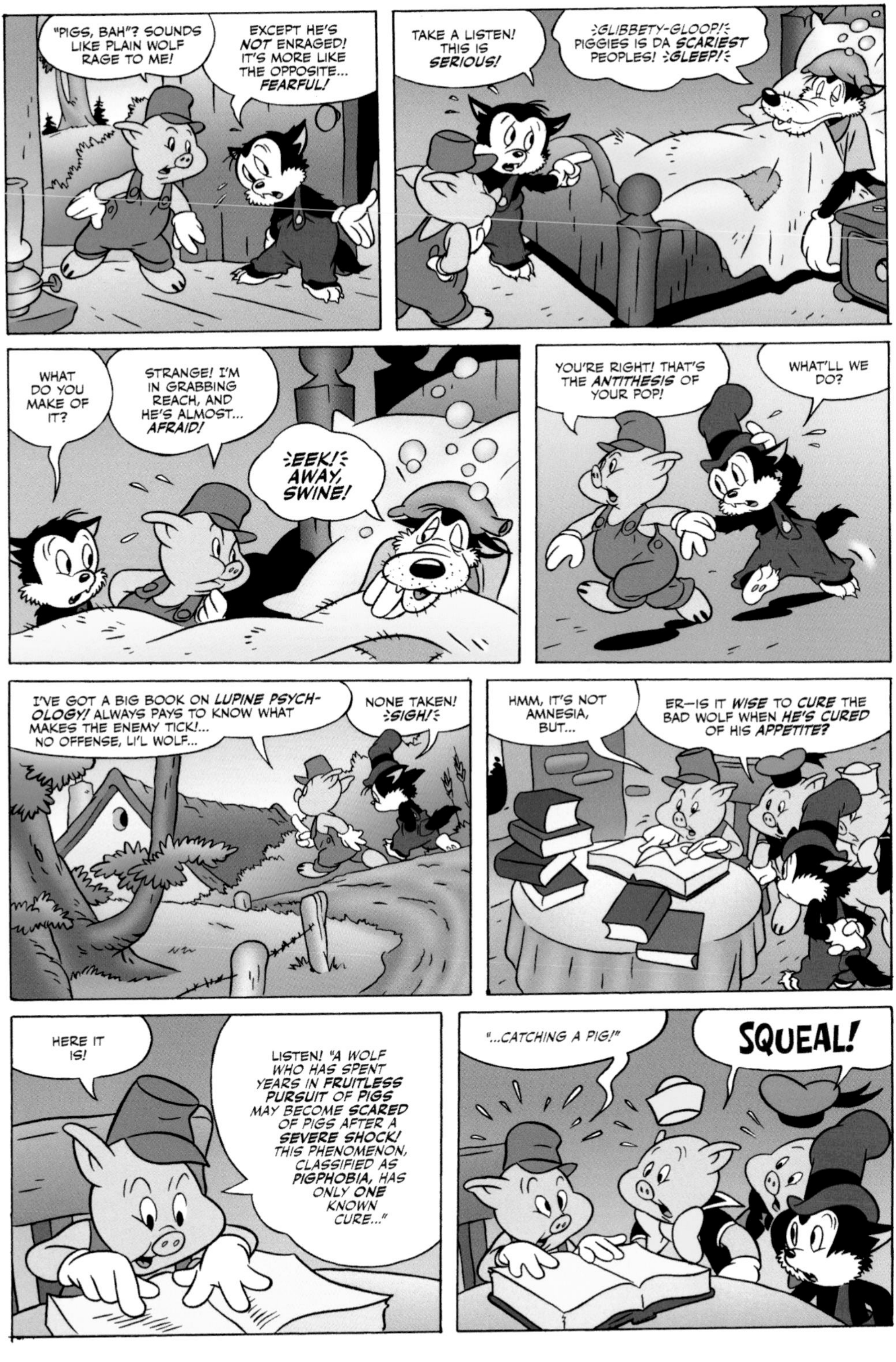
"PIGS, BAH"? SOUNDS LIKE PLAIN WOLF RAGE TO ME!
EXCEPT HE'S NOT ENRAGED! IT'S MORE LIKE THE OPPOSITE... FEARFUL!
TAKE A LISTEN! THIS IS SERIOUS!
GLIBBETY-GLOOP! PIGGIES IS DA SCARIEST PEOPLES! GLEEP!
WHAT DO YOU MAKE OF IT?
STRANGE! I'M IN GRABBING REACH, AND HE'S ALMOST... AFRAID!
EEK! AWAY, SWINE!
YOU'RE RIGHT! THAT'S THE ANTITHESIS OF YOUR POP!
WHAT'LL WE DO?
I'VE GOT A BIG BOOK ON LUPINE PSYCHOLOGY! ALWAYS PAYS TO KNOW WHAT MAKES THE ENEMY TICK!... NO OFFENSE, LI'L WOLF...
NONE TAKEN! SIGH!
HMM, IT'S NOT AMNESIA, BUT...
ER—IS IT WISE TO CURE THE BAD WOLF WHEN HE'S CURED OF HIS APPETITE?
HERE IT IS!
LISTEN! "A WOLF WHO HAS SPENT YEARS IN FRUITLESS PURSUIT OF PIGS MAY BECOME SCARED OF PIGS AFTER A SEVERE SHOCK! THIS PHENOMENON, CLASSIFIED AS PIGPHOBIA, HAS ONLY ONE KNOWN CURE..."
"...CATCHING A PIG!"
SQUEAL!

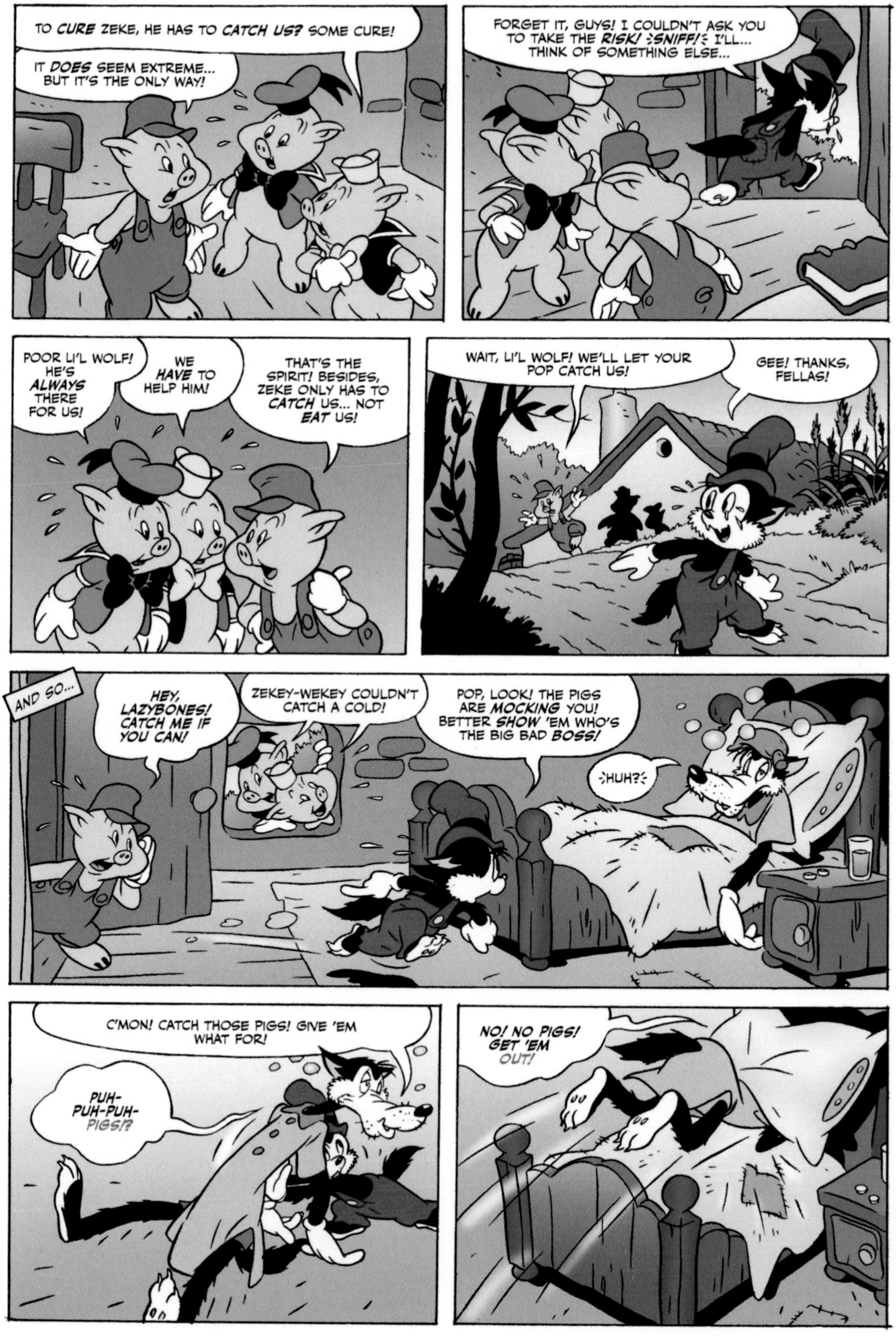
TO CURE ZEKE, HE HAS TO CATCH US? SOME CURE!
IT DOES SEEM EXTREME... BUT IT'S THE ONLY WAY!
FORGET IT, GUYS! I COULDN'T ASK YOU TO TAKE THE RISK! SNIFF! I'LL... THINK OF SOMETHING ELSE...
POOR LI'L WOLF! HE'S ALWAYS THERE FOR US!
WE HAVE TO HELP HIM!
THAT'S THE SPIRIT! BESIDES, ZEKE ONLY HAS TO CATCH US... NOT EAT US!
WAIT, LI'L WOLF! WE'LL LET YOUR POP CATCH US!
GEE! THANKS, FELLAS!
AND SO...
HEY, LAZYBONES! CATCH ME IF YOU CAN!
ZEKEY-WEKEY COULDN'T CATCH A COLD!
POP, LOOK! THE PIGS ARE MOCKING YOU! BETTER SHOW 'EM WHO'S THE BIG BAD BOSS!
HUH?
C'MON! CATCH THOSE PIGS! GIVE 'EM WHAT FOR!
PUH-PUH-PUH-PIGS!?
NO! NO PIGS! GET 'EM OUT!

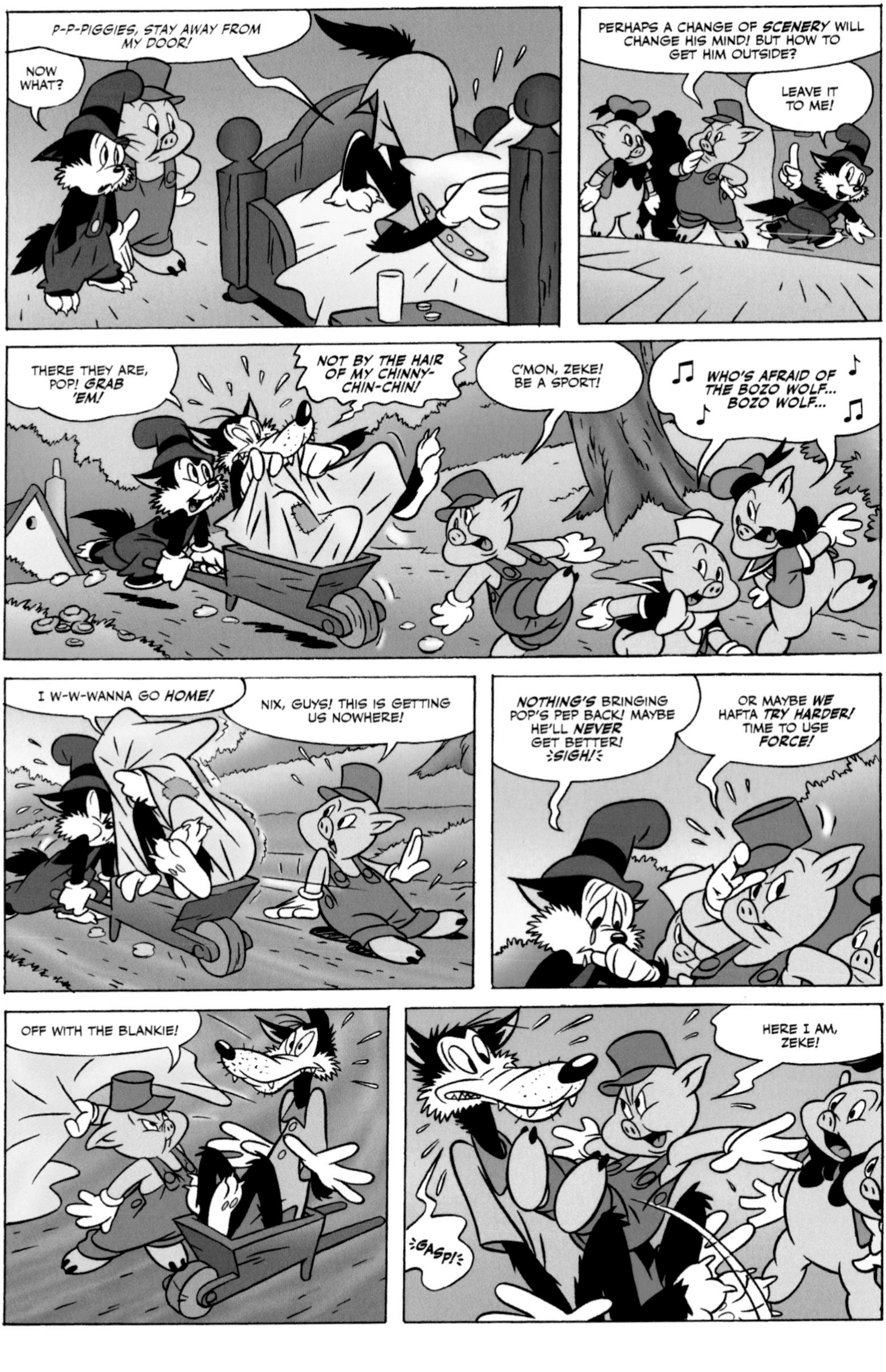

P-P-PIGGIES, STAY AWAY FROM MY DOOR!
NOW WHAT?
PERHAPS A CHANGE OF SCENERY WILL CHANGE HIS MIND! BUT HOW TO GET HIM OUTSIDE?
LEAVE IT TO ME!
THERE THEY ARE, POP! GRAB 'EM!
NOT BY THE HAIR OF MY CHINNY-CHIN-CHIN!
C'MON, ZEKE! BE A SPORT!
WHO'S AFRAID OF THE BOZO WOLF... BOZO WOLF...
I W-W-WANNA GO HOME!
NIX, GUYS! THIS IS GETTING US NOWHERE!
NOTHING'S BRINGING POP'S PEP BACK! MAYBE HE'LL NEVER GET BETTER! SIGH!
OR MAYBE WE HAFTA TRY HARDER! TIME TO USE FORCE!
OFF WITH THE BLANKIE!
HERE I AM, ZEKE!
GASP!

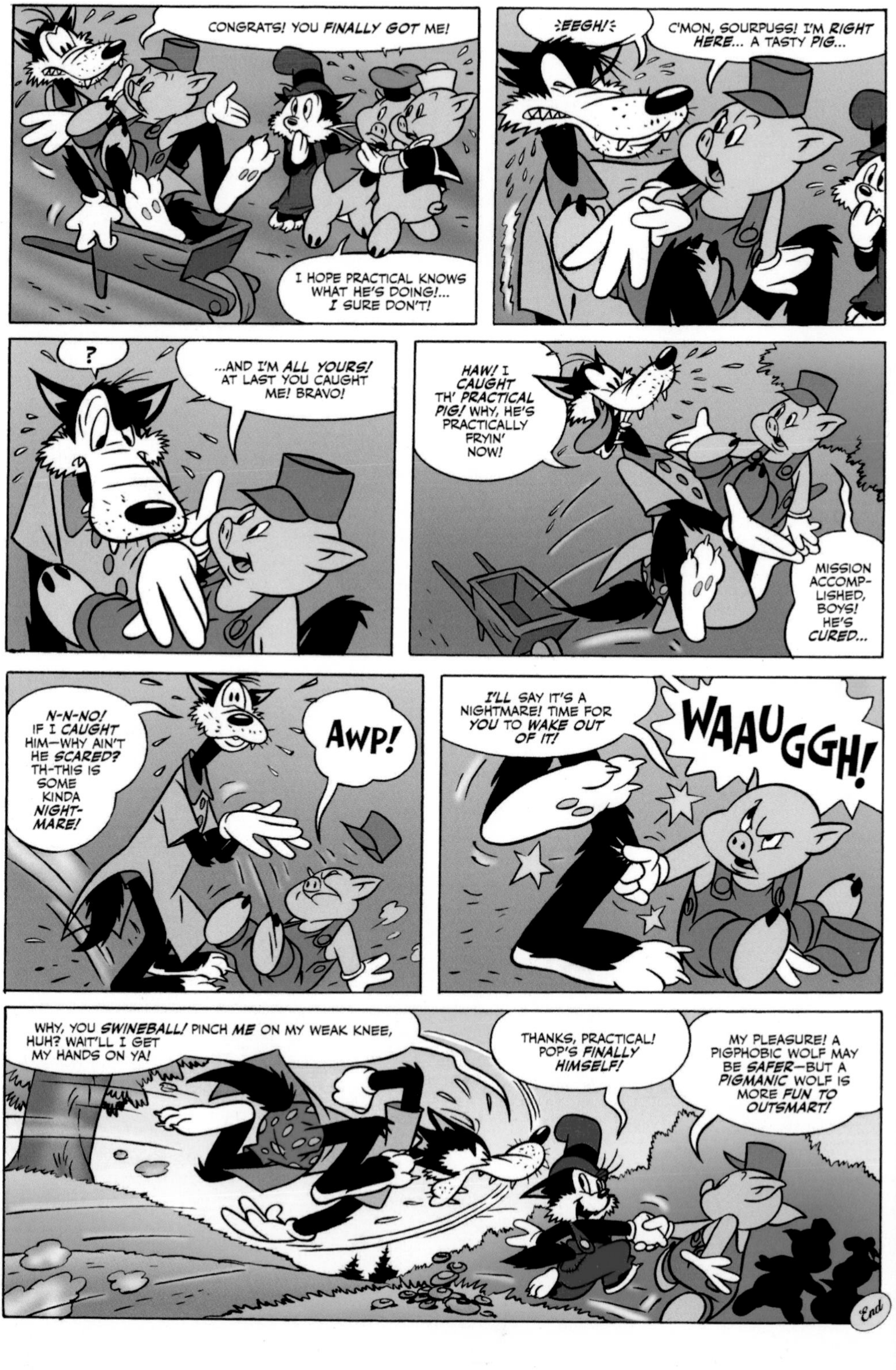
CONGRATS! YOU FINALLY GOT ME!
I HOPE PRACTICAL KNOWS WHAT HE'S DOING!... I SURE DON'T!
EEGH!
C'MON, SOURPUSS! I'M RIGHT HERE... A TASTY PIG...
?
...AND I'M ALL YOURS! AT LAST YOU CAUGHT ME! BRAVO!
HAW! I CAUGHT TH' PRACTICAL PIG! WHY, HE'S PRACTICALLY FRYIN' NOW!
MISSION ACCOMP- LISHED, BOYS! HE'S CURED...
N-N-NO! IF I CAUGHT HIM—WHY AIN'T HE SCARED? TH-THIS IS SOME KINDA NIGHT- MARE!
AWP!
I'LL SAY IT'S A NIGHTMARE! TIME FOR YOU TO WAKE OUT OF IT!
WAAUGGH!
WHY, YOU SWINEBALL! PINCH ME ON MY WEAK KNEE, HUH? WAIT'LL I GET MY HANDS ON YA!
THANKS, PRACTICAL! POP'S FINALLY HIMSELF!
MY PLEASURE! A PIGPHOBIC WOLF MAY BE SAFER—BUT A PIGMANIC WOLF IS MORE FUN TO OUTSMART!
End

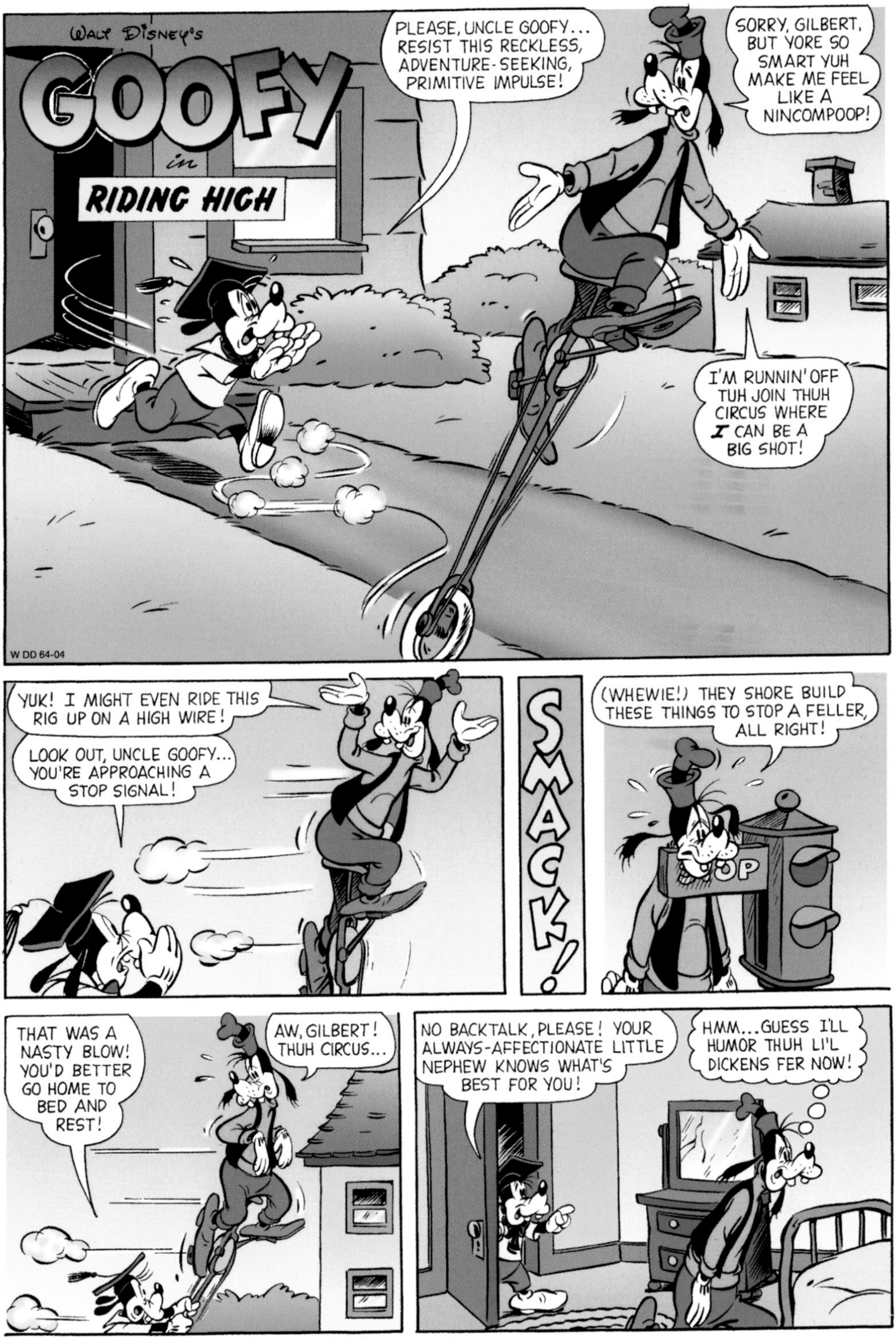
WALT DISNEY'S
GOOFY
in
RIDING HIGH
PLEASE, UNCLE GOOFY... RESIST THIS RECKLESS, ADVENTURE-SEEKING, PRIMITIVE IMPULSE!
SORRY, GILBERT, BUT YORE SO SMART YUH MAKE ME FEEL LIKE A NINCOMPOOP!
I'M RUNNIN' OFF TUH JOIN THUH CIRCUS WHERE I CAN BE A BIG SHOT!
W DD 64-04
YUK! I MIGHT EVEN RIDE THIS RIG UP ON A HIGH WIRE!
LOOK OUT, UNCLE GOOFY... YOU'RE APPROACHING A STOP SIGNAL!
SMACK!
(WHEWIE!) THEY SHORE BUILD THESE THINGS TO STOP A FELLER, ALL RIGHT!
OP
THAT WAS A NASTY BLOW! YOU'D BETTER GO HOME TO BED AND REST!
AW, GILBERT! THUH CIRCUS...
NO BACKTALK, PLEASE! YOUR ALWAYS-AFFECTIONATE LITTLE NEPHEW KNOWS WHAT'S BEST FOR YOU!
HMM...GUESS I'LL HUMOR THUH LI'L DICKENS FER NOW!

Originally published in *Donald Duck* #64 (USA, 1959)

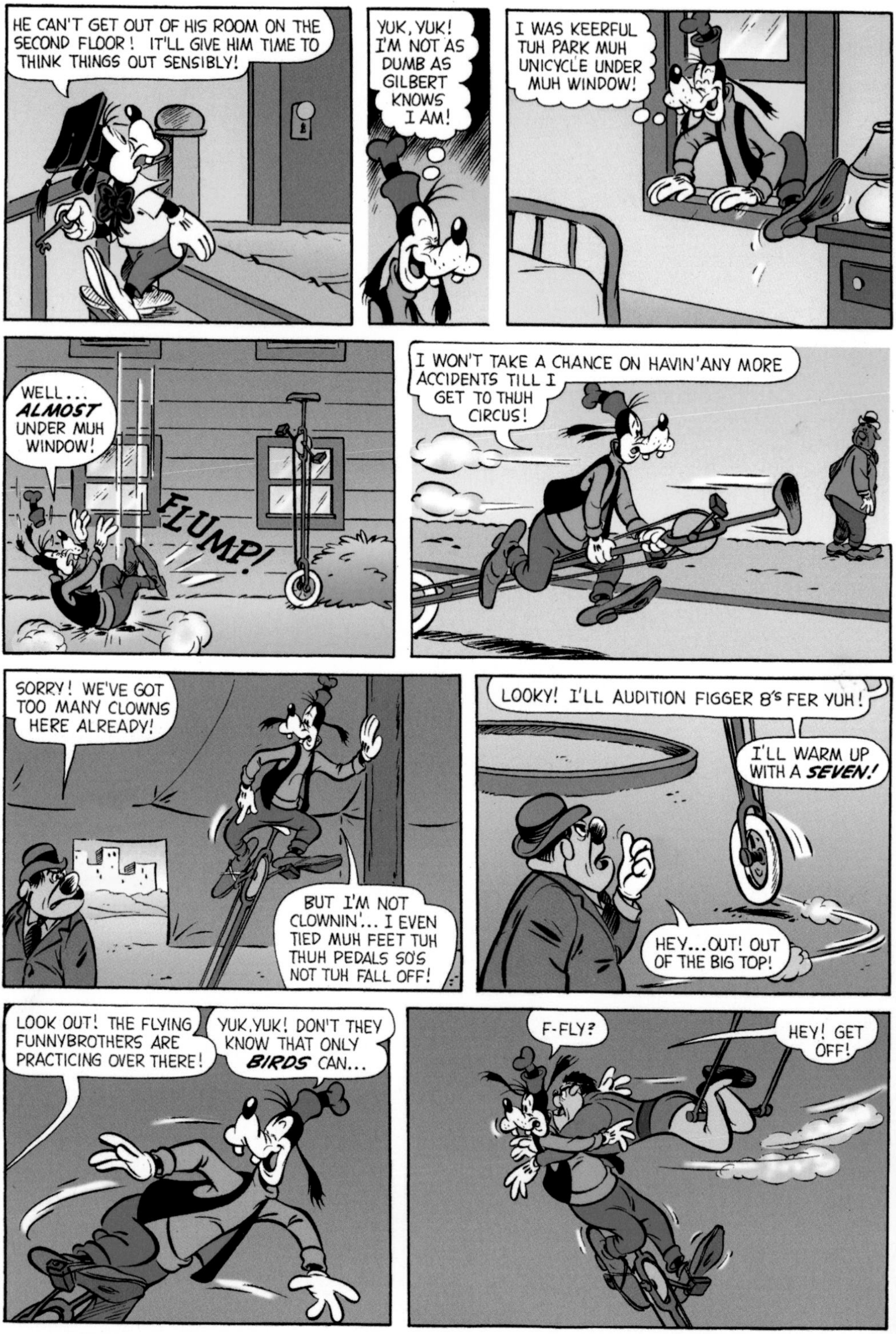
HE CAN'T GET OUT OF HIS ROOM ON THE SECOND FLOOR! IT'LL GIVE HIM TIME TO THINK THINGS OUT SENSIBLY!
YUK, YUK! I'M NOT AS DUMB AS GILBERT KNOWS I AM!
I WAS KEERFUL TUH PARK MUH UNICYCLE UNDER MUH WINDOW!
WELL... ALMOST UNDER MUH WINDOW!
FLUMP!
I WON'T TAKE A CHANCE ON HAVIN' ANY MORE ACCIDENTS TILL I GET TO THUH CIRCUS!
SORRY! WE'VE GOT TOO MANY CLOWNS HERE ALREADY!
BUT I'M NOT CLOWNIN'... I EVEN TIED MUH FEET TUH THUH PEDALS SO'S NOT TUH FALL OFF!
LOOKY! I'LL AUDITION FIGGER 8's FER YUH!
I'LL WARM UP WITH A SEVEN!
HEY...OUT! OUT OF THE BIG TOP!
LOOK OUT! THE FLYING FUNNYBROTHERS ARE PRACTICING OVER THERE!
YUK, YUK! DON'T THEY KNOW THAT ONLY BIRDS CAN...
F-FLY?
HEY! GET OFF!

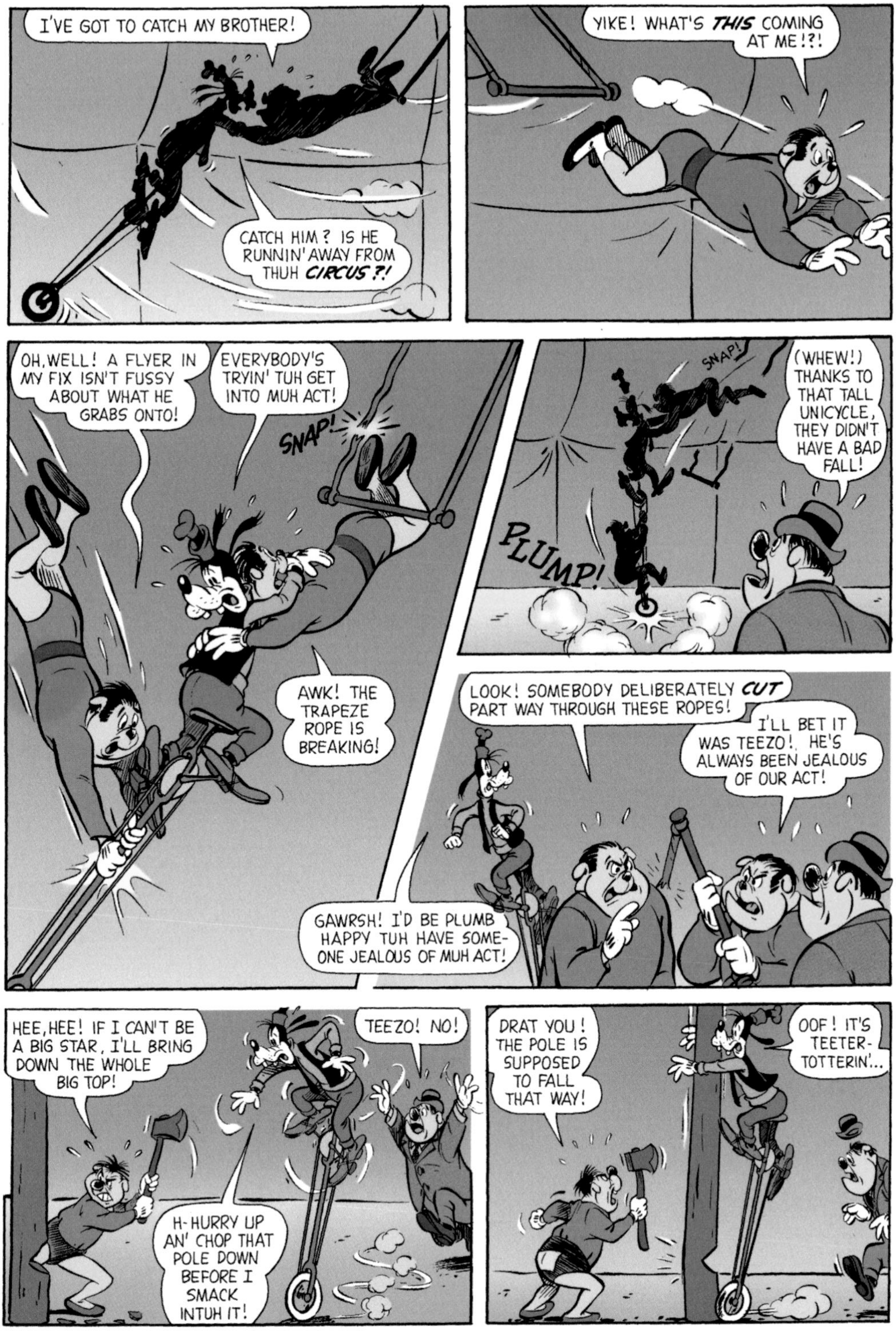
I'VE GOT TO CATCH MY BROTHER!
CATCH HIM? IS HE RUNNIN' AWAY FROM THUH CIRCUS?!
YIKE! WHAT'S THIS COMING AT ME!?!
OH, WELL! A FLYER IN MY FIX ISN'T FUSSY ABOUT WHAT HE GRABS ONTO!
EVERYBODY'S TRYIN' TUH GET INTO MUH ACT!
SNAP!
AWK! THE TRAPEZE ROPE IS BREAKING!
SNAP!
(WHEW!) THANKS TO THAT TALL UNICYCLE, THEY DIDN'T HAVE A BAD FALL!
PLUMP!
LOOK! SOMEBODY DELIBERATELY CUT PART WAY THROUGH THESE ROPES!
I'LL BET IT WAS TEEZO! HE'S ALWAYS BEEN JEALOUS OF OUR ACT!
GAWRSH! I'D BE PLUMB HAPPY TUH HAVE SOMEONE JEALOUS OF MUH ACT!
HEE, HEE! IF I CAN'T BE A BIG STAR, I'LL BRING DOWN THE WHOLE BIG TOP!
TEEZO! NO!
H-HURRY UP AN' CHOP THAT POLE DOWN BEFORE I SMACK INTUH IT!
DRAT YOU! THE POLE IS SUPPOSED TO FALL THAT WAY!
OOF! IT'S TEETER-TOTTERIN'...

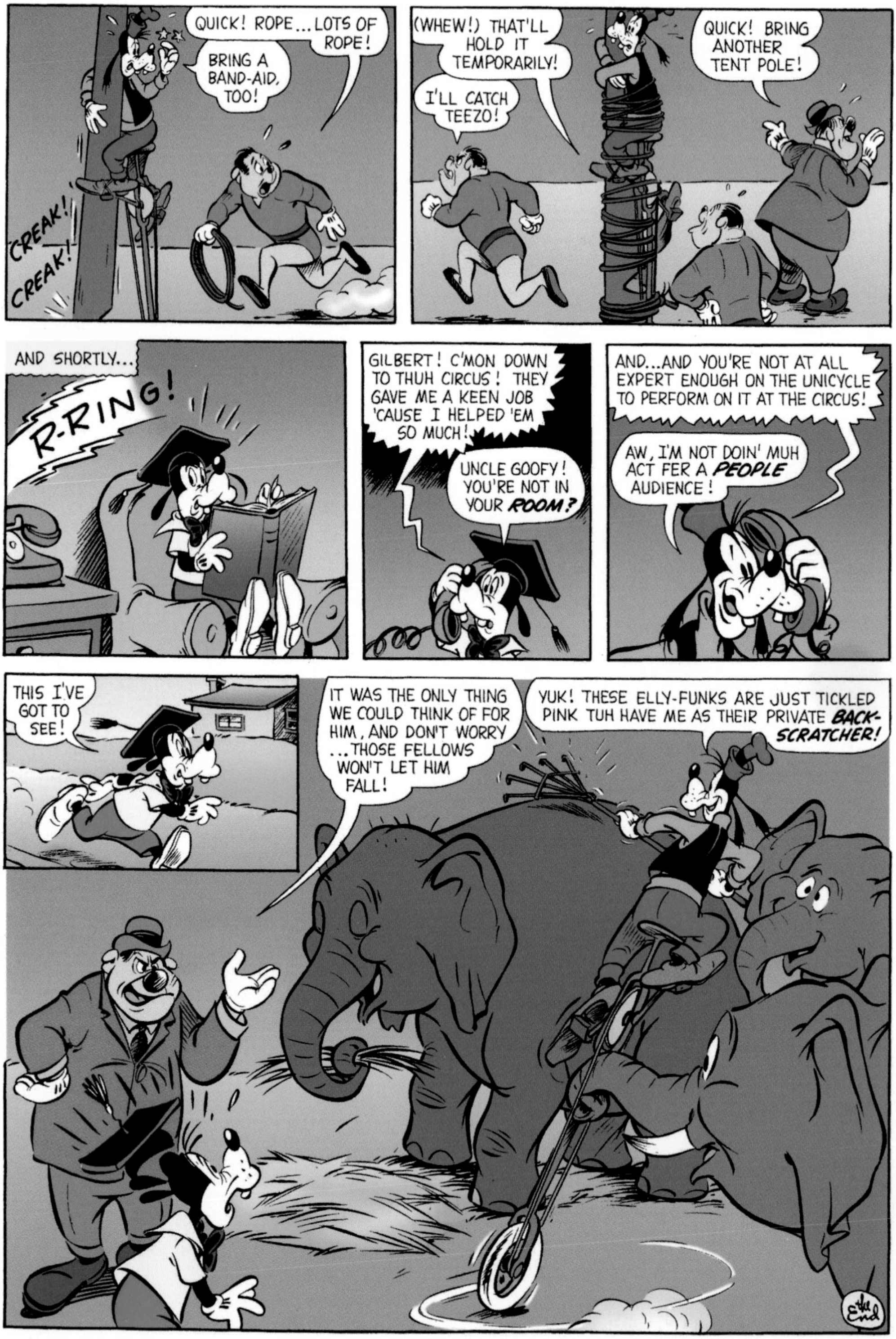

QUICK! ROPE... LOTS OF ROPE!
BRING A BAND-AID, TOO!
CREAK! CREAK!
(WHEW!) THAT'LL HOLD IT TEMPORARILY!
I'LL CATCH TEEZO!
QUICK! BRING ANOTHER TENT POLE!
AND SHORTLY...
R-RING!
GILBERT! C'MON DOWN TO THUH CIRCUS! THEY GAVE ME A KEEN JOB 'CAUSE I HELPED 'EM SO MUCH!
UNCLE GOOFY! YOU'RE NOT IN YOUR ROOM?
AND...AND YOU'RE NOT AT ALL EXPERT ENOUGH ON THE UNICYCLE TO PERFORM ON IT AT THE CIRCUS!
AW, I'M NOT DOIN' MUH ACT FER A PEOPLE AUDIENCE!
THIS I'VE GOT TO SEE!
IT WAS THE ONLY THING WE COULD THINK OF FOR HIM, AND DON'T WORRY ...THOSE FELLOWS WON'T LET HIM FALL!
YUK! THESE ELLY-FUNKS ARE JUST TICKLED PINK TUH HAVE ME AS THEIR PRIVATE BACK-SCRATCHER!
The End

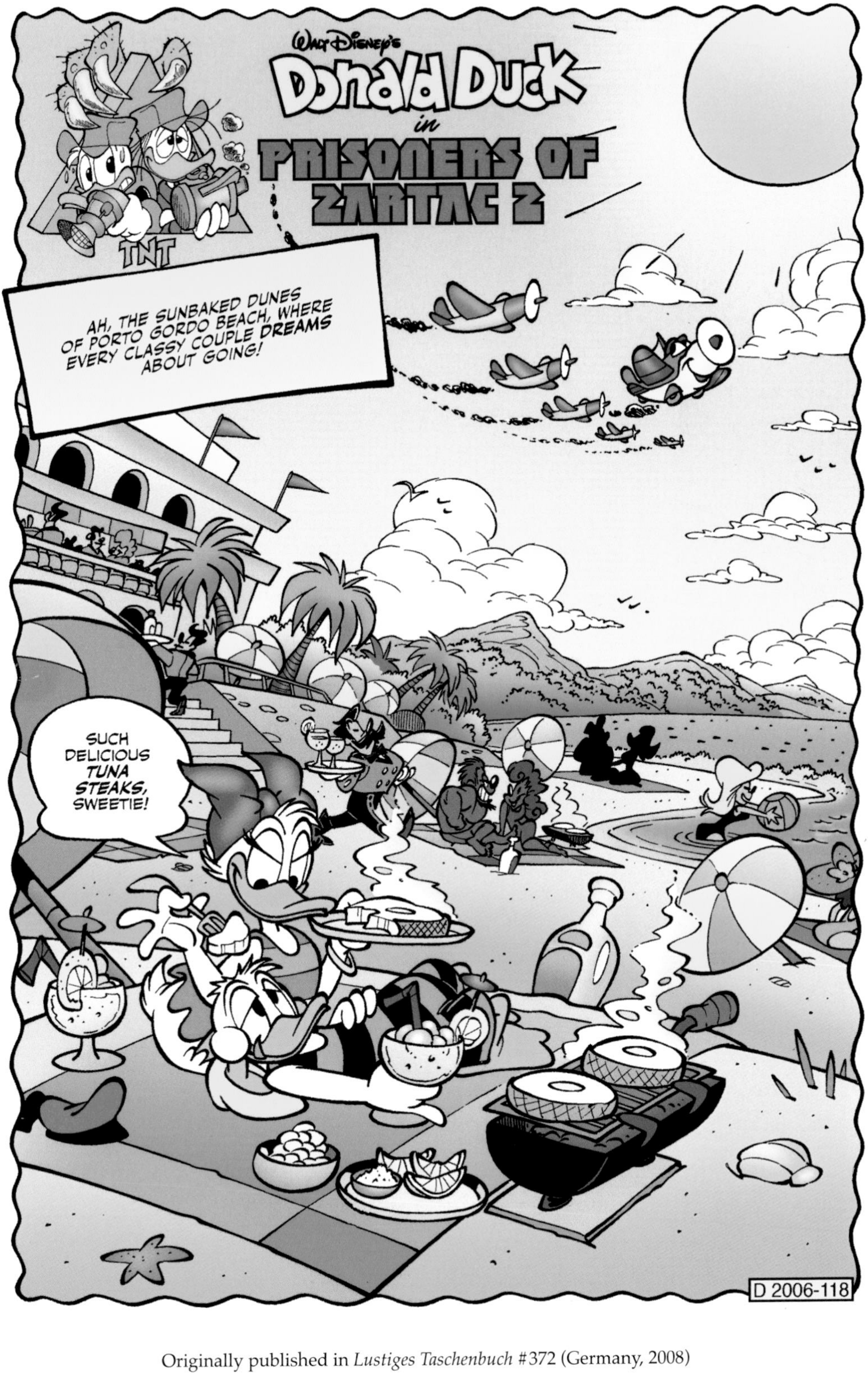
WALT DISNEY'S
Donald Duck
in
PRISONERS OF ZARTAC 2
TNT
AH, THE SUNBAKED DUNES OF PORTO GORDO BEACH, WHERE EVERY CLASSY COUPLE DREAMS ABOUT GOING!
SUCH DELICIOUS TUNA STEAKS, SWEETIE!
D 2006-118

Originally published in *Lustiges Taschenbuch* #372 (Germany, 2008)

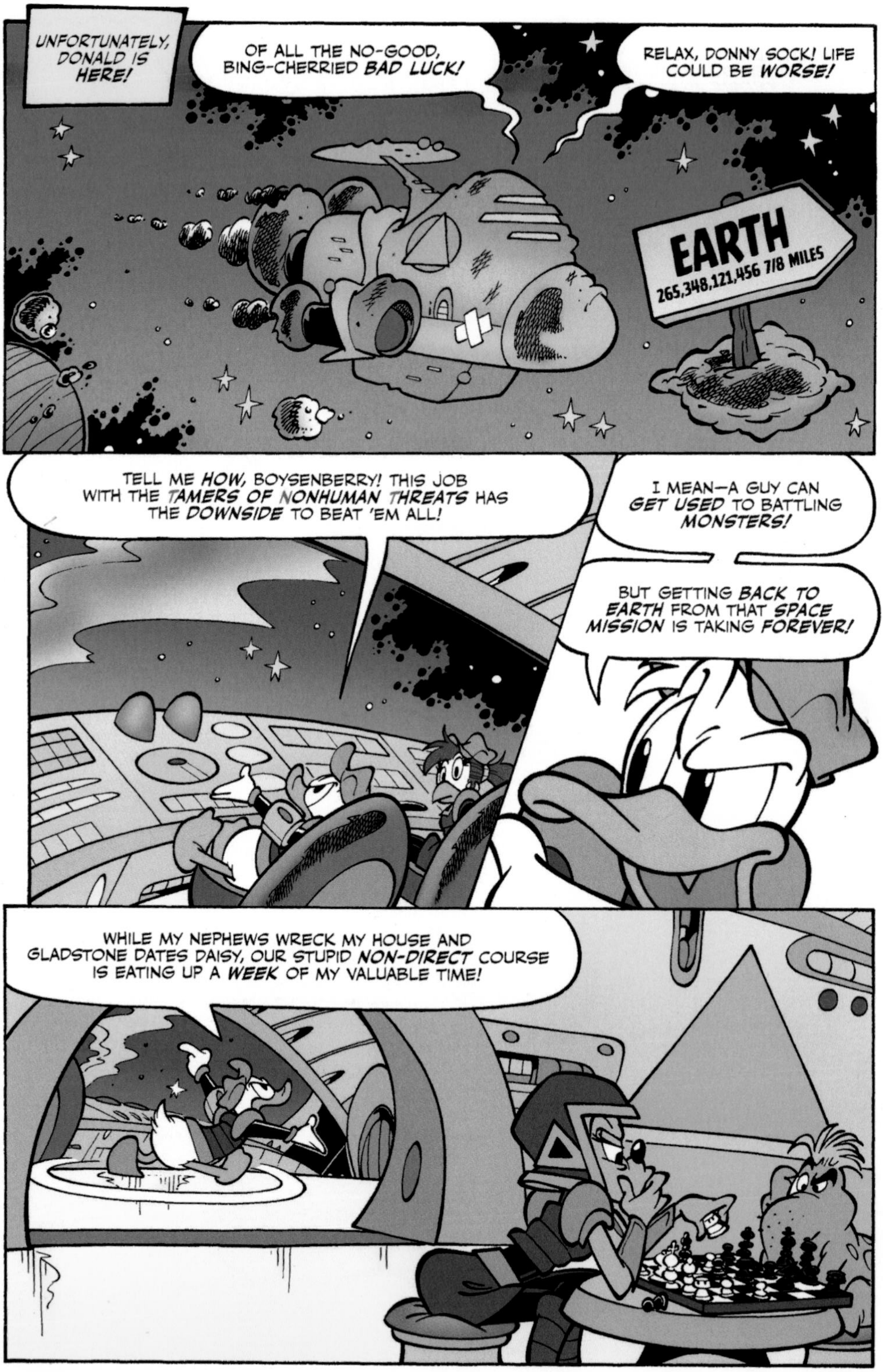
UNFORTUNATELY, DONALD IS HERE!
OF ALL THE NO-GOOD, BING-CHERRIED BAD LUCK!
RELAX, DONNY SOCK! LIFE COULD BE WORSE!
EARTH
265,348,121,456 7/8 MILES
TELL ME HOW, BOYSENBERRY! THIS JOB WITH THE TAMERS OF NONHUMAN THREATS HAS THE DOWNSIDE TO BEAT 'EM ALL!
I MEAN—A GUY CAN GET USED TO BATTLING MONSTERS!
BUT GETTING BACK TO EARTH FROM THAT SPACE MISSION IS TAKING FOREVER!
WHILE MY NEPHEWS WRECK MY HOUSE AND GLADSTONE DATES DAISY, OUR STUPID NON-DIRECT COURSE IS EATING UP A WEEK OF MY VALUABLE TIME!

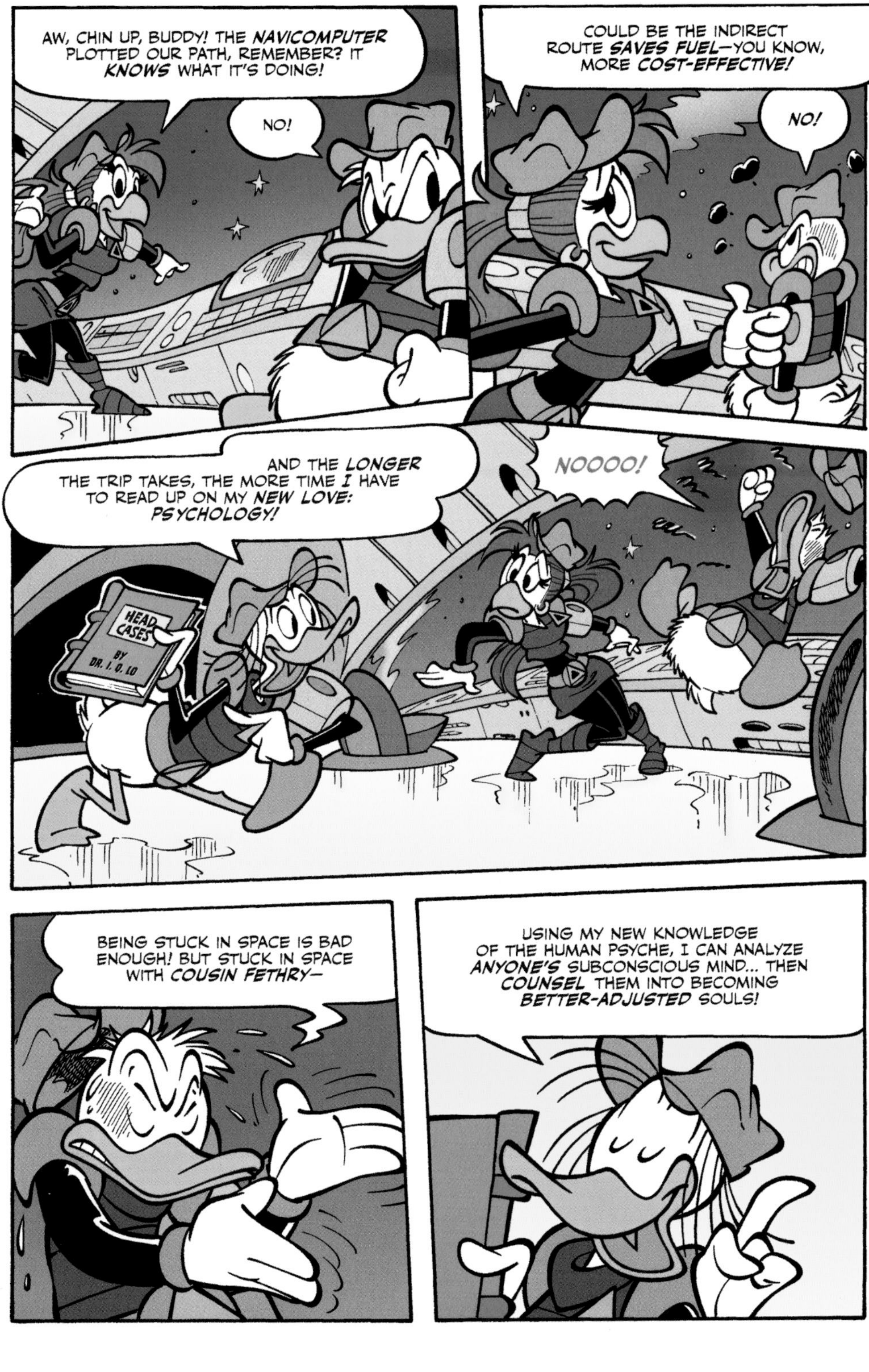
AW, CHIN UP, BUDDY! THE NAVICOMPUTER PLOTTED OUR PATH, REMEMBER? IT KNOWS WHAT IT'S DOING!
NO!
COULD BE THE INDIRECT ROUTE SAVES FUEL—YOU KNOW, MORE COST-EFFECTIVE!
NO!
AND THE LONGER THE TRIP TAKES, THE MORE TIME I HAVE TO READ UP ON MY NEW LOVE: PSYCHOLOGY!
HEAD CASES BY DR. I. O. LO
NOOOO!
BEING STUCK IN SPACE IS BAD ENOUGH! BUT STUCK IN SPACE WITH COUSIN FETHRY—
USING MY NEW KNOWLEDGE OF THE HUMAN PSYCHE, I CAN ANALYZE ANYONE'S SUBCONSCIOUS MIND... THEN COUNSEL THEM INTO BECOMING BETTER-ADJUSTED SOULS!

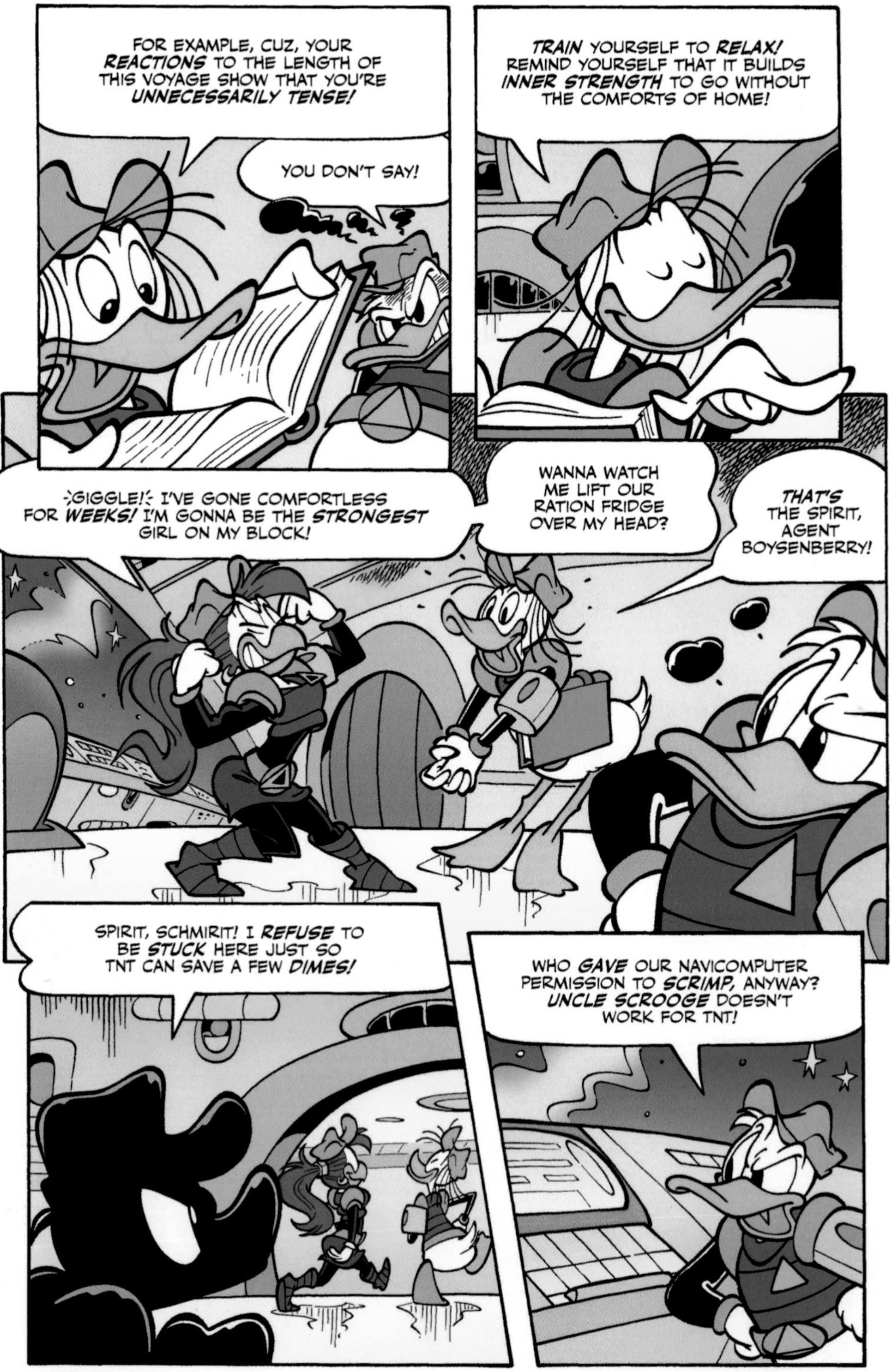
FOR EXAMPLE, CUZ, YOUR REACTIONS TO THE LENGTH OF THIS VOYAGE SHOW THAT YOU'RE UNNECESSARILY TENSE!
YOU DON'T SAY!
TRAIN YOURSELF TO RELAX! REMIND YOURSELF THAT IT BUILDS INNER STRENGTH TO GO WITHOUT THE COMFORTS OF HOME!
GIGGLE! I'VE GONE COMFORTLESS FOR WEEKS! I'M GONNA BE THE STRONGEST GIRL ON MY BLOCK!
WANNA WATCH ME LIFT OUR RATION FRIDGE OVER MY HEAD?
THAT'S THE SPIRIT, AGENT BOYSENBERRY!
SPIRIT, SCHMIRIT! I REFUSE TO BE STUCK HERE JUST SO TNT CAN SAVE A FEW DIMES!
WHO GAVE OUR NAVICOMPUTER PERMISSION TO SCRIMP, ANYWAY? UNCLE SCROOGE DOESN'T WORK FOR TNT!

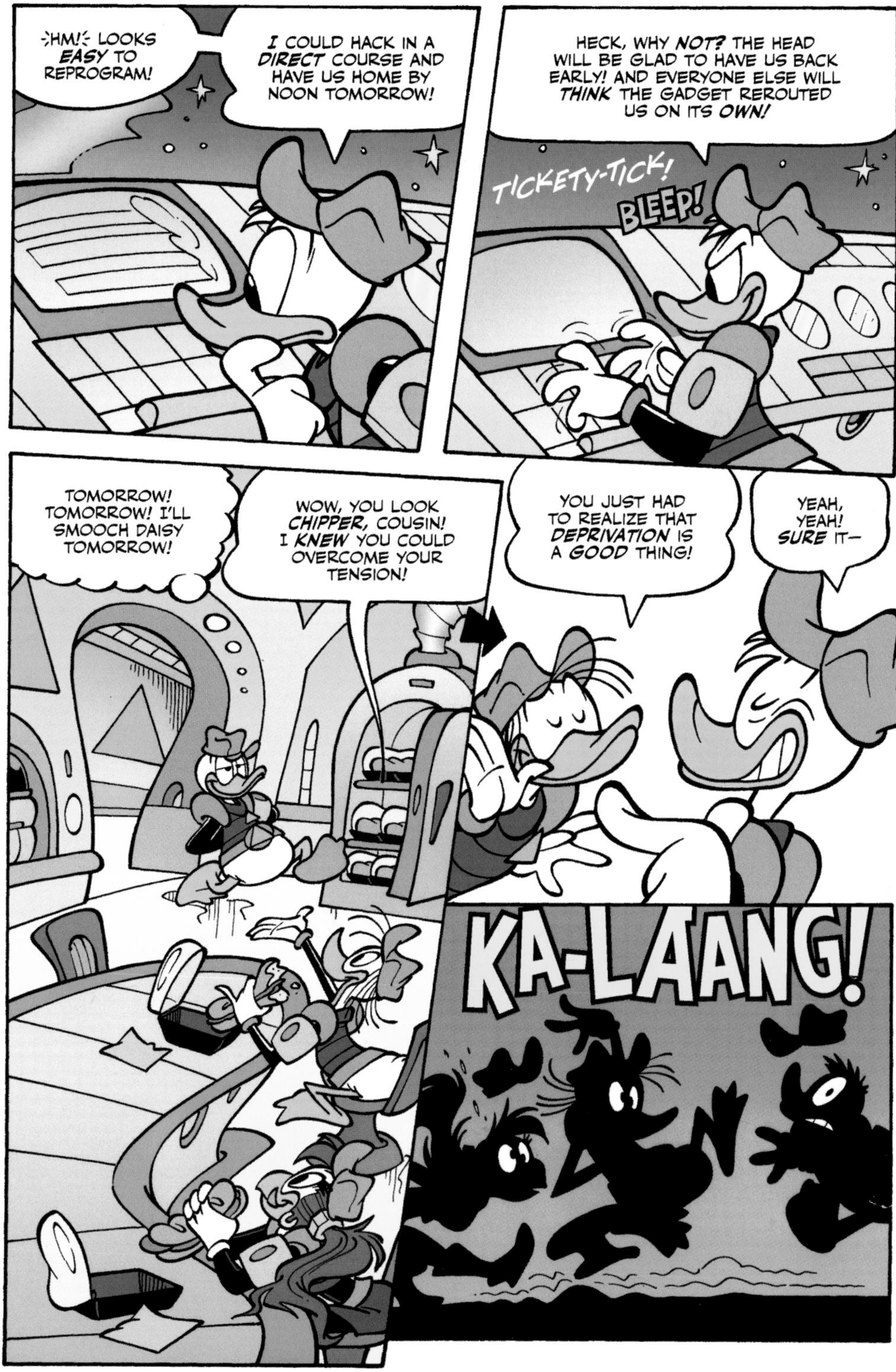

-HM!- LOOKS EASY TO REPROGRAM!
I COULD HACK IN A DIRECT COURSE AND HAVE US HOME BY NOON TOMORROW!
HECK, WHY NOT? THE HEAD WILL BE GLAD TO HAVE US BACK EARLY! AND EVERYONE ELSE WILL THINK THE GADGET REROUTED US ON ITS OWN!
TICKETY-TICK!
BLEEP!
TOMORROW! TOMORROW! I'LL SMOOCH DAISY TOMORROW!
WOW, YOU LOOK CHIPPER, COUSIN! I KNEW YOU COULD OVERCOME YOUR TENSION!
YOU JUST HAD TO REALIZE THAT DEPRIVATION IS A GOOD THING!
YEAH, YEAH! SURE IT—
KA-LAANG!

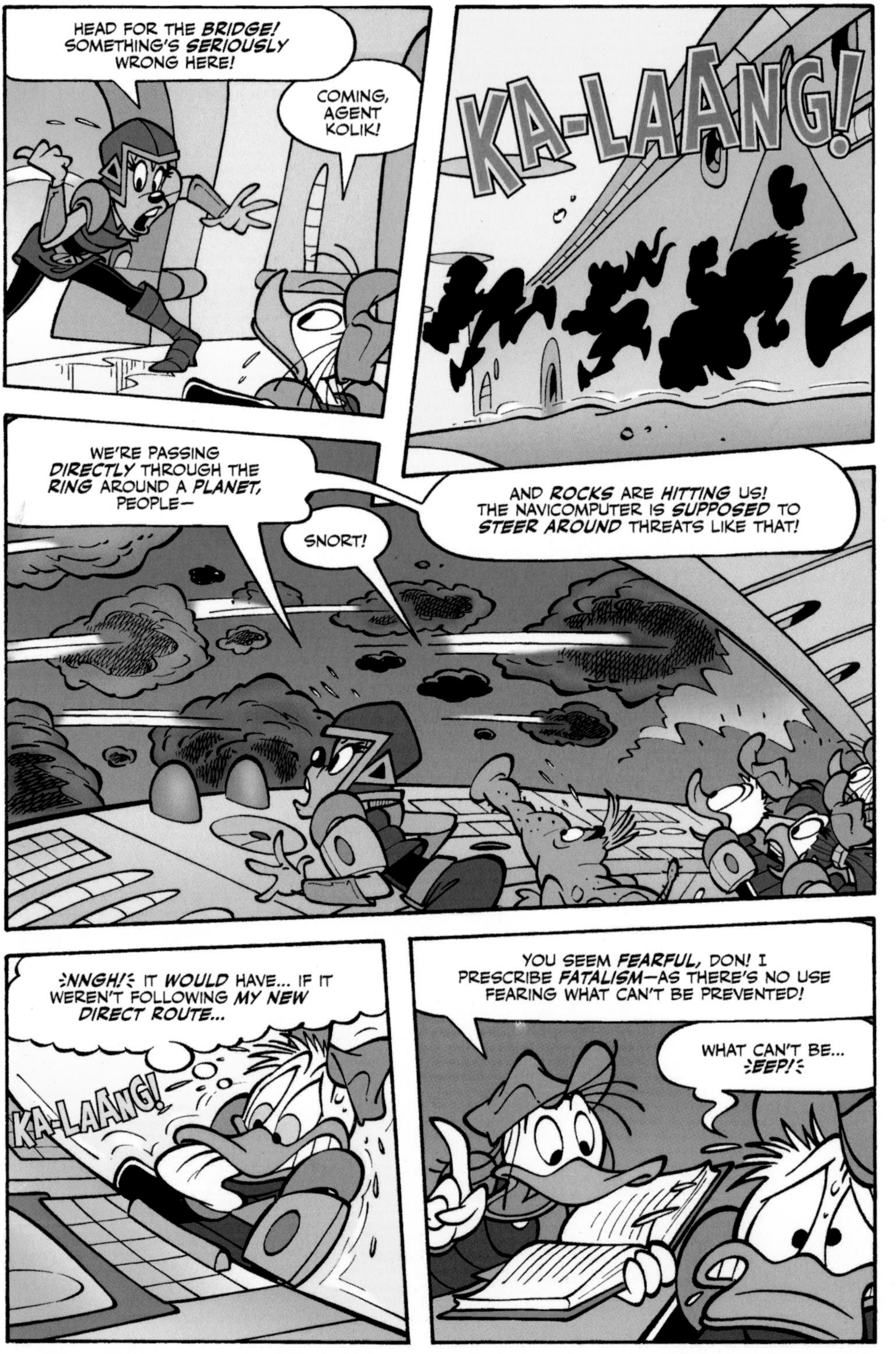
HEAD FOR THE BRIDGE! SOMETHING'S SERIOUSLY WRONG HERE!
COMING, AGENT KOLIK!
KA-LAANG!
WE'RE PASSING DIRECTLY THROUGH THE RING AROUND A PLANET, PEOPLE—
AND ROCKS ARE HITTING US! THE NAVICOMPUTER IS SUPPOSED TO STEER AROUND THREATS LIKE THAT!
SNORT!
NNGH! IT WOULD HAVE... IF IT WEREN'T FOLLOWING MY NEW DIRECT ROUTE...
KA-LAANG!
YOU SEEM FEARFUL, DON! I PRESCRIBE FATALISM—AS THERE'S NO USE FEARING WHAT CAN'T BE PREVENTED!
WHAT CAN'T BE... EEP!

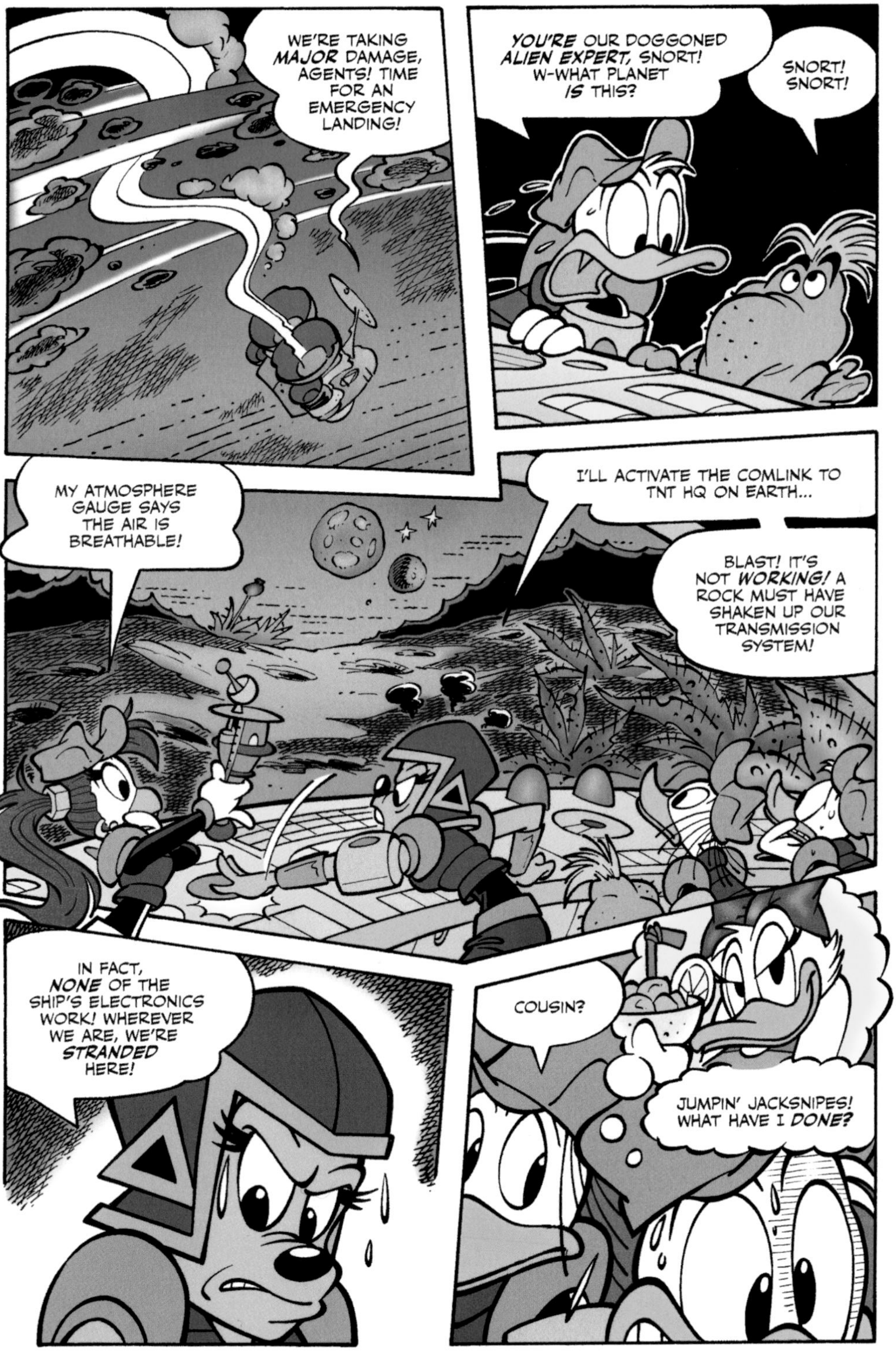
WE'RE TAKING MAJOR DAMAGE, AGENTS! TIME FOR AN EMERGENCY LANDING!
YOU'RE OUR DOGGONED ALIEN EXPERT, SNORT! W-WHAT PLANET IS THIS?
SNORT! SNORT!
MY ATMOSPHERE GAUGE SAYS THE AIR IS BREATHABLE!
I'LL ACTIVATE THE COMLINK TO TNT HQ ON EARTH...
BLAST! IT'S NOT WORKING! A ROCK MUST HAVE SHAKEN UP OUR TRANSMISSION SYSTEM!
IN FACT, NONE OF THE SHIP'S ELECTRONICS WORK! WHEREVER WE ARE, WE'RE STRANDED HERE!
COUSIN?
JUMPIN' JACKSNIPES! WHAT HAVE I DONE?

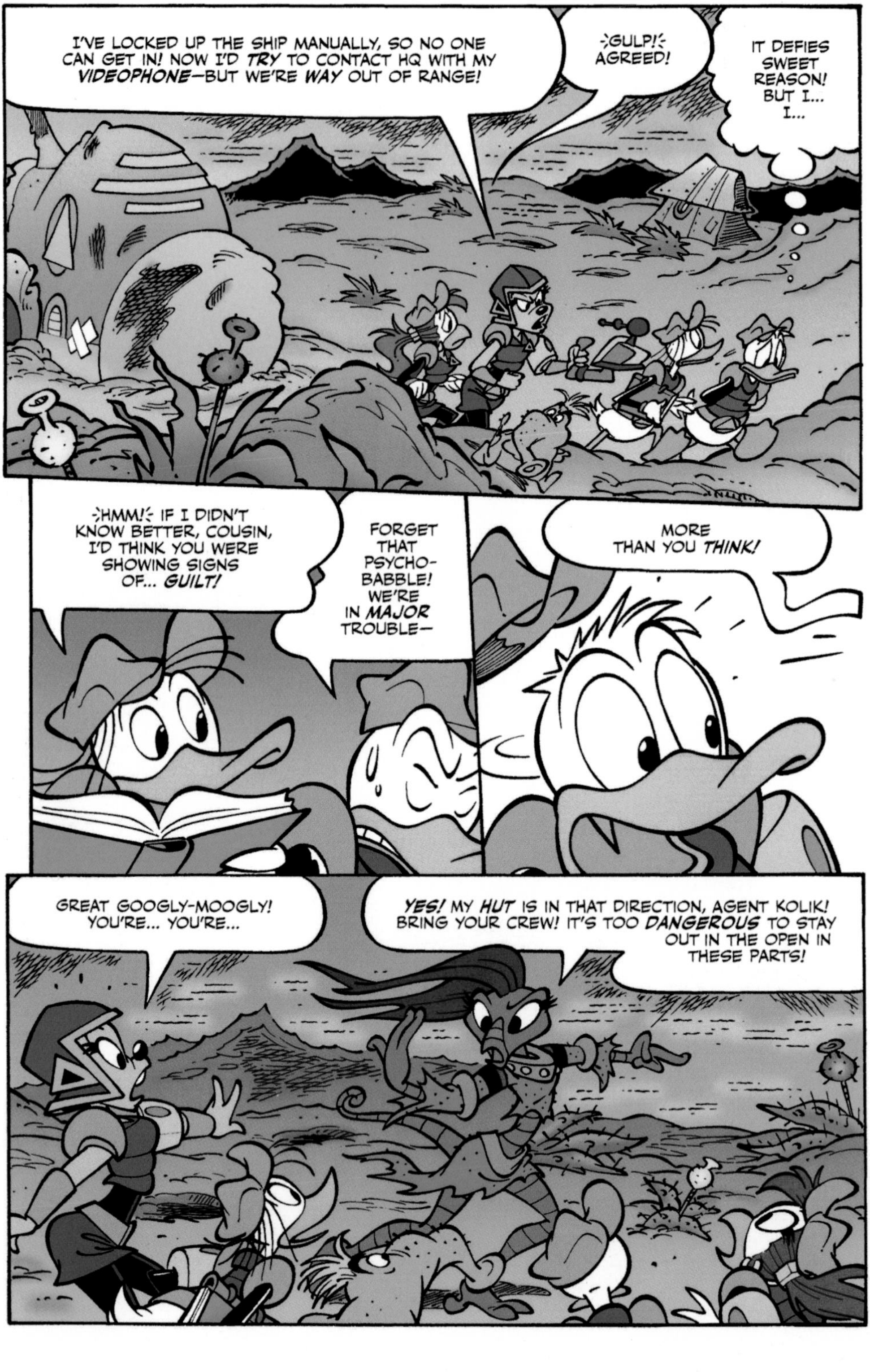
I'VE LOCKED UP THE SHIP MANUALLY, SO NO ONE CAN GET IN! NOW I'D TRY TO CONTACT HQ WITH MY VIDEOPHONE—BUT WE'RE WAY OUT OF RANGE!
-GULP!- AGREED!
IT DEFIES SWEET REASON! BUT I... I...
-HMM!- IF I DIDN'T KNOW BETTER, COUSIN, I'D THINK YOU WERE SHOWING SIGNS OF... GUILT!
FORGET THAT PSYCHO-BABBLE! WE'RE IN MAJOR TROUBLE—
MORE THAN YOU THINK!
GREAT GOOGLY-MOOGLY! YOU'RE... YOU'RE...
YES! MY HUT IS IN THAT DIRECTION, AGENT KOLIK! BRING YOUR CREW! IT'S TOO DANGEROUS TO STAY OUT IN THE OPEN IN THESE PARTS!

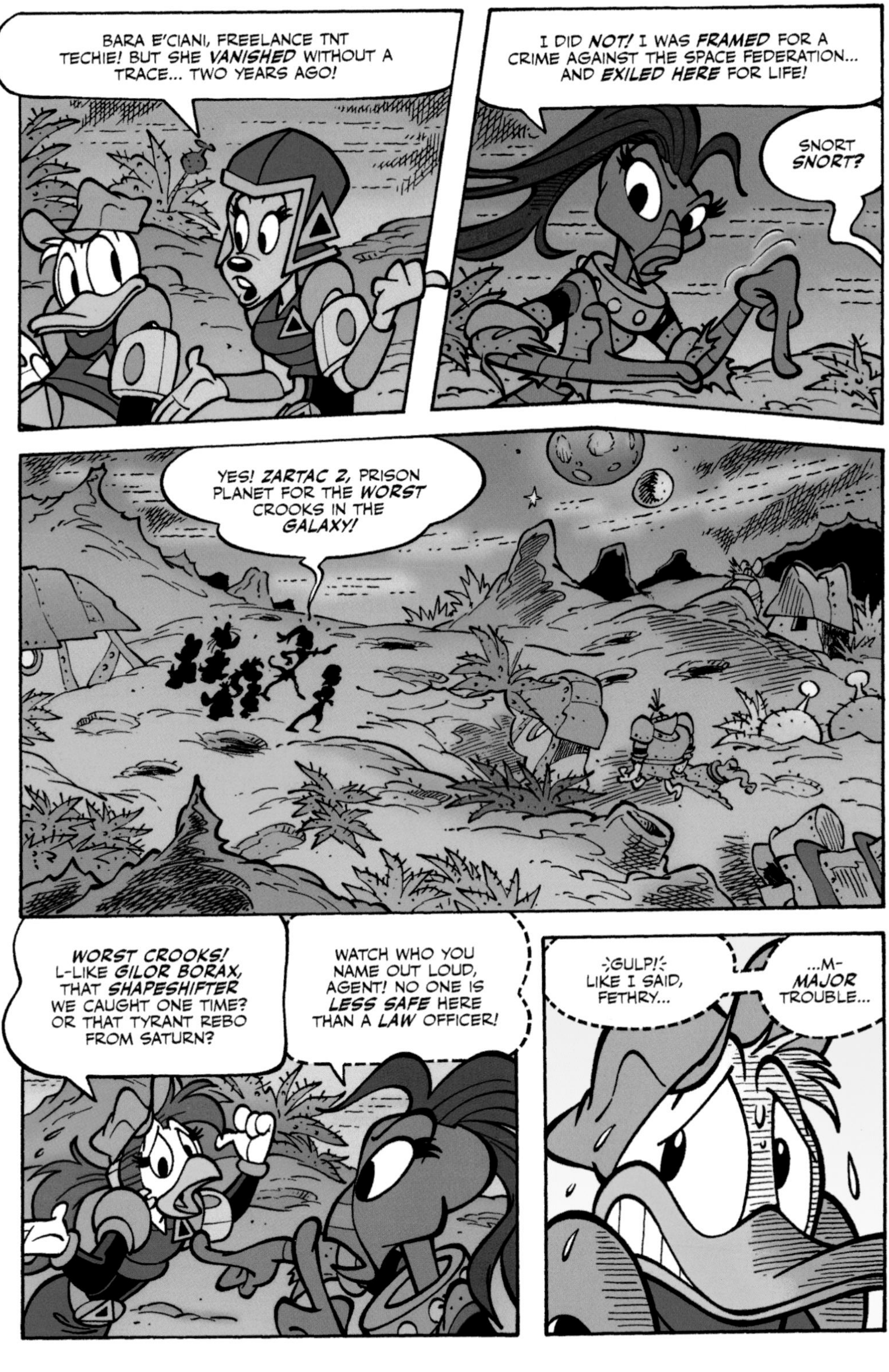
BARA E'CIANI, FREELANCE TNT TECHIE! BUT SHE VANISHED WITHOUT A TRACE... TWO YEARS AGO!
I DID NOT! I WAS FRAMED FOR A CRIME AGAINST THE SPACE FEDERATION... AND EXILED HERE FOR LIFE!
SNORT SNORT?
YES! ZARTAC 2, PRISON PLANET FOR THE WORST CROOKS IN THE GALAXY!
WORST CROOKS! L-LIKE GILOR BORAX, THAT SHAPESHIFTER WE CAUGHT ONE TIME? OR THAT TYRANT REBO FROM SATURN?
WATCH WHO YOU NAME OUT LOUD, AGENT! NO ONE IS LESS SAFE HERE THAN A LAW OFFICER!
-GULP!- LIKE I SAID, FETHRY...
...M-MAJOR TROUBLE...

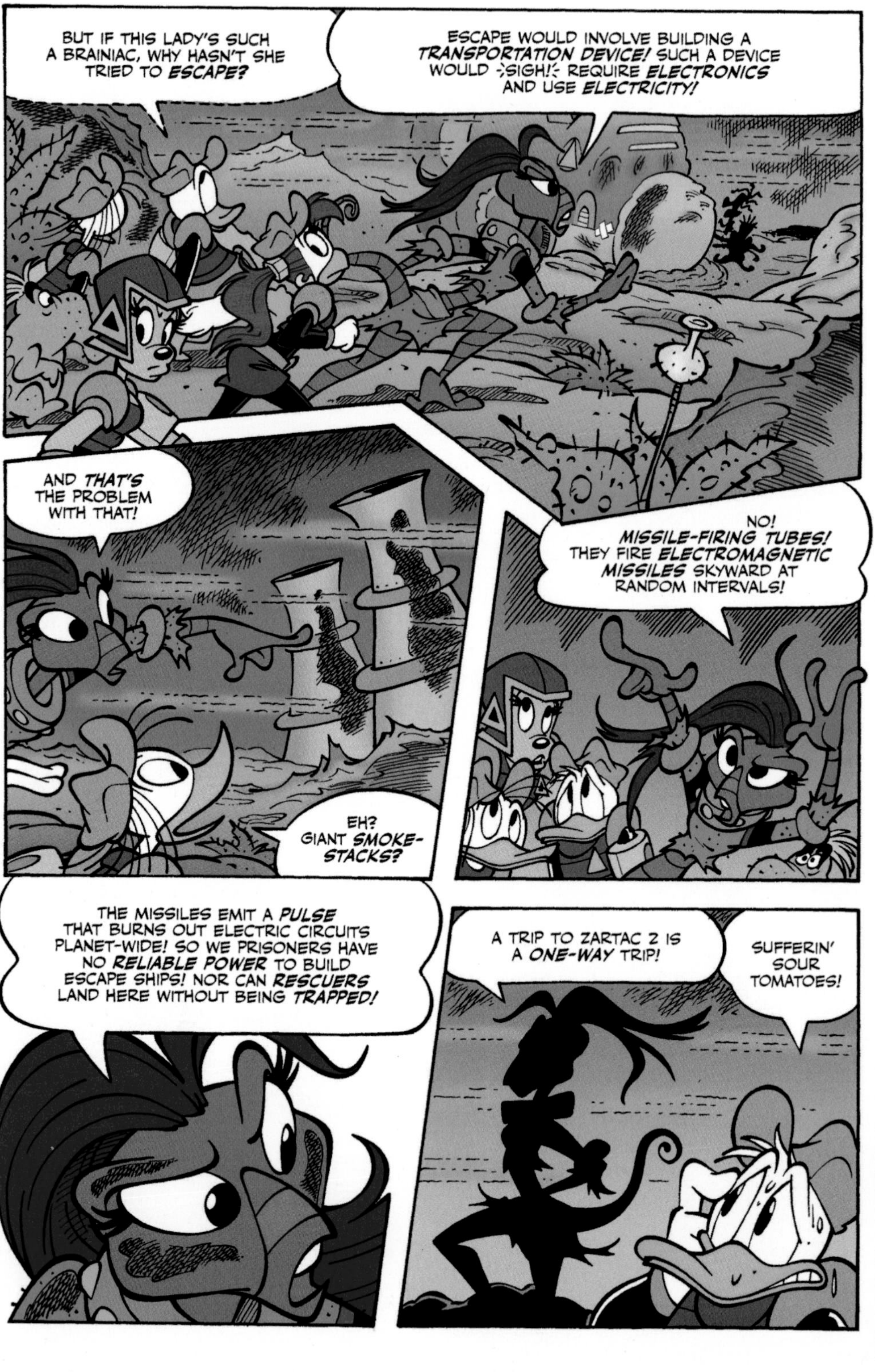
BUT IF THIS LADY'S SUCH A BRAINIAC, WHY HASN'T SHE TRIED TO ESCAPE?
ESCAPE WOULD INVOLVE BUILDING A TRANSPORTATION DEVICE! SUCH A DEVICE WOULD -SIGH!- REQUIRE ELECTRONICS AND USE ELECTRICITY!
AND THAT'S THE PROBLEM WITH THAT!
EH? GIANT SMOKE-STACKS?
NO! MISSILE-FIRING TUBES! THEY FIRE ELECTROMAGNETIC MISSILES SKYWARD AT RANDOM INTERVALS!
THE MISSILES EMIT A PULSE THAT BURNS OUT ELECTRIC CIRCUITS PLANET-WIDE! SO WE PRISONERS HAVE NO RELIABLE POWER TO BUILD ESCAPE SHIPS! NOR CAN RESCUERS LAND HERE WITHOUT BEING TRAPPED!
A TRIP TO ZARTAC 2 IS A ONE-WAY TRIP!
SUFFERIN' SOUR TOMATOES!

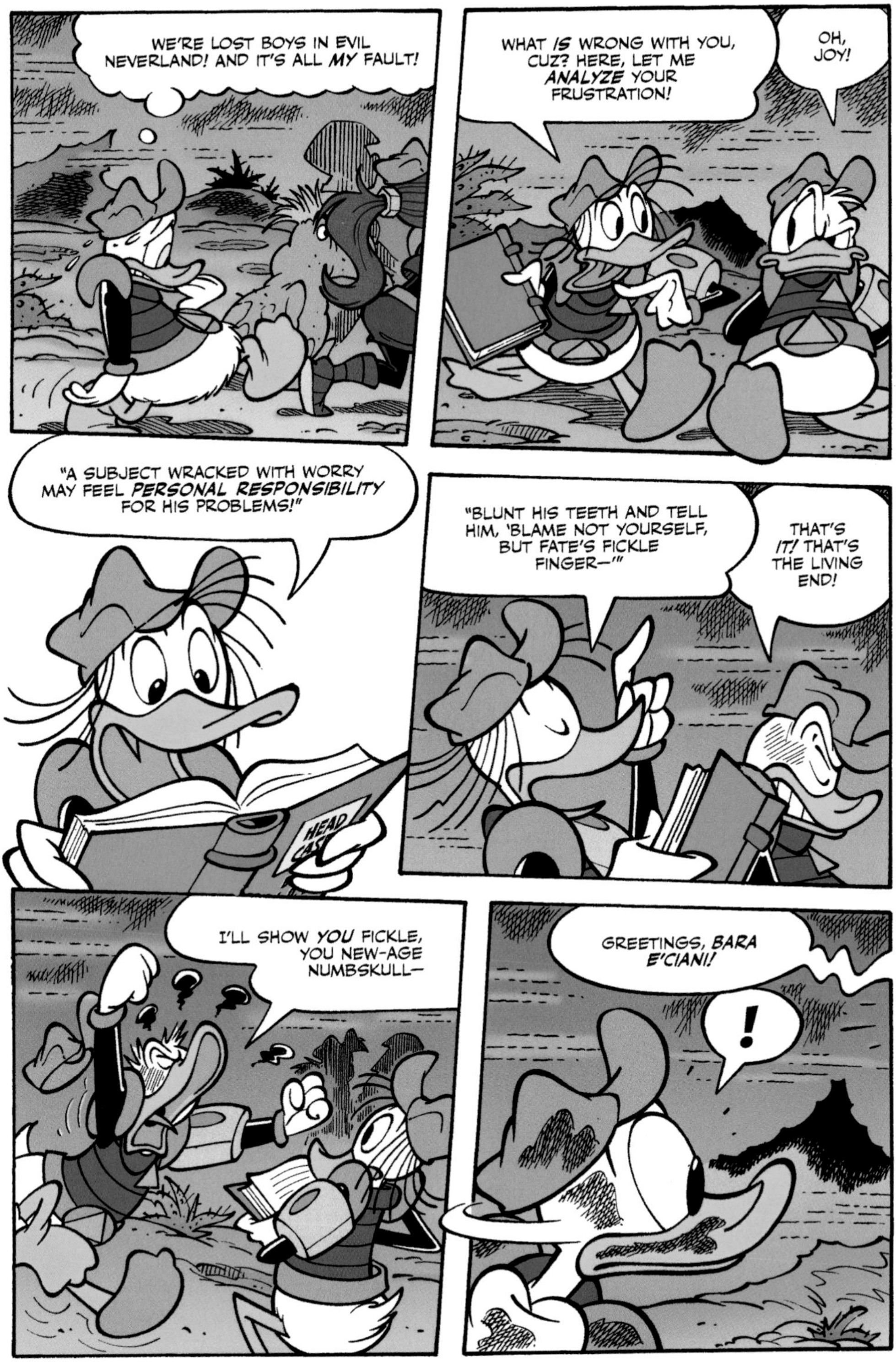
WE'RE LOST BOYS IN EVIL NEVERLAND! AND IT'S ALL MY FAULT!
WHAT IS WRONG WITH YOU, CUZ? HERE, LET ME ANALYZE YOUR FRUSTRATION!
OH, JOY!
"A SUBJECT WRACKED WITH WORRY MAY FEEL PERSONAL RESPONSIBILITY FOR HIS PROBLEMS!"
HEAD CASE
"BLUNT HIS TEETH AND TELL HIM, 'BLAME NOT YOURSELF, BUT FATE'S FICKLE FINGER—'"
THAT'S IT! THAT'S THE LIVING END!
I'LL SHOW YOU FICKLE, YOU NEW-AGE NUMBSKULL—
GREETINGS, BARA E'CIANI!
!

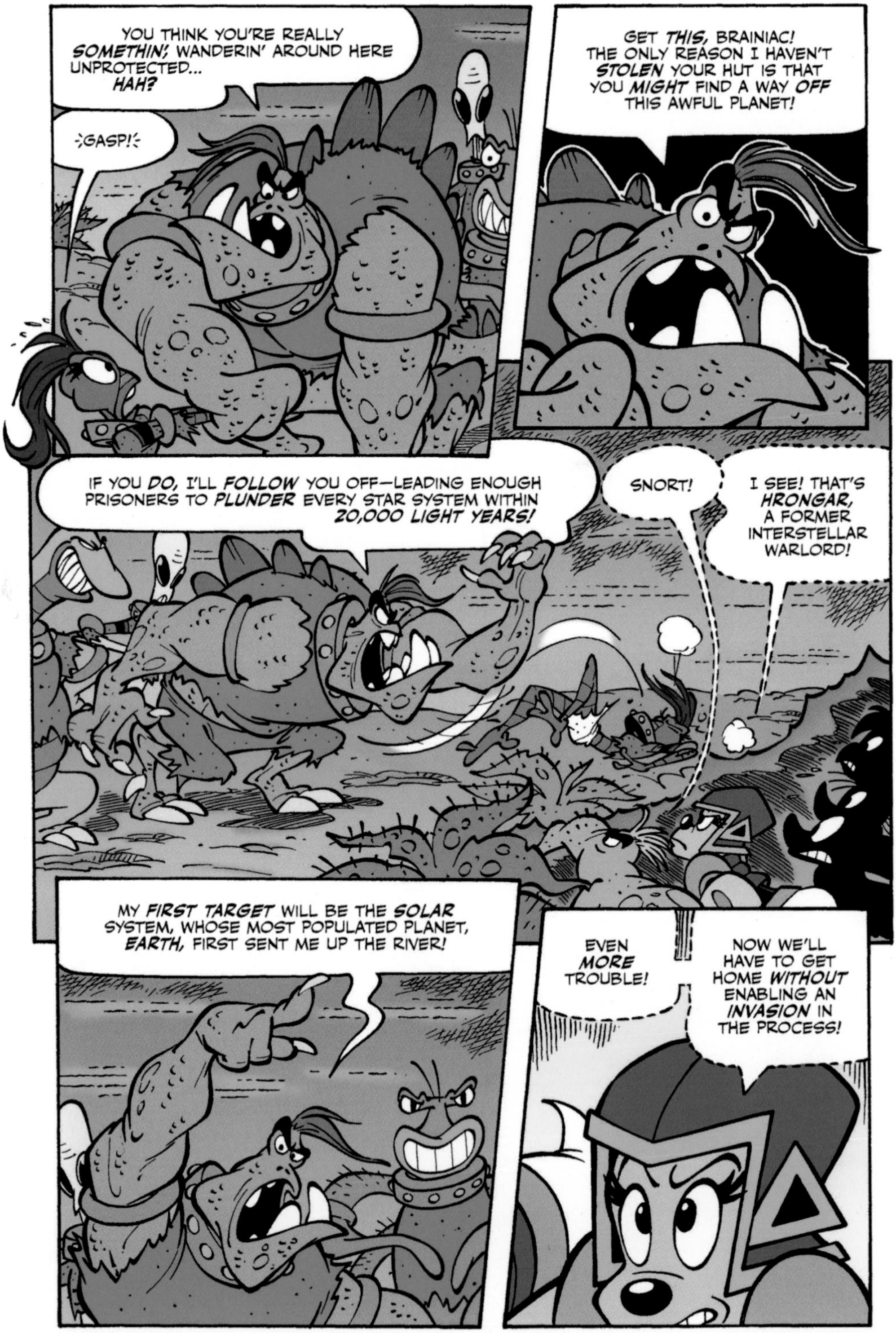
YOU THINK YOU'RE REALLY SOMETHIN', WANDERIN' AROUND HERE UNPROTECTED... HAH?
GASP!
GET THIS, BRAINIAC! THE ONLY REASON I HAVEN'T STOLEN YOUR HUT IS THAT YOU MIGHT FIND A WAY OFF THIS AWFUL PLANET!
IF YOU DO, I'LL FOLLOW YOU OFF—LEADING ENOUGH PRISONERS TO PLUNDER EVERY STAR SYSTEM WITHIN 20,000 LIGHT YEARS!
SNORT!
I SEE! THAT'S HRONGAR, A FORMER INTERSTELLAR WARLORD!
MY FIRST TARGET WILL BE THE SOLAR SYSTEM, WHOSE MOST POPULATED PLANET, EARTH, FIRST SENT ME UP THE RIVER!
EVEN MORE TROUBLE!
NOW WE'LL HAVE TO GET HOME WITHOUT ENABLING AN INVASION IN THE PROCESS!

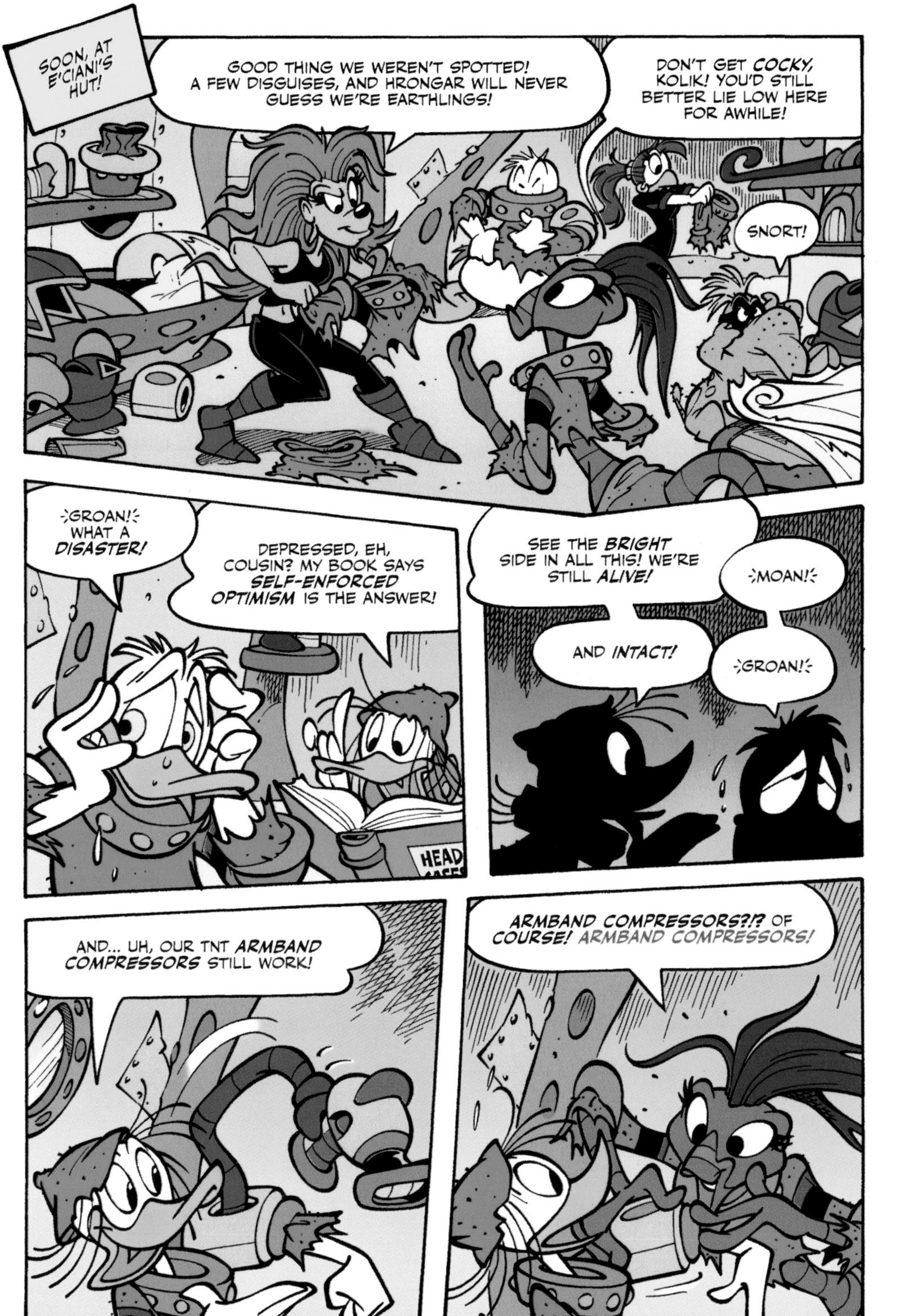
SOON, AT E'CIANI'S HUT!
GOOD THING WE WEREN'T SPOTTED! A FEW DISGUISES, AND HRONGAR WILL NEVER GUESS WE'RE EARTHLINGS!
DON'T GET COCKY, KOLIK! YOU'D STILL BETTER LIE LOW HERE FOR AWHILE!
SNORT!
GROAN! WHAT A DISASTER!
DEPRESSED, EH, COUSIN? MY BOOK SAYS SELF-ENFORCED OPTIMISM IS THE ANSWER!
HEAD
SEE THE BRIGHT SIDE IN ALL THIS! WE'RE STILL ALIVE!
MOAN!
AND INTACT!
GROAN!
AND... UH, OUR TNT ARMBAND COMPRESSORS STILL WORK!
ARMBAND COMPRESSORS?!? OF COURSE! ARMBAND COMPRESSORS!

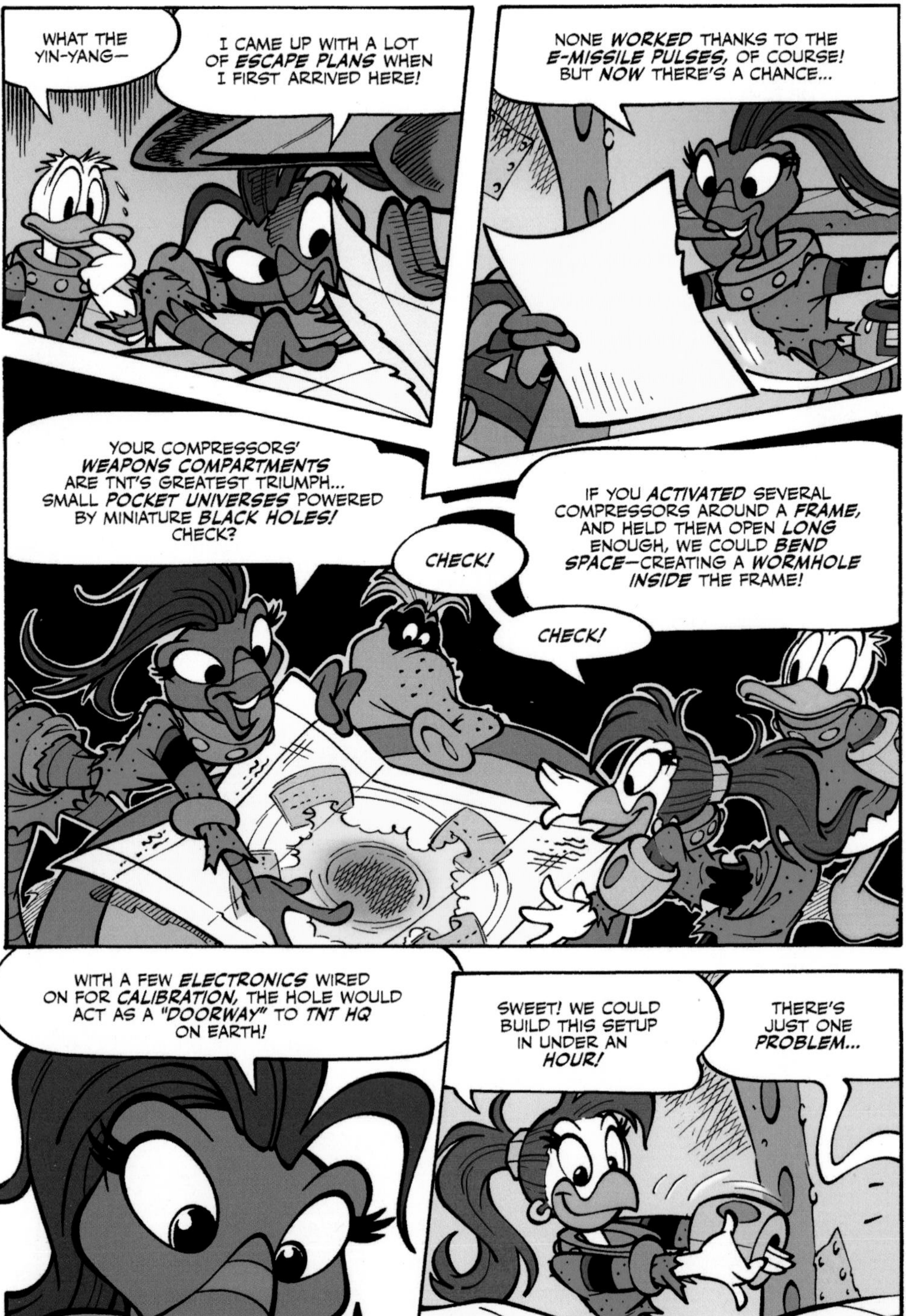
WHAT THE YIN-YANG—
I CAME UP WITH A LOT OF ESCAPE PLANS WHEN I FIRST ARRIVED HERE!
NONE WORKED THANKS TO THE E-MISSILE PULSES, OF COURSE! BUT NOW THERE'S A CHANCE...
YOUR COMPRESSORS' WEAPONS COMPARTMENTS ARE TNT'S GREATEST TRIUMPH... SMALL POCKET UNIVERSES POWERED BY MINIATURE BLACK HOLES! CHECK?
CHECK!
IF YOU ACTIVATED SEVERAL COMPRESSORS AROUND A FRAME, AND HELD THEM OPEN LONG ENOUGH, WE COULD BEND SPACE—CREATING A WORMHOLE INSIDE THE FRAME!
CHECK!
WITH A FEW ELECTRONICS WIRED ON FOR CALIBRATION, THE HOLE WOULD ACT AS A "DOORWAY" TO TNT HQ ON EARTH!
SWEET! WE COULD BUILD THIS SETUP IN UNDER AN HOUR!
THERE'S JUST ONE PROBLEM...

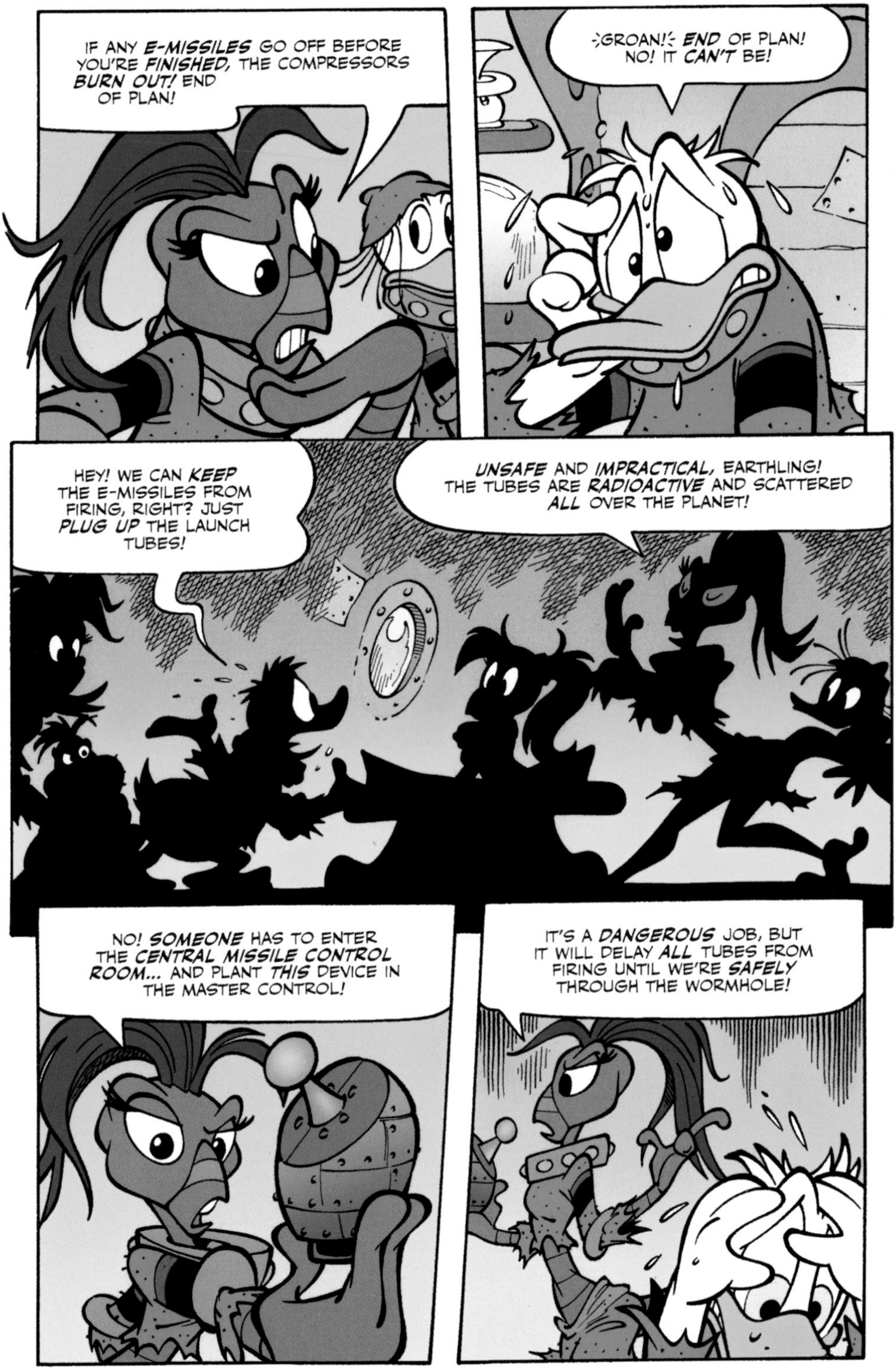
IF ANY E-MISSILES GO OFF BEFORE YOU'RE FINISHED, THE COMPRESSORS BURN OUT! END OF PLAN!
-GROAN!- END OF PLAN! NO! IT CAN'T BE!
HEY! WE CAN KEEP THE E-MISSILES FROM FIRING, RIGHT? JUST PLUG UP THE LAUNCH TUBES!
UNSAFE AND IMPRACTICAL, EARTHLING! THE TUBES ARE RADIOACTIVE AND SCATTERED ALL OVER THE PLANET!
NO! SOMEONE HAS TO ENTER THE CENTRAL MISSILE CONTROL ROOM... AND PLANT THIS DEVICE IN THE MASTER CONTROL!
IT'S A DANGEROUS JOB, BUT IT WILL DELAY ALL TUBES FROM FIRING UNTIL WE'RE SAFELY THROUGH THE WORMHOLE!

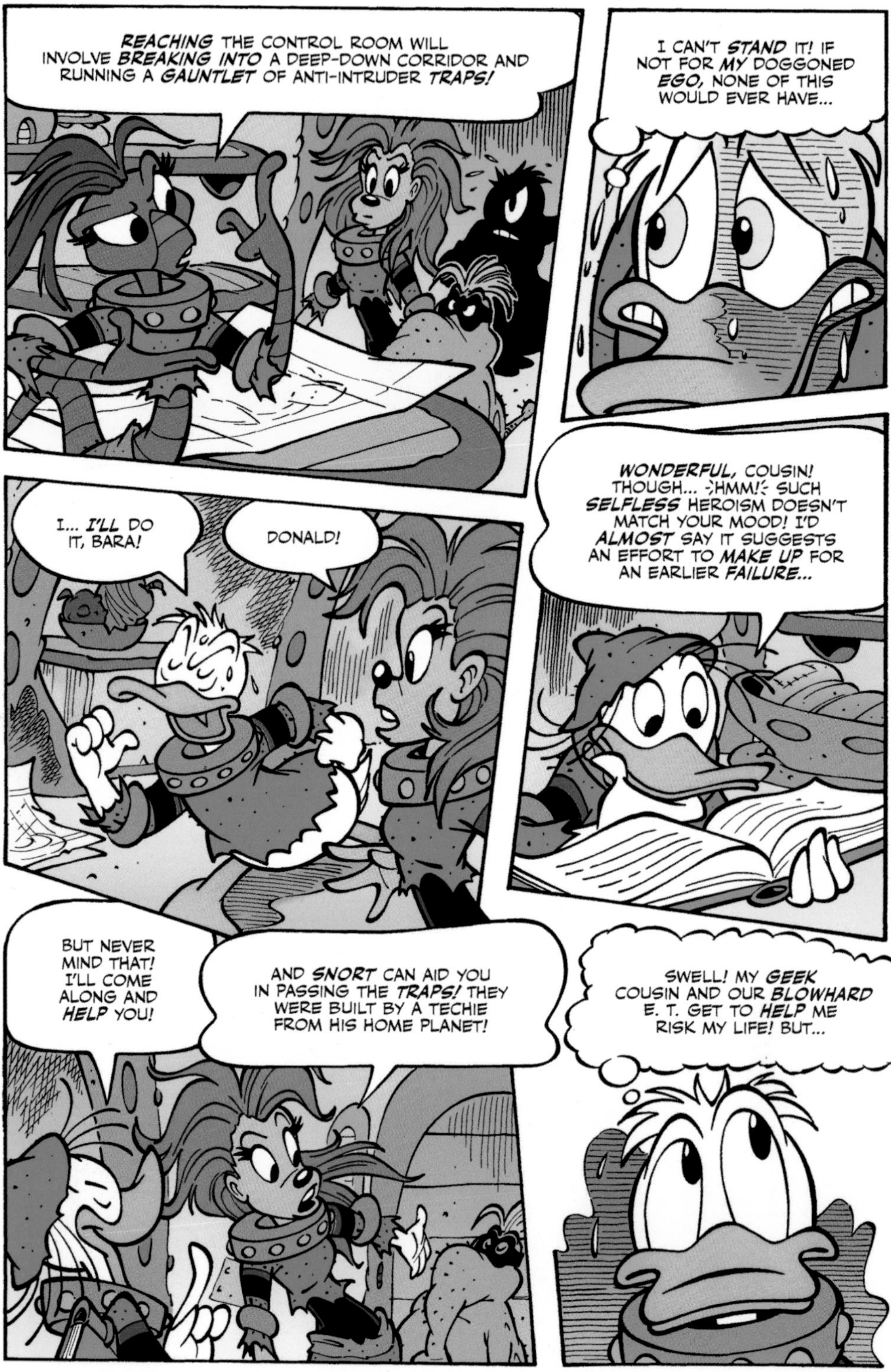
REACHING THE CONTROL ROOM WILL INVOLVE BREAKING INTO A DEEP-DOWN CORRIDOR AND RUNNING A GAUNTLET OF ANTI-INTRUDER TRAPS!
I CAN'T STAND IT! IF NOT FOR MY DOGGONED EGO, NONE OF THIS WOULD EVER HAVE...
I... I'LL DO IT, BARA!
DONALD!
WONDERFUL, COUSIN! THOUGH... -HMM!- SUCH SELFLESS HEROISM DOESN'T MATCH YOUR MOOD! I'D ALMOST SAY IT SUGGESTS AN EFFORT TO MAKE UP FOR AN EARLIER FAILURE...
BUT NEVER MIND THAT! I'LL COME ALONG AND HELP YOU!
AND SNORT CAN AID YOU IN PASSING THE TRAPS! THEY WERE BUILT BY A TECHIE FROM HIS HOME PLANET!
SWELL! MY GEEK COUSIN AND OUR BLOWHARD E. T. GET TO HELP ME RISK MY LIFE! BUT...

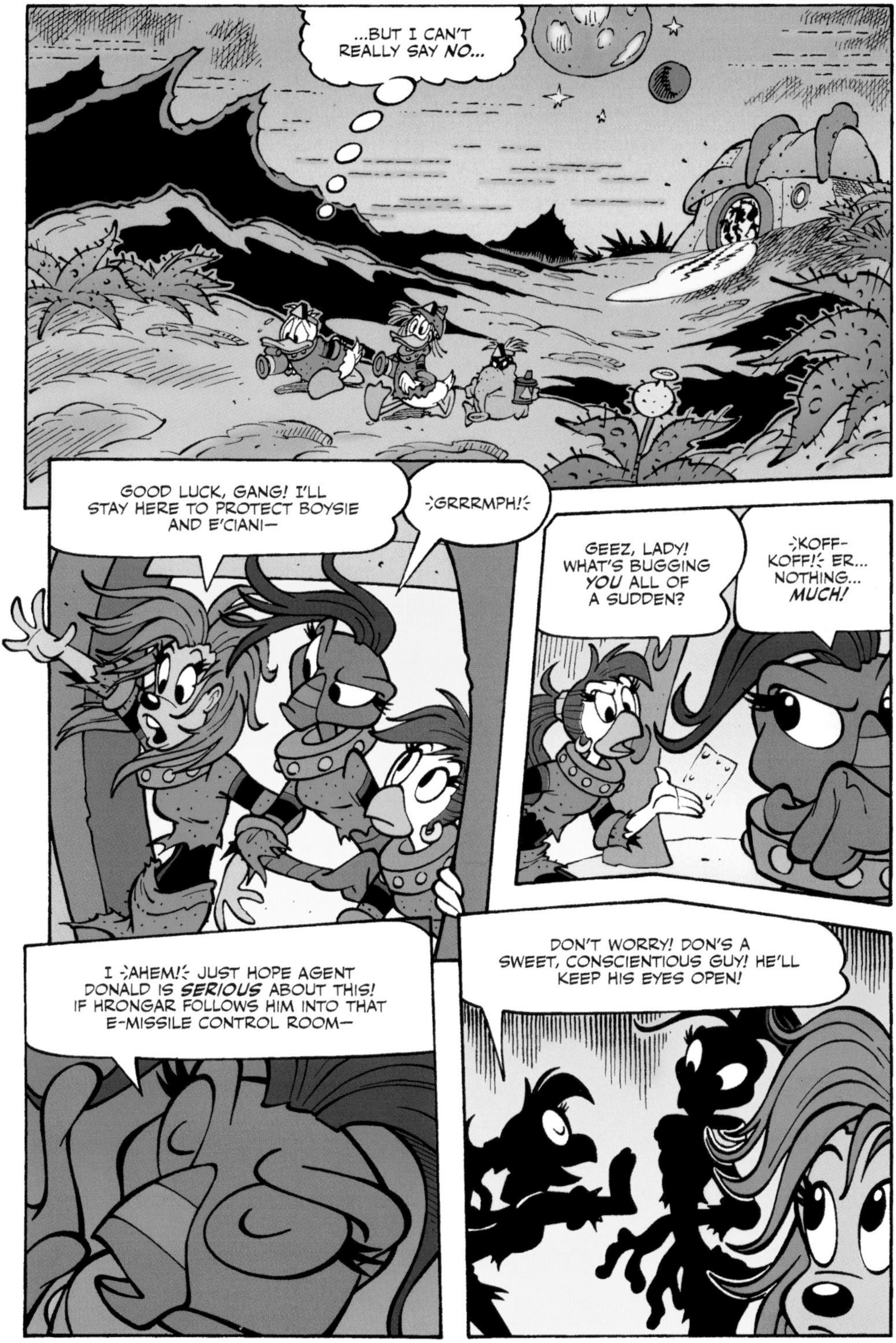
...BUT I CAN'T REALLY SAY *NO*...
GOOD LUCK, GANG! I'LL STAY HERE TO PROTECT BOYSIE AND E'CIANI—
GRRRMPH!
GEEZ, LADY! WHAT'S BUGGING *YOU* ALL OF A SUDDEN?
KOFF-KOFF! ER... NOTHING... *MUCH!*
I AHEM! JUST HOPE AGENT DONALD IS *SERIOUS* ABOUT THIS! IF HRONGAR FOLLOWS HIM INTO THAT E-MISSILE CONTROL ROOM—
DON'T WORRY! DON'S A SWEET, CONSCIENTIOUS GUY! HE'LL KEEP HIS EYES OPEN!

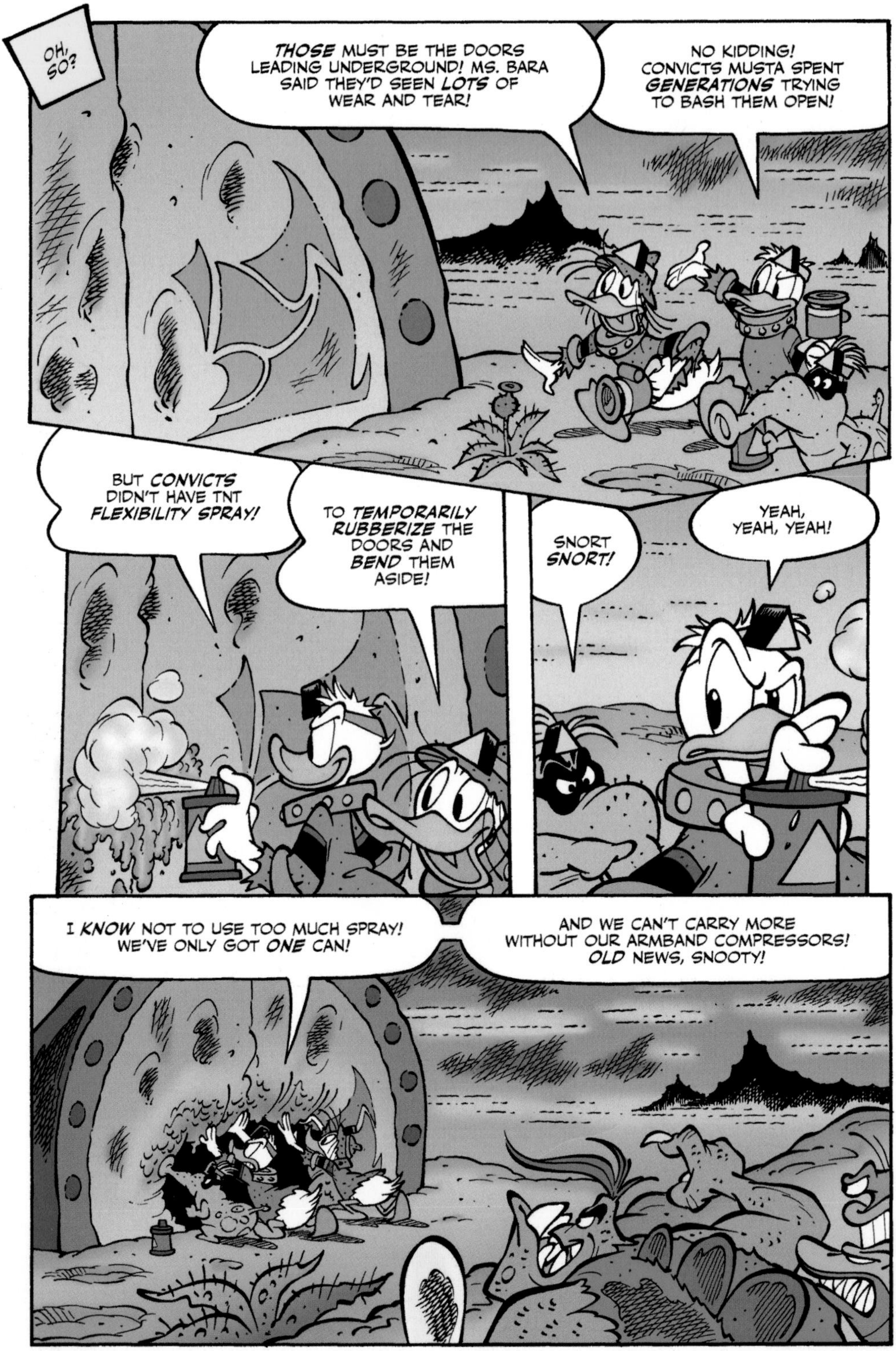
OH, SO?
THOSE MUST BE THE DOORS LEADING UNDERGROUND! MS. BARA SAID THEY'D SEEN LOTS OF WEAR AND TEAR!
NO KIDDING! CONVICTS MUSTA SPENT GENERATIONS TRYING TO BASH THEM OPEN!
BUT CONVICTS DIDN'T HAVE TNT FLEXIBILITY SPRAY!
TO TEMPORARILY RUBBERIZE THE DOORS AND BEND THEM ASIDE!
SNORT SNORT!
YEAH, YEAH, YEAH!
I KNOW NOT TO USE TOO MUCH SPRAY! WE'VE ONLY GOT ONE CAN!
AND WE CAN'T CARRY MORE WITHOUT OUR ARMBAND COMPRESSORS! OLD NEWS, SNOOTY!

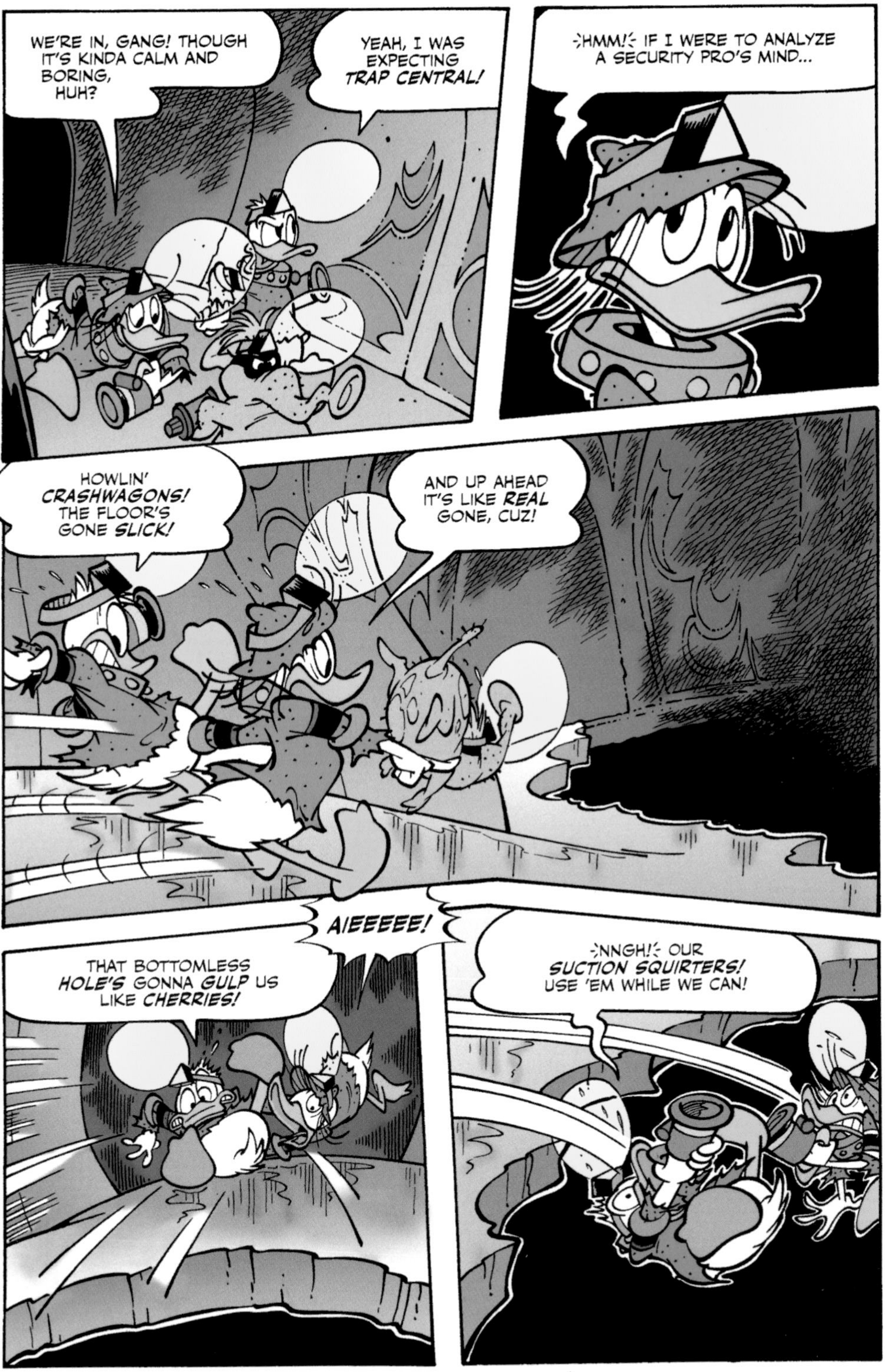
WE'RE IN, GANG! THOUGH IT'S KINDA CALM AND BORING, HUH?
YEAH, I WAS EXPECTING TRAP CENTRAL!
HMM! IF I WERE TO ANALYZE A SECURITY PRO'S MIND...
HOWLIN' CRASHWAGONS! THE FLOOR'S GONE SLICK!
AND UP AHEAD IT'S LIKE REAL GONE, CUZ!
AIEEEEE!
THAT BOTTOMLESS HOLE'S GONNA GULP US LIKE CHERRIES!
NNGH! OUR SUCTION SQUIRTERS! USE 'EM WHILE WE CAN!

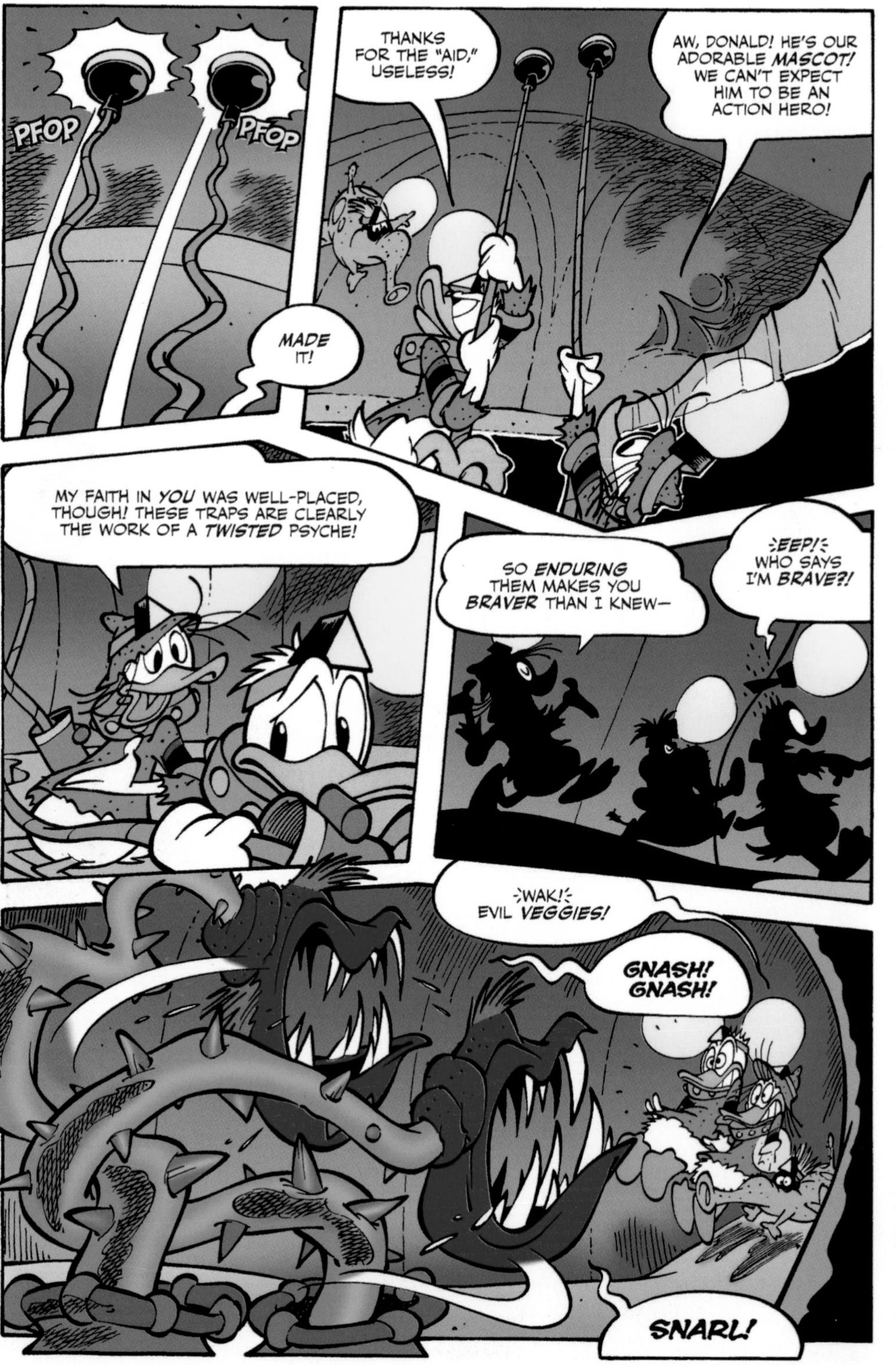
PFOP
PFOP
THANKS FOR THE "AID," USELESS!
AW, DONALD! HE'S OUR ADORABLE MASCOT! WE CAN'T EXPECT HIM TO BE AN ACTION HERO!
MADE IT!
MY FAITH IN YOU WAS WELL-PLACED, THOUGH! THESE TRAPS ARE CLEARLY THE WORK OF A TWISTED PSYCHE!
SO ENDURING THEM MAKES YOU BRAVER THAN I KNEW—
EEP! WHO SAYS I'M BRAVE?!
WAK! EVIL VEGGIES!
GNASH! GNASH!
SNARL!

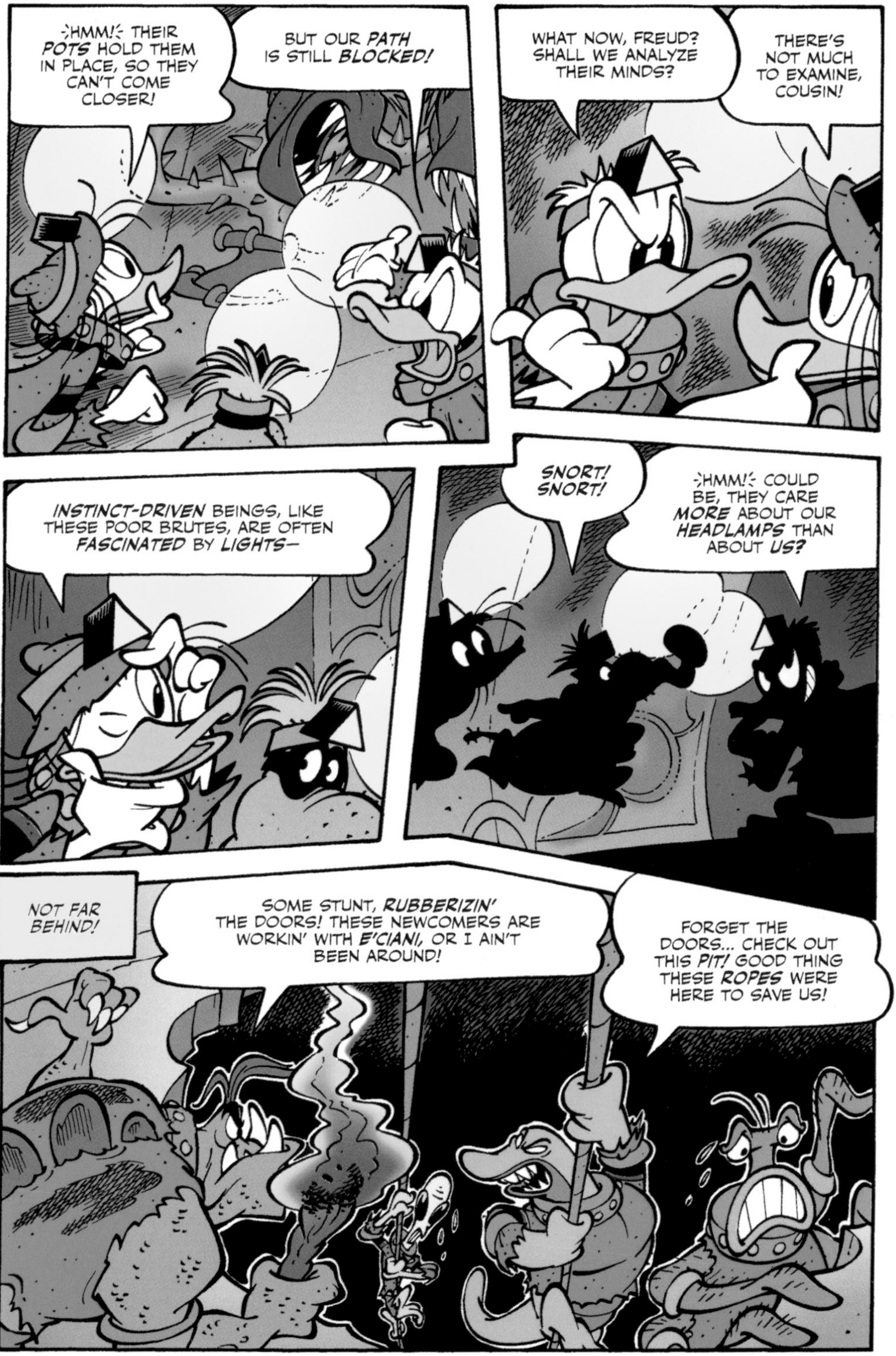
-HMM!- THEIR POTS HOLD THEM IN PLACE, SO THEY CAN'T COME CLOSER!
BUT OUR PATH IS STILL BLOCKED!
WHAT NOW, FREUD? SHALL WE ANALYZE THEIR MINDS?
THERE'S NOT MUCH TO EXAMINE, COUSIN!
INSTINCT-DRIVEN BEINGS, LIKE THESE POOR BRUTES, ARE OFTEN FASCINATED BY LIGHTS—
SNORT! SNORT!
-HMM!- COULD BE, THEY CARE MORE ABOUT OUR HEADLAMPS THAN ABOUT US?
NOT FAR BEHIND!
SOME STUNT, RUBBERIZIN' THE DOORS! THESE NEWCOMERS ARE WORKIN' WITH E'CIANI, OR I AIN'T BEEN AROUND!
FORGET THE DOORS... CHECK OUT THIS PIT! GOOD THING THESE ROPES WERE HERE TO SAVE US!

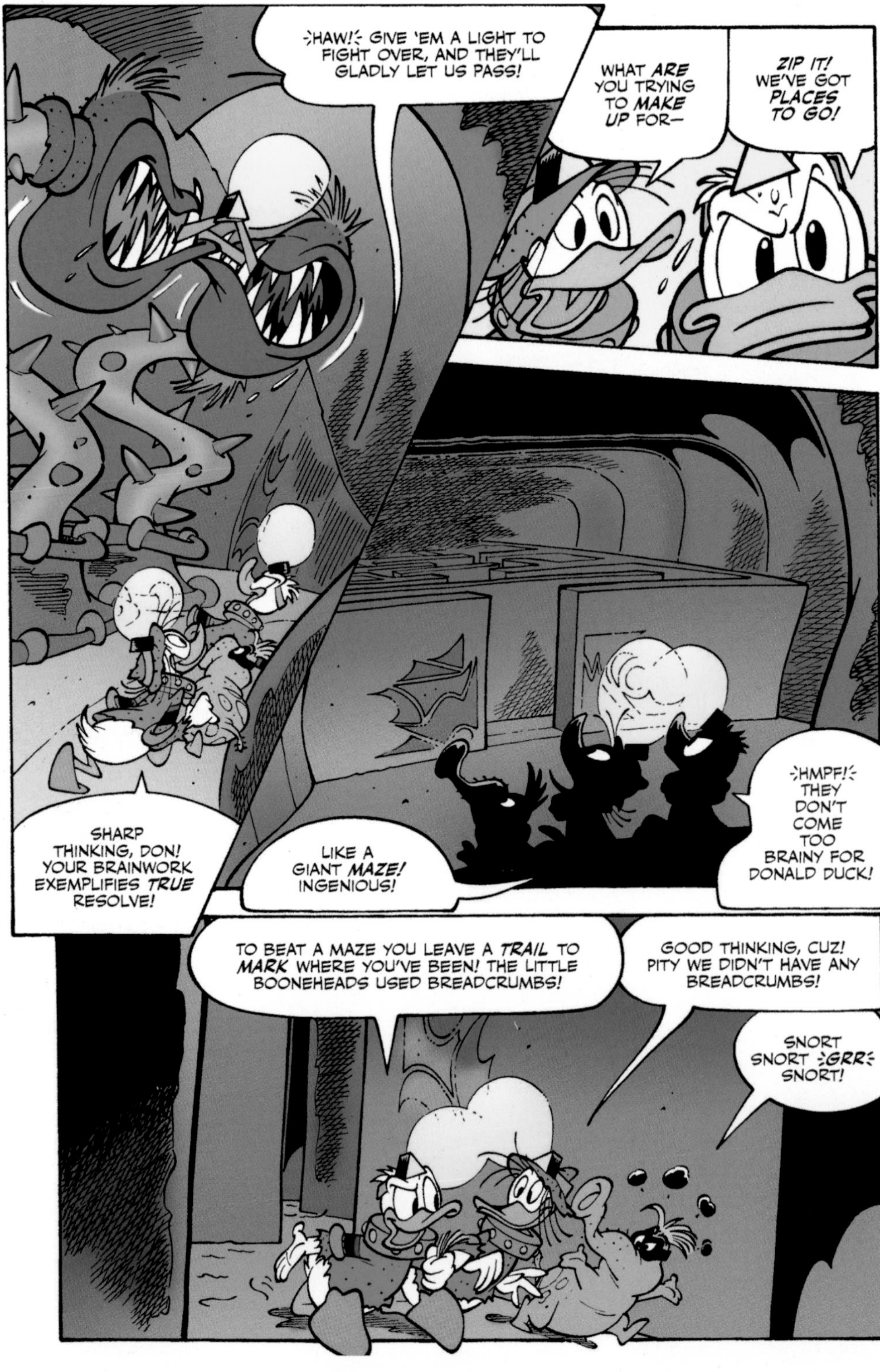

⁝HAW!⁝ GIVE 'EM A LIGHT TO FIGHT OVER, AND THEY'LL GLADLY LET US PASS!
WHAT ARE YOU TRYING TO MAKE UP FOR—
ZIP IT! WE'VE GOT PLACES TO GO!
SHARP THINKING, DON! YOUR BRAINWORK EXEMPLIFIES TRUE RESOLVE!
LIKE A GIANT MAZE! INGENIOUS!
⁝HMPF!⁝ THEY DON'T COME TOO BRAINY FOR DONALD DUCK!
TO BEAT A MAZE YOU LEAVE A TRAIL TO MARK WHERE YOU'VE BEEN! THE LITTLE BOONEHEADS USED BREADCRUMBS!
GOOD THINKING, CUZ! PITY WE DIDN'T HAVE ANY BREADCRUMBS!
SNORT SNORT ⁝GRR⁝ SNORT!

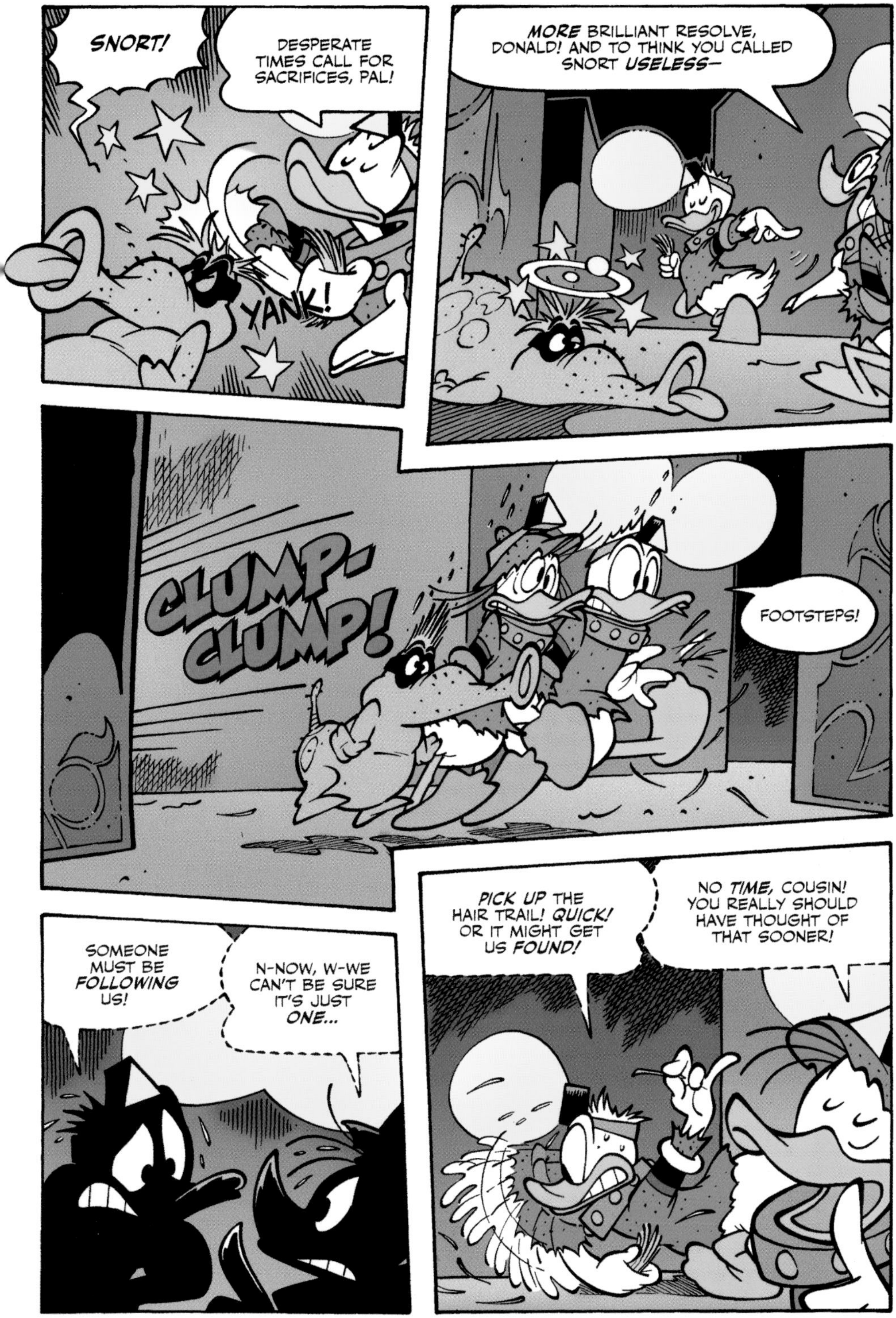
SNORT!
DESPERATE TIMES CALL FOR SACRIFICES, PAL!
YANK!
MORE BRILLIANT RESOLVE, DONALD! AND TO THINK YOU CALLED SNORT USELESS—
CLUMP-CLUMP!
FOOTSTEPS!
SOMEONE MUST BE FOLLOWING US!
N-NOW, W-WE CAN'T BE SURE IT'S JUST ONE...
PICK UP THE HAIR TRAIL! QUICK! OR IT MIGHT GET US FOUND!
NO TIME, COUSIN! YOU REALLY SHOULD HAVE THOUGHT OF THAT SOONER!

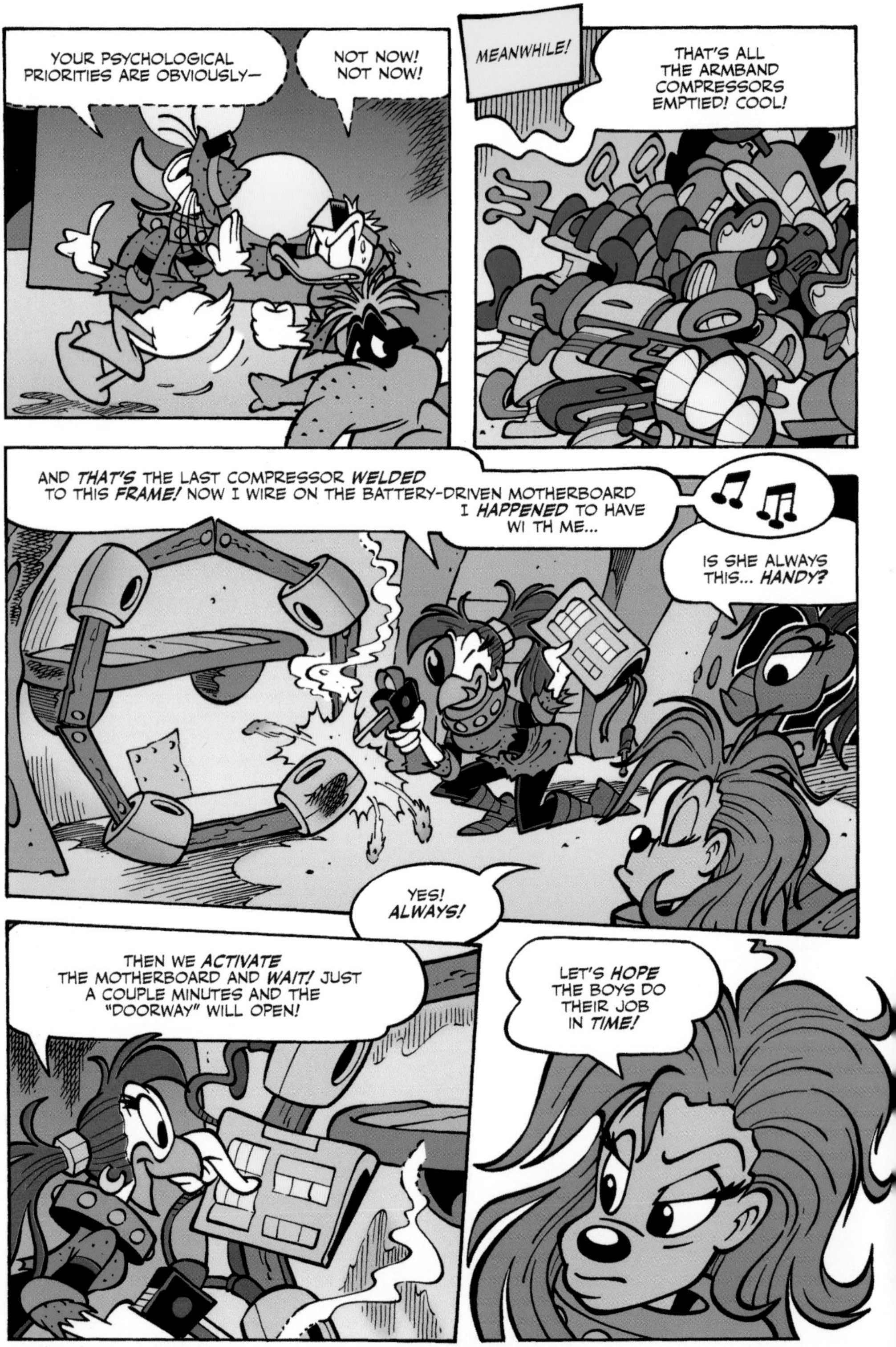
YOUR PSYCHOLOGICAL PRIORITIES ARE OBVIOUSLY—
NOT NOW! NOT NOW!
MEANWHILE!
THAT'S ALL THE ARMBAND COMPRESSORS EMPTIED! COOL!
AND *THAT'S* THE LAST COMPRESSOR *WELDED* TO THIS *FRAME!* NOW I WIRE ON THE BATTERY-DRIVEN MOTHERBOARD I *HAPPENED* TO HAVE WI TH ME...
IS SHE ALWAYS THIS... *HANDY?*
YES! *ALWAYS!*
THEN WE *ACTIVATE* THE MOTHERBOARD AND *WAIT!* JUST A COUPLE MINUTES AND THE "DOORWAY" WILL OPEN!
LET'S *HOPE* THE BOYS DO THEIR JOB IN *TIME!*

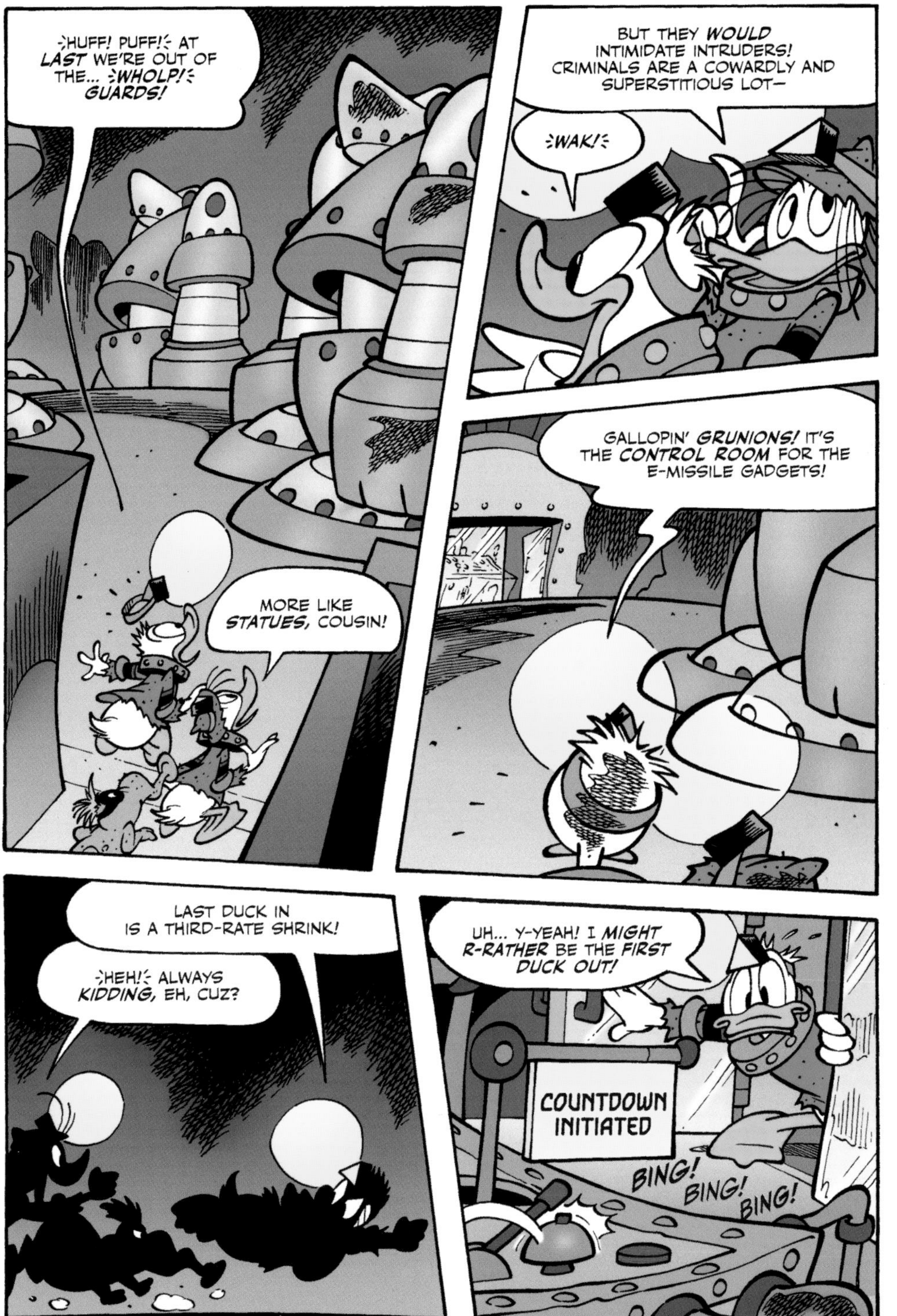

HUFF! PUFF! AT LAST WE'RE OUT OF THE... WHOLP! GUARDS!
MORE LIKE STATUES, COUSIN!
BUT THEY WOULD INTIMIDATE INTRUDERS! CRIMINALS ARE A COWARDLY AND SUPERSTITIOUS LOT—
WAK!
GALLOPIN' GRUNIONS! IT'S THE CONTROL ROOM FOR THE E-MISSILE GADGETS!
LAST DUCK IN IS A THIRD-RATE SHRINK!
HEH! ALWAYS KIDDING, EH, CUZ?
UH... Y-YEAH! I MIGHT R-RATHER BE THE FIRST DUCK OUT!
COUNTDOWN INITIATED
BING! BING! BING!

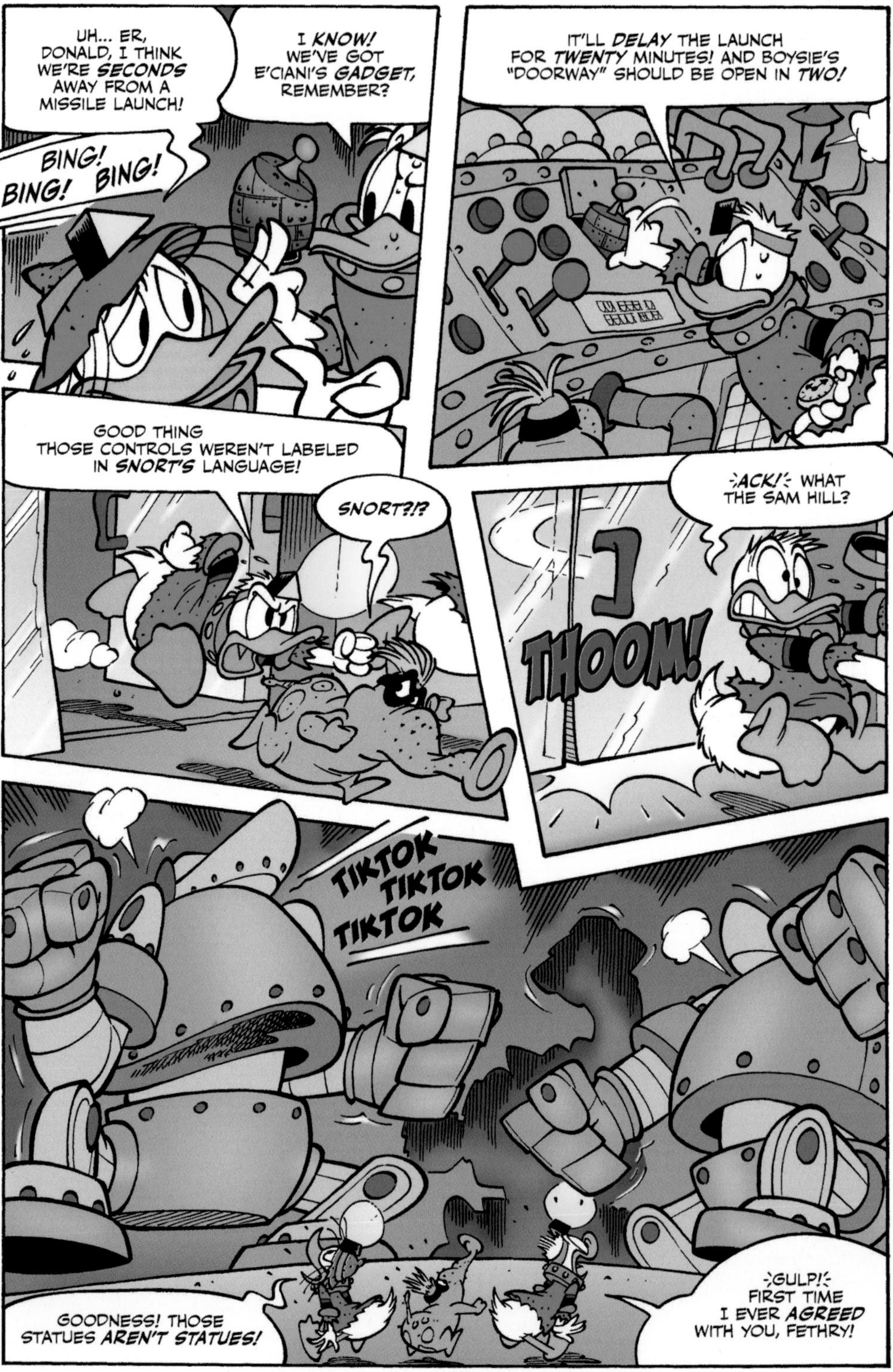
UH... ER, DONALD, I THINK WE'RE SECONDS AWAY FROM A MISSILE LAUNCH!
I KNOW! WE'VE GOT E'CIANI'S GADGET, REMEMBER?
BING! BING! BING!
IT'LL DELAY THE LAUNCH FOR TWENTY MINUTES! AND BOYSIE'S "DOORWAY" SHOULD BE OPEN IN TWO!
GOOD THING THOSE CONTROLS WEREN'T LABELED IN SNORT'S LANGUAGE!
SNORT?!?
ACK! WHAT THE SAM HILL?
THOOM!
TIKTOK TIKTOK TIKTOK
GOODNESS! THOSE STATUES AREN'T STATUES!
GULP! FIRST TIME I EVER AGREED WITH YOU, FETHRY!

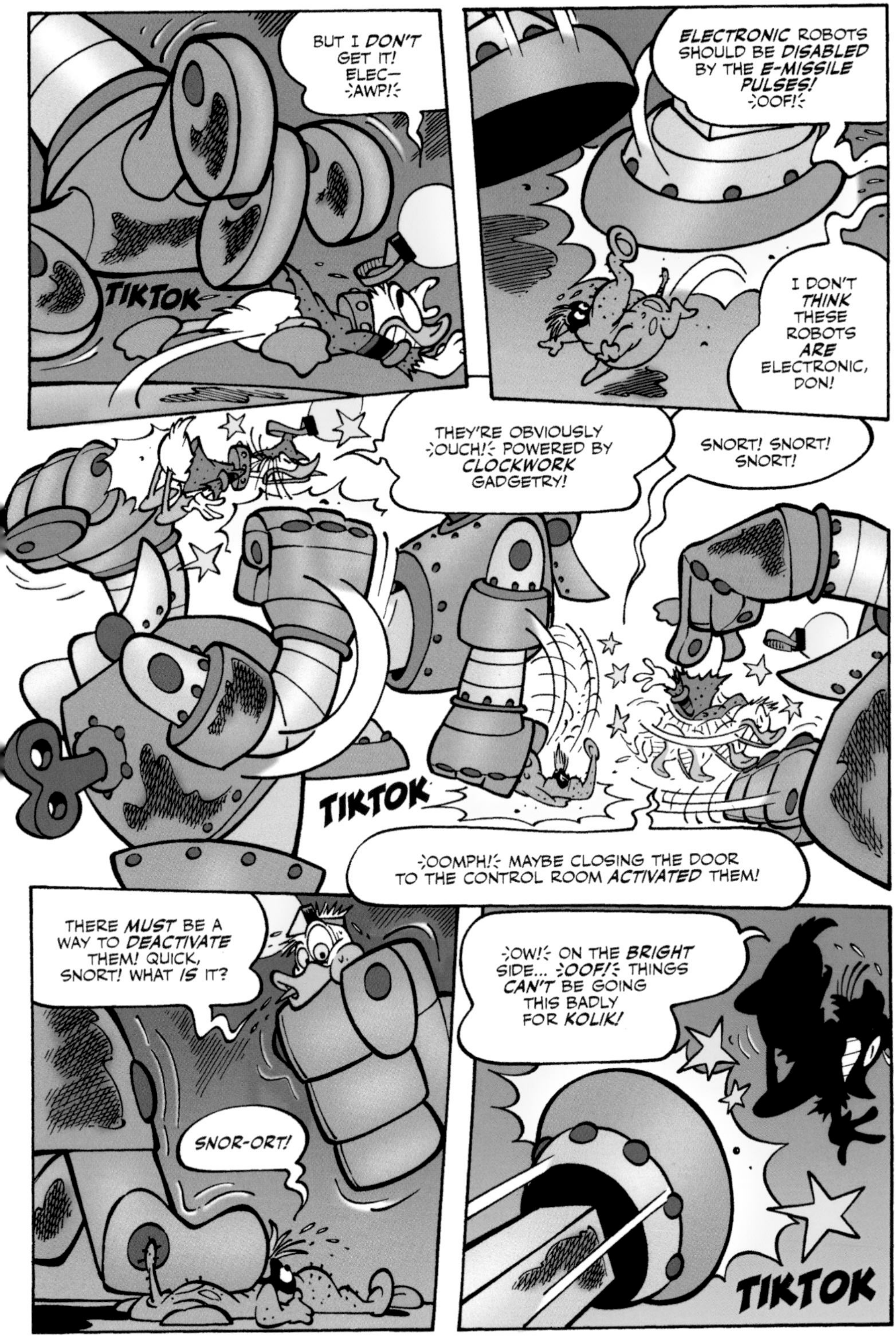
BUT I DON'T GET IT! ELEC— -AWP!-
TIKTOK
ELECTRONIC ROBOTS SHOULD BE DISABLED BY THE E-MISSILE PULSES! -OOF!-
I DON'T THINK THESE ROBOTS ARE ELECTRONIC, DON!
THEY'RE OBVIOUSLY -OUCH!- POWERED BY CLOCKWORK GADGETRY!
SNORT! SNORT! SNORT!
TIKTOK
-OOMPH!- MAYBE CLOSING THE DOOR TO THE CONTROL ROOM ACTIVATED THEM!
THERE MUST BE A WAY TO DEACTIVATE THEM! QUICK, SNORT! WHAT IS IT?
SNOR-ORT!
-OW!- ON THE BRIGHT SIDE... -OOF!- THINGS CAN'T BE GOING THIS BADLY FOR KOLIK!
TIKTOK

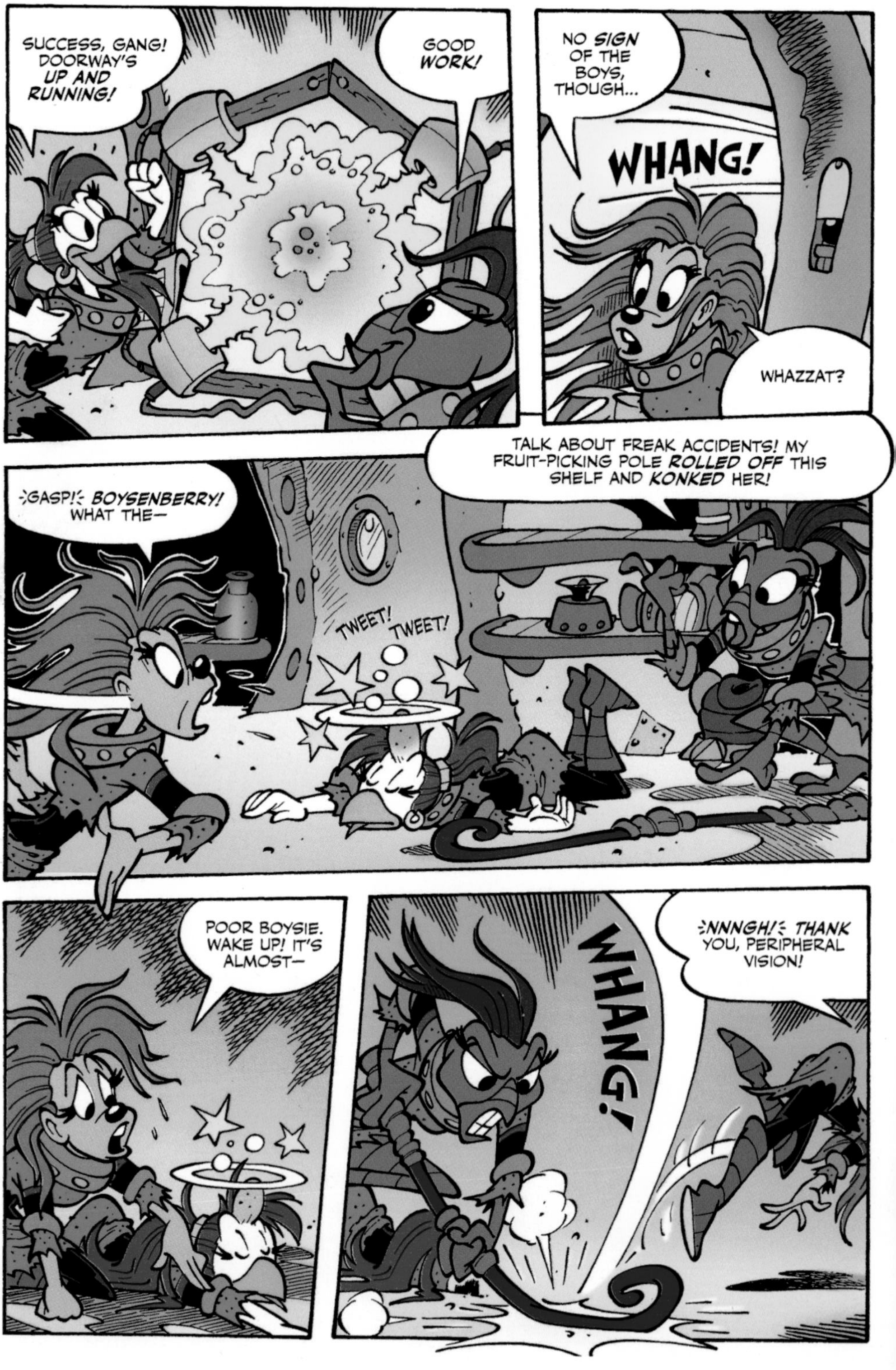
SUCCESS, GANG! DOORWAY'S UP AND RUNNING!
GOOD WORK!
NO SIGN OF THE BOYS, THOUGH...
WHANG!
WHAZZAT?
TALK ABOUT FREAK ACCIDENTS! MY FRUIT-PICKING POLE ROLLED OFF THIS SHELF AND KONKED HER!
GASP! BOYSENBERRY! WHAT THE—
TWEET! TWEET!
POOR BOYSIE. WAKE UP! IT'S ALMOST—
WHANG!
NNNGH! THANK YOU, PERIPHERAL VISION!

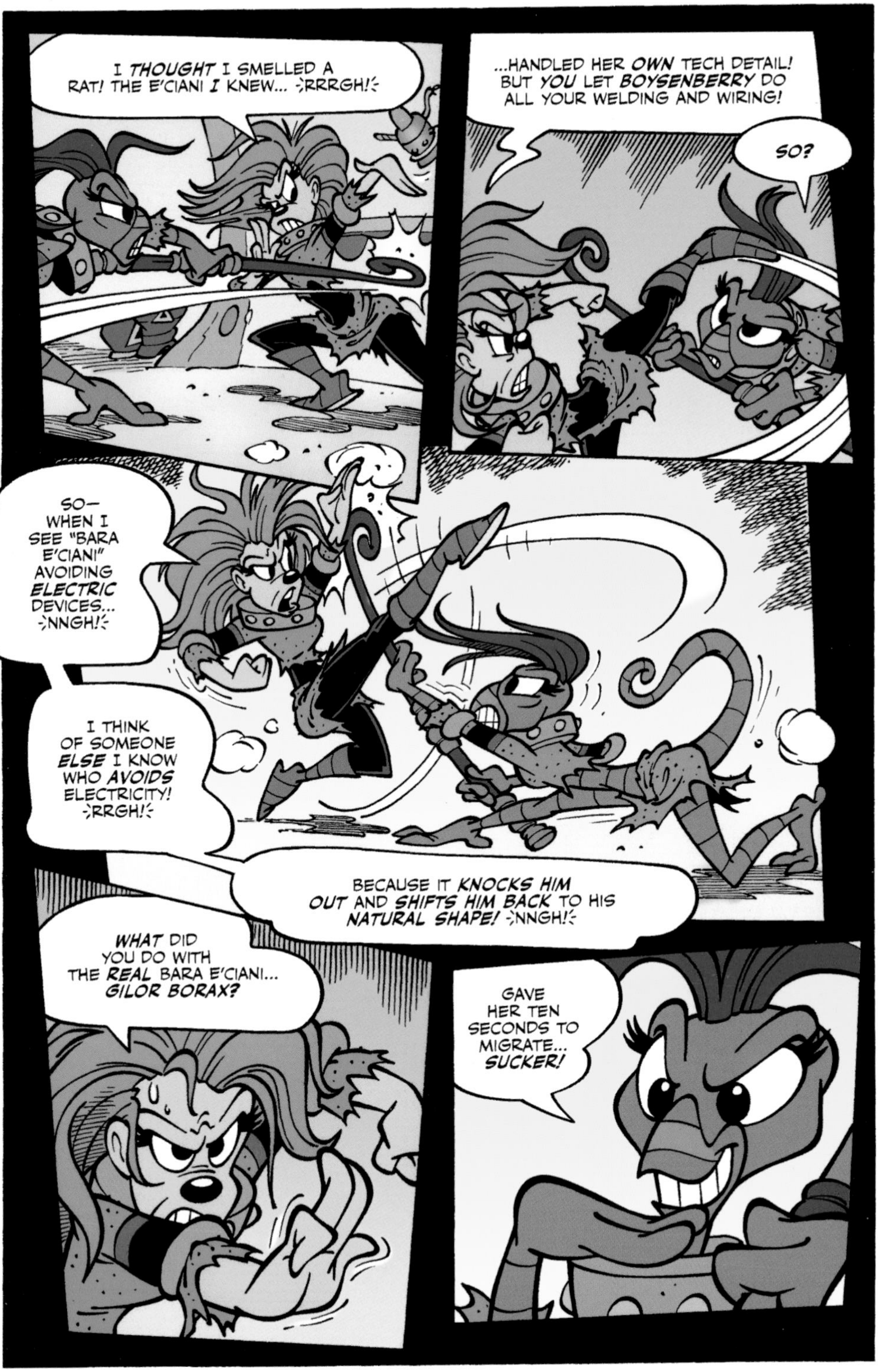
I THOUGHT I SMELLED A RAT! THE E'CIANI I KNEW... RRRGH!
...HANDLED HER OWN TECH DETAIL! BUT YOU LET BOYSENBERRY DO ALL YOUR WELDING AND WIRING!
SO?
SO— WHEN I SEE "BARA E'CIANI" AVOIDING ELECTRIC DEVICES... NNGH!
I THINK OF SOMEONE ELSE I KNOW WHO AVOIDS ELECTRICITY! RRGH!
BECAUSE IT KNOCKS HIM OUT AND SHIFTS HIM BACK TO HIS NATURAL SHAPE! NNGH!
WHAT DID YOU DO WITH THE REAL BARA E'CIANI... GILOR BORAX?
GAVE HER TEN SECONDS TO MIGRATE... SUCKER!

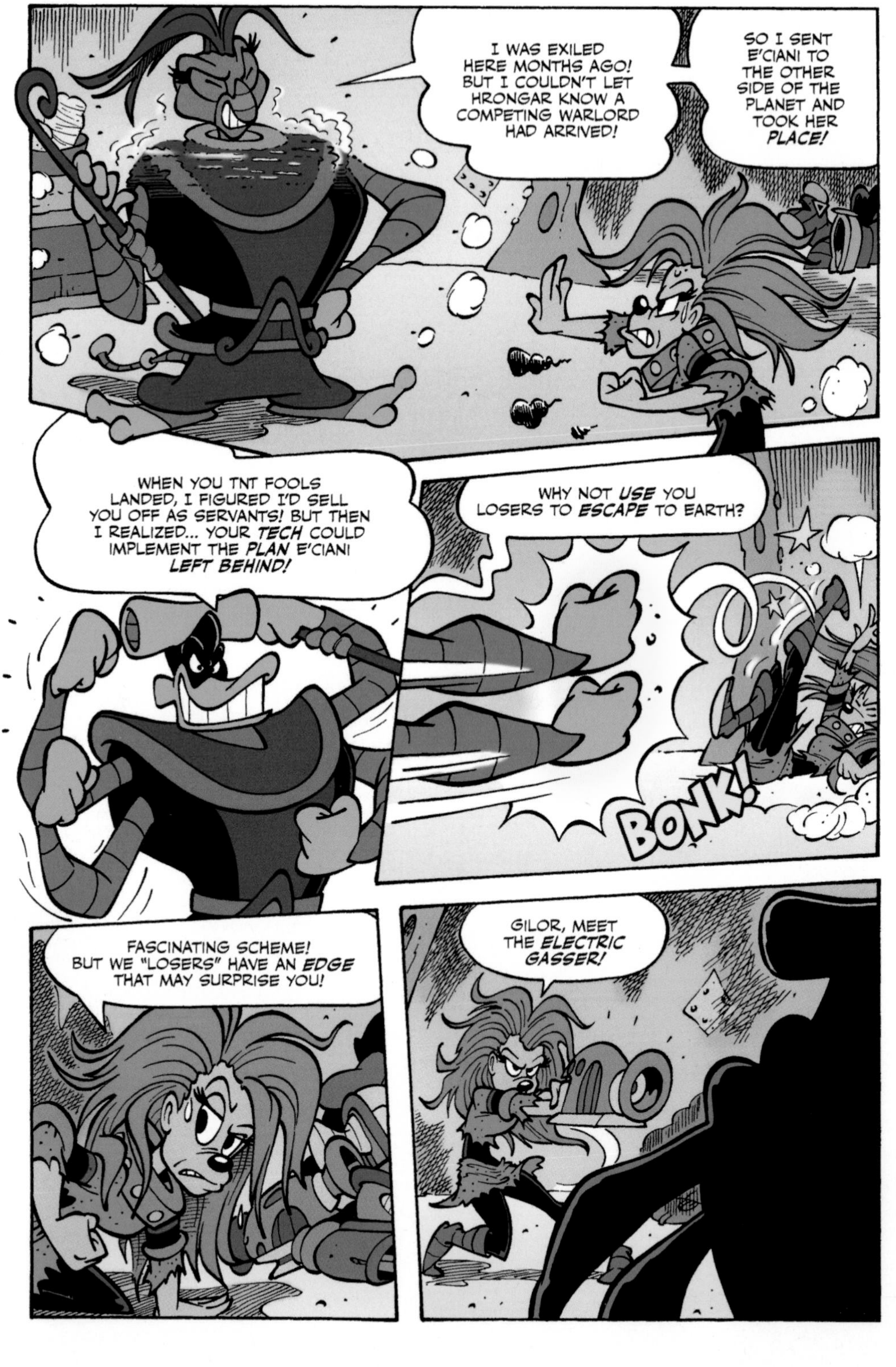
I WAS EXILED HERE MONTHS AGO! BUT I COULDN'T LET HRONGAR KNOW A COMPETING WARLORD HAD ARRIVED!
SO I SENT E'CIANI TO THE OTHER SIDE OF THE PLANET AND TOOK HER PLACE!
WHEN YOU TNT FOOLS LANDED, I FIGURED I'D SELL YOU OFF AS SERVANTS! BUT THEN I REALIZED... YOUR TECH COULD IMPLEMENT THE PLAN E'CIANI LEFT BEHIND!
WHY NOT USE YOU LOSERS TO ESCAPE TO EARTH?
BONK!
FASCINATING SCHEME! BUT WE "LOSERS" HAVE AN EDGE THAT MAY SURPRISE YOU!
GILOR, MEET THE ELECTRIC GASSER!

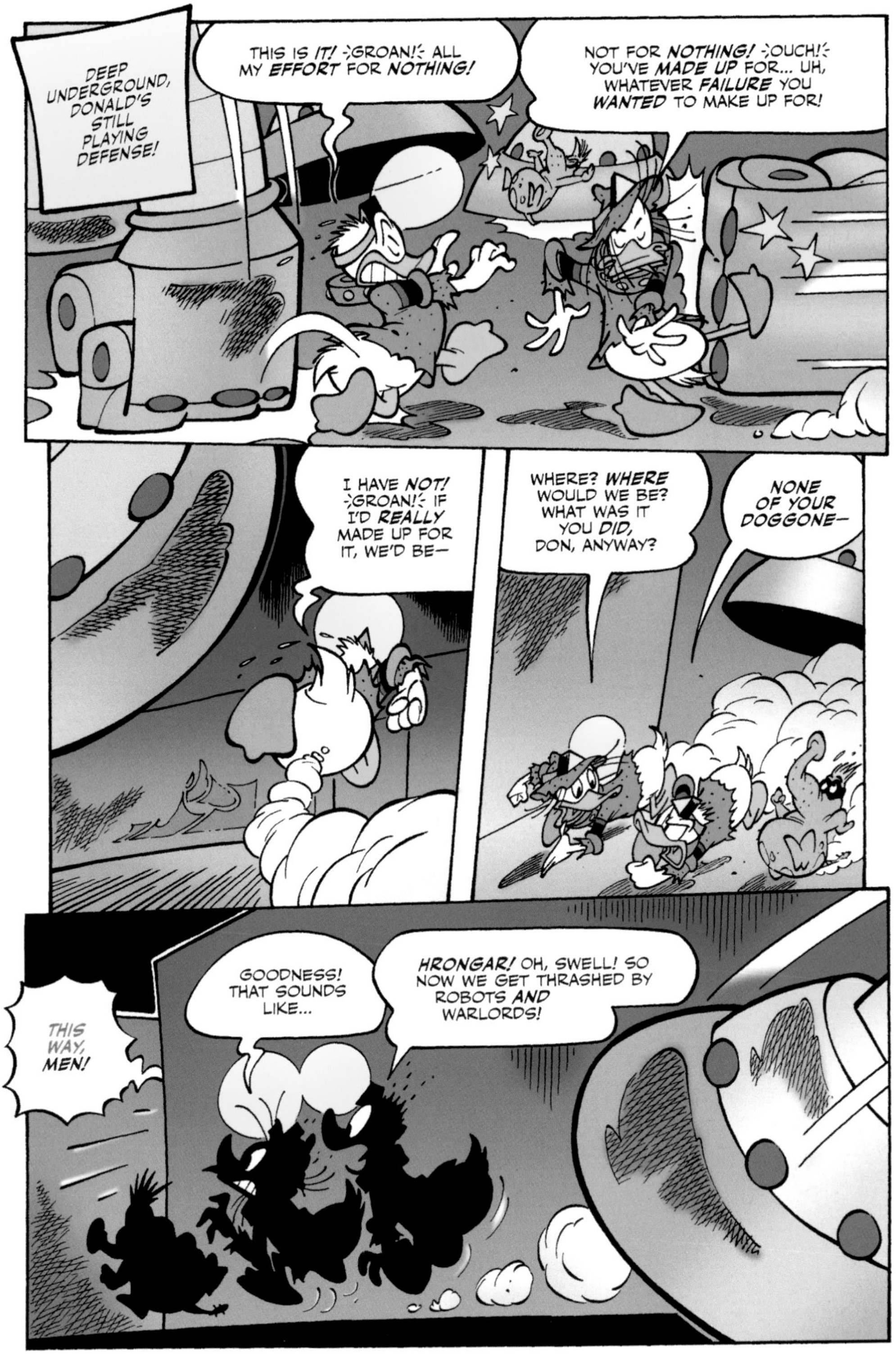
DEEP UNDERGROUND, DONALD'S STILL PLAYING DEFENSE!
THIS IS *IT!* -GROAN!- ALL MY ***EFFORT*** FOR ***NOTHING!***
NOT FOR ***NOTHING!*** -OUCH!- YOU'VE ***MADE UP*** FOR... UH, WHATEVER ***FAILURE*** YOU ***WANTED*** TO MAKE UP FOR!
I HAVE ***NOT!*** -GROAN!- IF I'D ***REALLY*** MADE UP FOR IT, WE'D BE—
WHERE? ***WHERE*** WOULD WE BE? WHAT WAS IT YOU ***DID,*** DON, ANYWAY?
NONE OF YOUR DOGGONE—
THIS WAY, ***MEN!***
GOODNESS! THAT SOUNDS LIKE...
HRONGAR! OH, SWELL! SO NOW WE GET THRASHED BY ROBOTS ***AND*** WARLORDS!

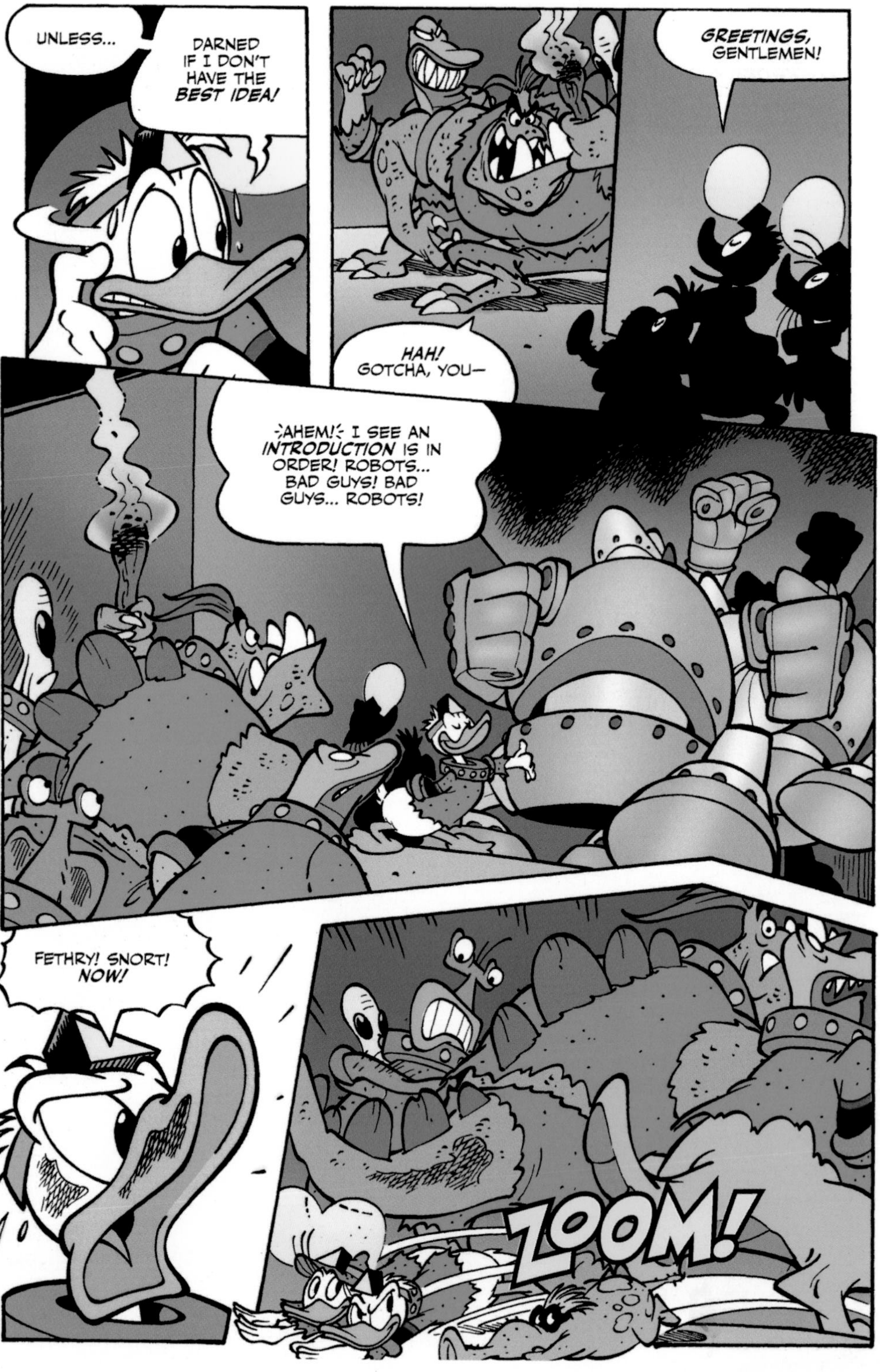
UNLESS...
DARNED IF I DON'T HAVE THE BEST IDEA!
GREETINGS, GENTLEMEN!
HAH! GOTCHA, YOU—
AHEM! I SEE AN INTRODUCTION IS IN ORDER! ROBOTS... BAD GUYS! BAD GUYS... ROBOTS!
FETHRY! SNORT! NOW!
ZOOM!

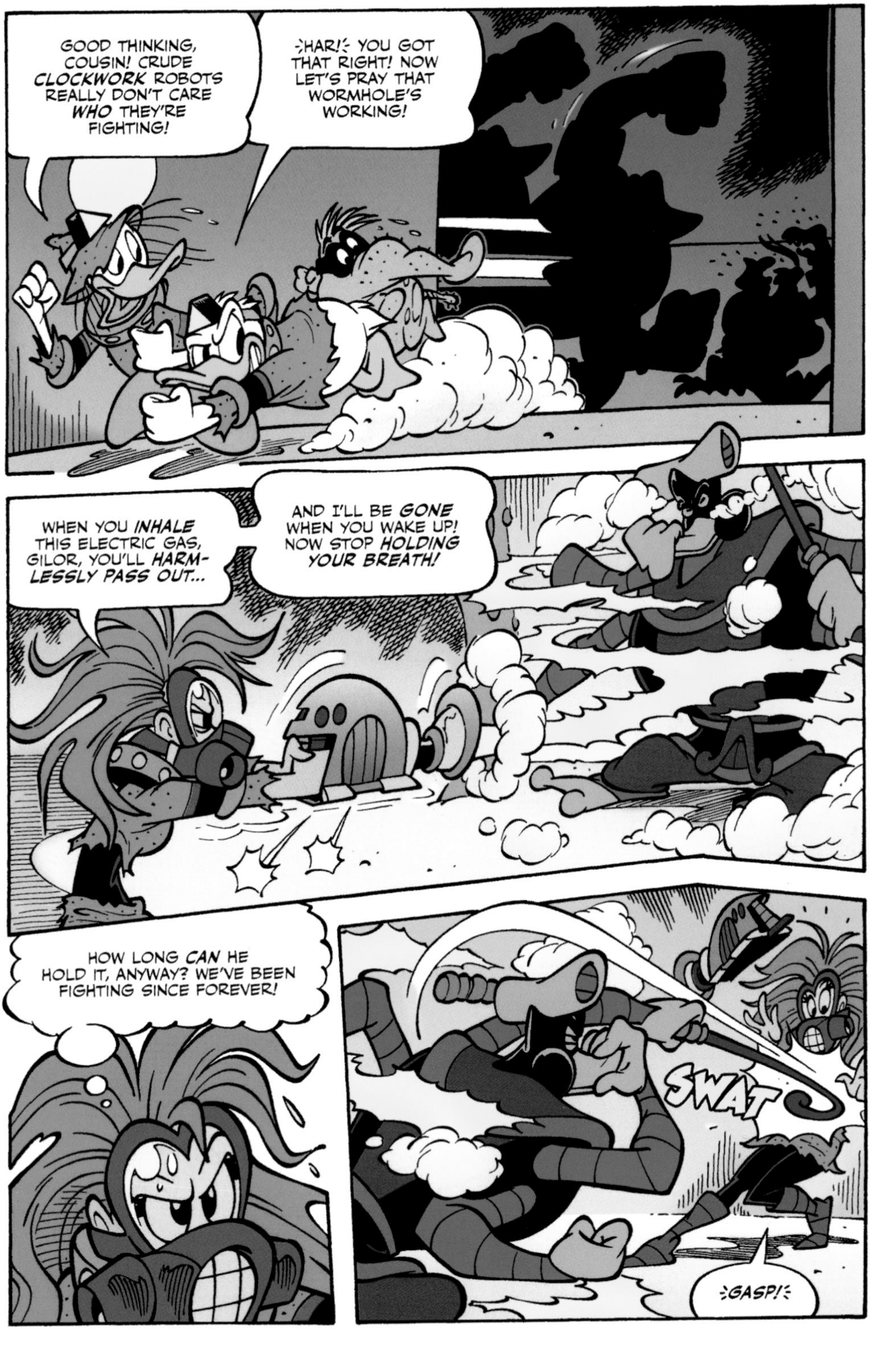
GOOD THINKING, COUSIN! CRUDE CLOCKWORK ROBOTS REALLY DON'T CARE WHO THEY'RE FIGHTING!
HAR! YOU GOT THAT RIGHT! NOW LET'S PRAY THAT WORMHOLE'S WORKING!
WHEN YOU INHALE THIS ELECTRIC GAS, GILOR, YOU'LL HARMLESSLY PASS OUT...
AND I'LL BE GONE WHEN YOU WAKE UP! NOW STOP HOLDING YOUR BREATH!
HOW LONG CAN HE HOLD IT, ANYWAY? WE'VE BEEN FIGHTING SINCE FOREVER!
SWAT
GASP!

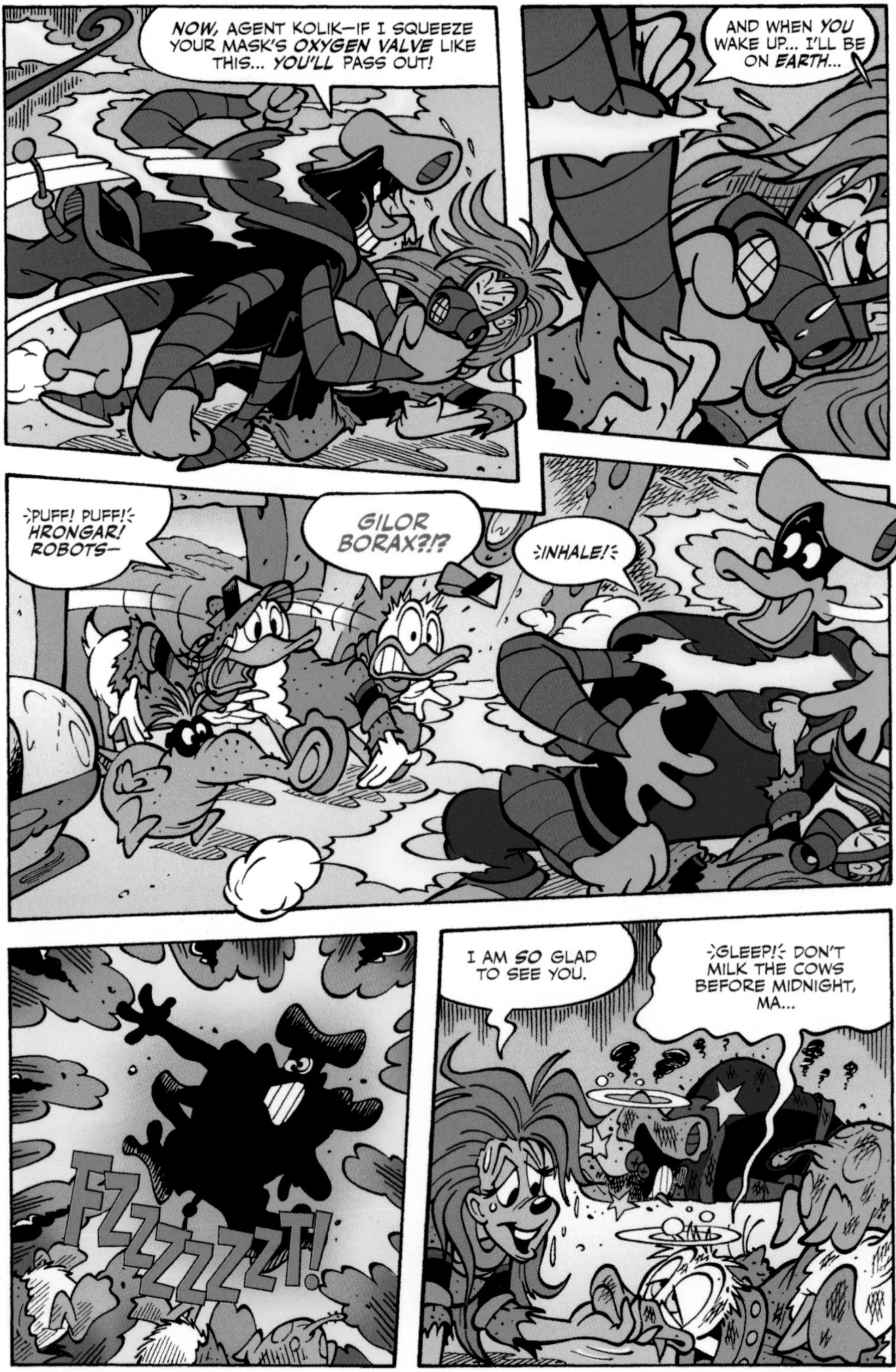
NOW, AGENT KOLIK—IF I SQUEEZE YOUR MASK'S OXYGEN VALVE LIKE THIS... YOU'LL PASS OUT!
AND WHEN YOU WAKE UP... I'LL BE ON EARTH...
-PUFF! PUFF!- HRONGAR! ROBOTS—
GILOR BORAX?!?
-INHALE!-
FZZZZZZZT!
I AM SO GLAD TO SEE YOU.
-GLEEP!- DON'T MILK THE COWS BEFORE MIDNIGHT, MA...

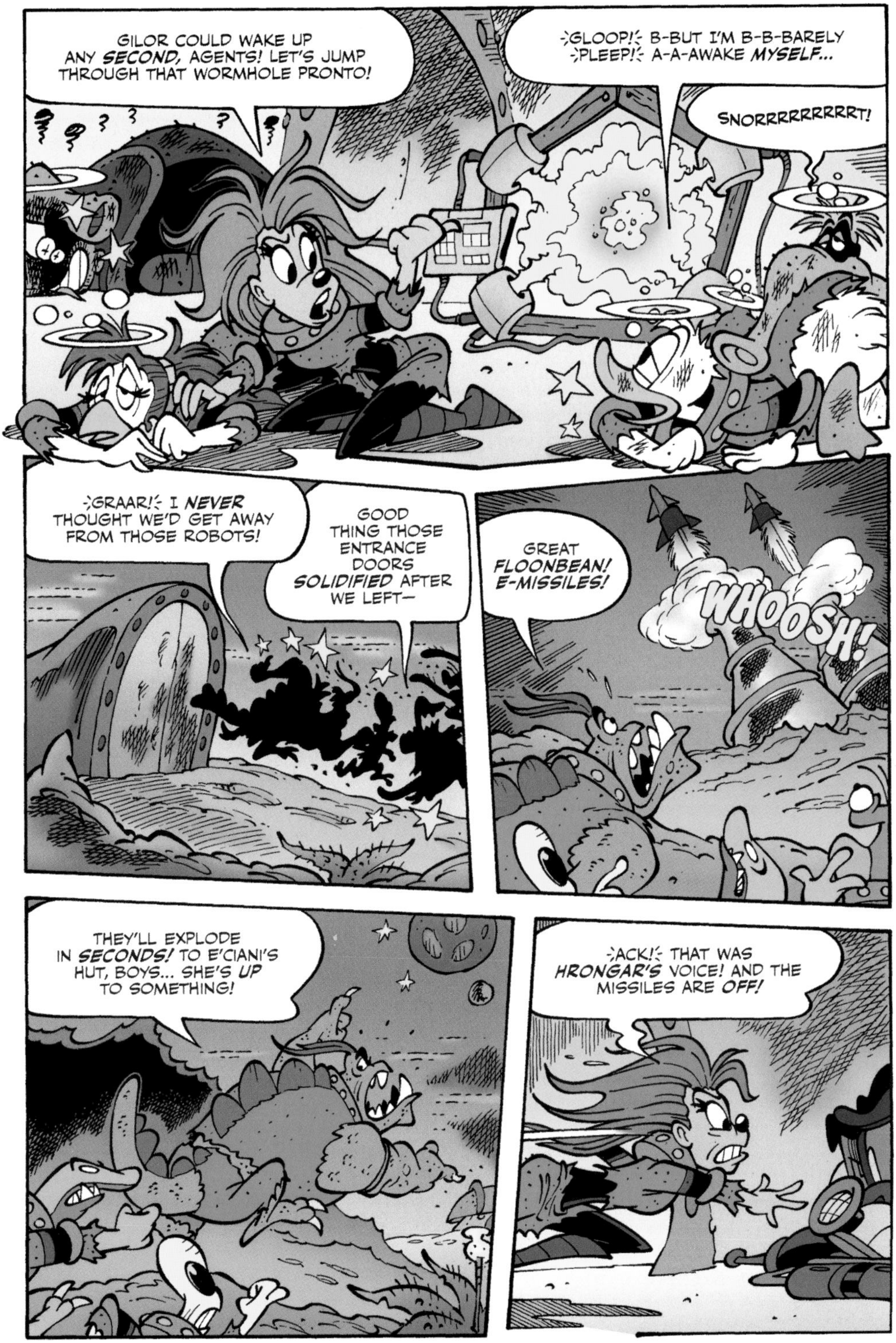
GILOR COULD WAKE UP ANY SECOND, AGENTS! LET'S JUMP THROUGH THAT WORMHOLE PRONTO!
GLOOP! B-BUT I'M B-B-BARELY PLEEP! A-A-AWAKE MYSELF...
SNORRRRRRRRT!
GRAAR! I NEVER THOUGHT WE'D GET AWAY FROM THOSE ROBOTS!
GOOD THING THOSE ENTRANCE DOORS SOLIDIFIED AFTER WE LEFT—
GREAT FLOONBEAN! E-MISSILES!
WHOOSH!
THEY'LL EXPLODE IN SECONDS! TO E'CIANI'S HUT, BOYS... SHE'S UP TO SOMETHING!
ACK! THAT WAS HRONGAR'S VOICE! AND THE MISSILES ARE OFF!

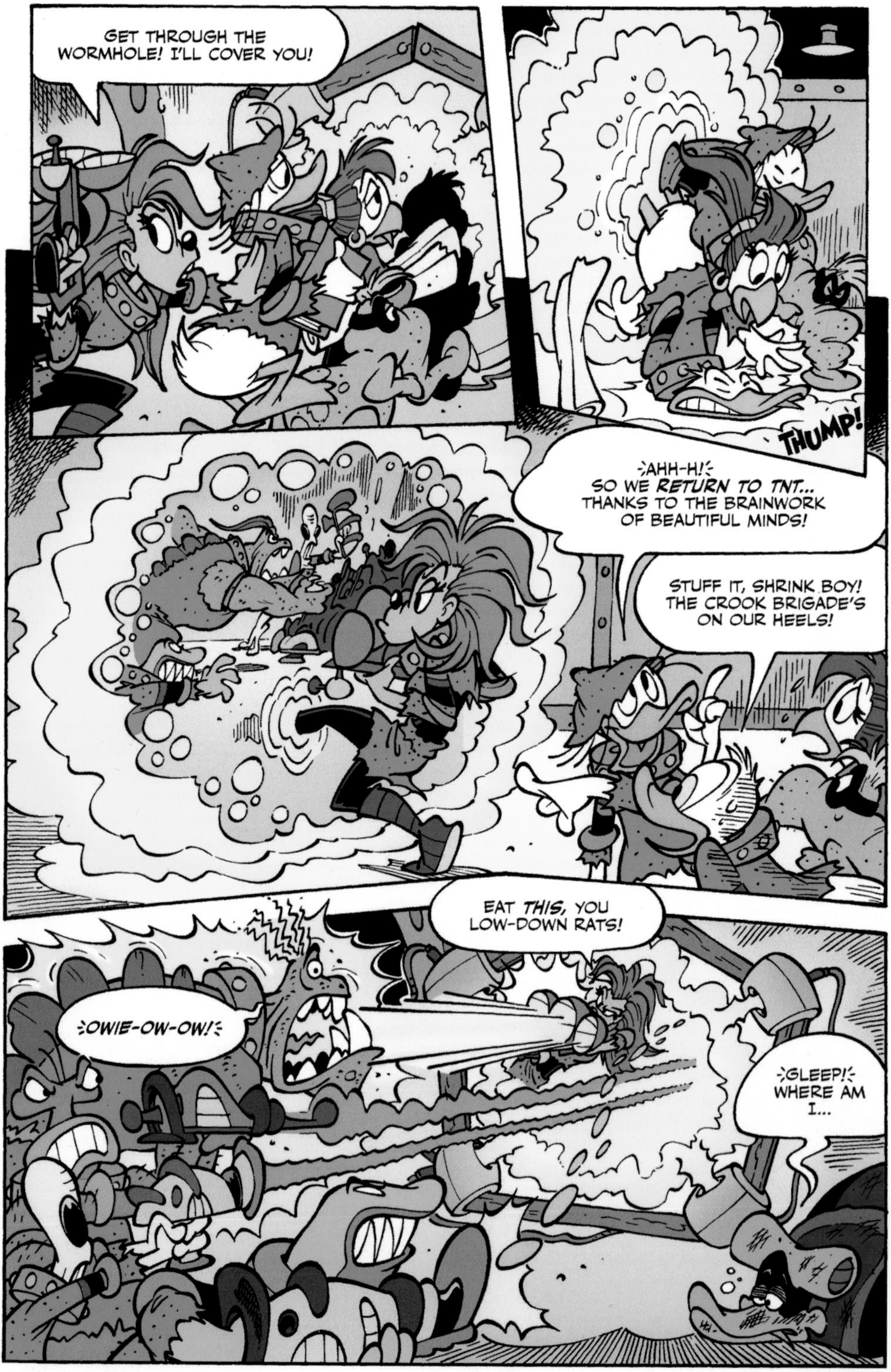

GET THROUGH THE WORMHOLE! I'LL COVER YOU!
THUMP!
-AHH-H!- SO WE RETURN TO TNT... THANKS TO THE BRAINWORK OF BEAUTIFUL MINDS!
STUFF IT, SHRINK BOY! THE CROOK BRIGADE'S ON OUR HEELS!
EAT THIS, YOU LOW-DOWN RATS!
-OWIE-OW-OW!-
-GLEEP!- WHERE AM I...

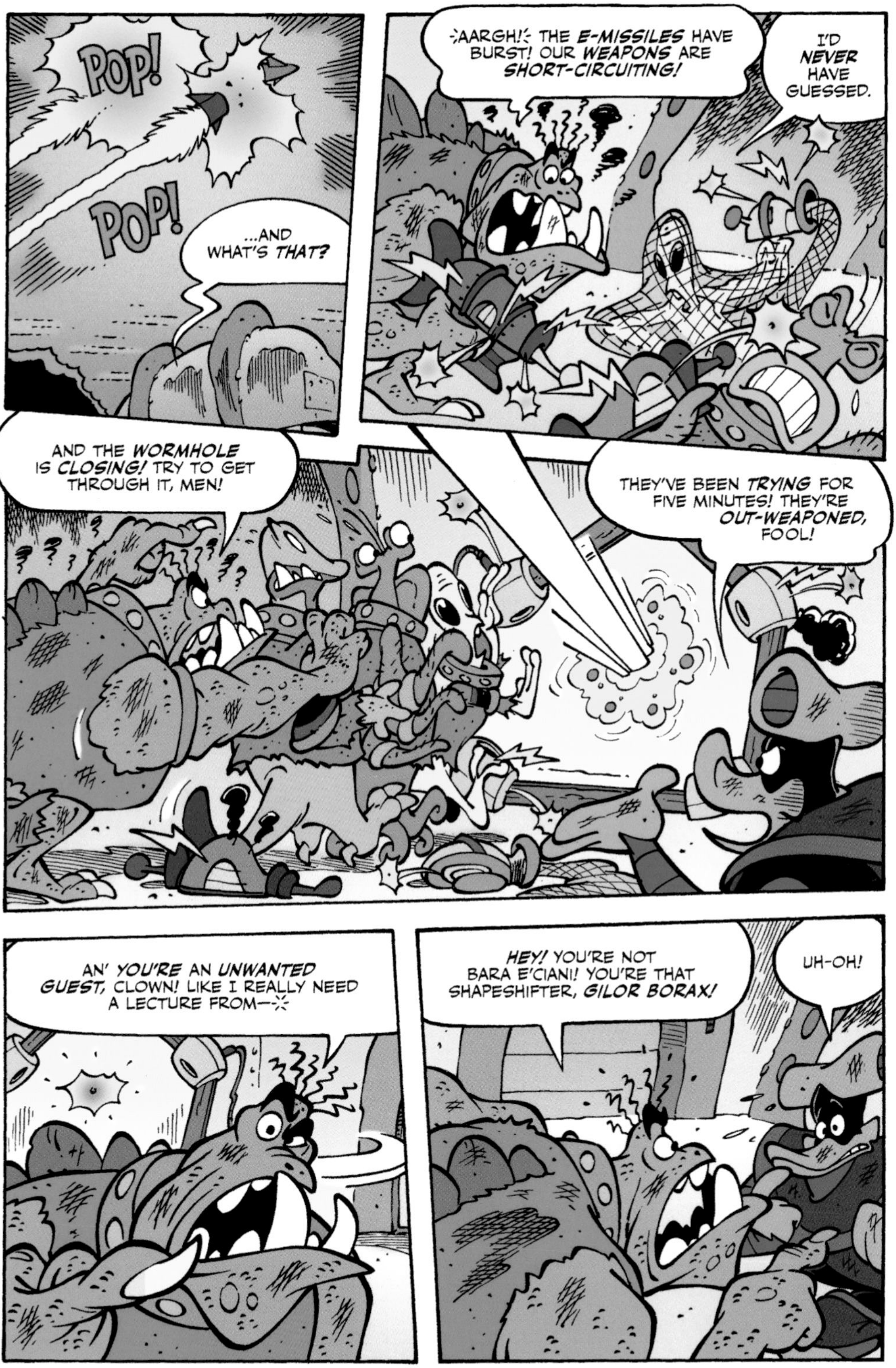
POP!
POP!
...AND WHAT'S THAT?
-AARGH!- THE E-MISSILES HAVE BURST! OUR WEAPONS ARE SHORT-CIRCUITING!
I'D NEVER HAVE GUESSED.
AND THE WORMHOLE IS CLOSING! TRY TO GET THROUGH IT, MEN!
THEY'VE BEEN TRYING FOR FIVE MINUTES! THEY'RE OUT-WEAPONED, FOOL!
AN' YOU'RE AN UNWANTED GUEST, CLOWN! LIKE I REALLY NEED A LECTURE FROM—
HEY! YOU'RE NOT BARA E'CIANI! YOU'RE THAT SHAPESHIFTER, GILOR BORAX!
UH-OH!

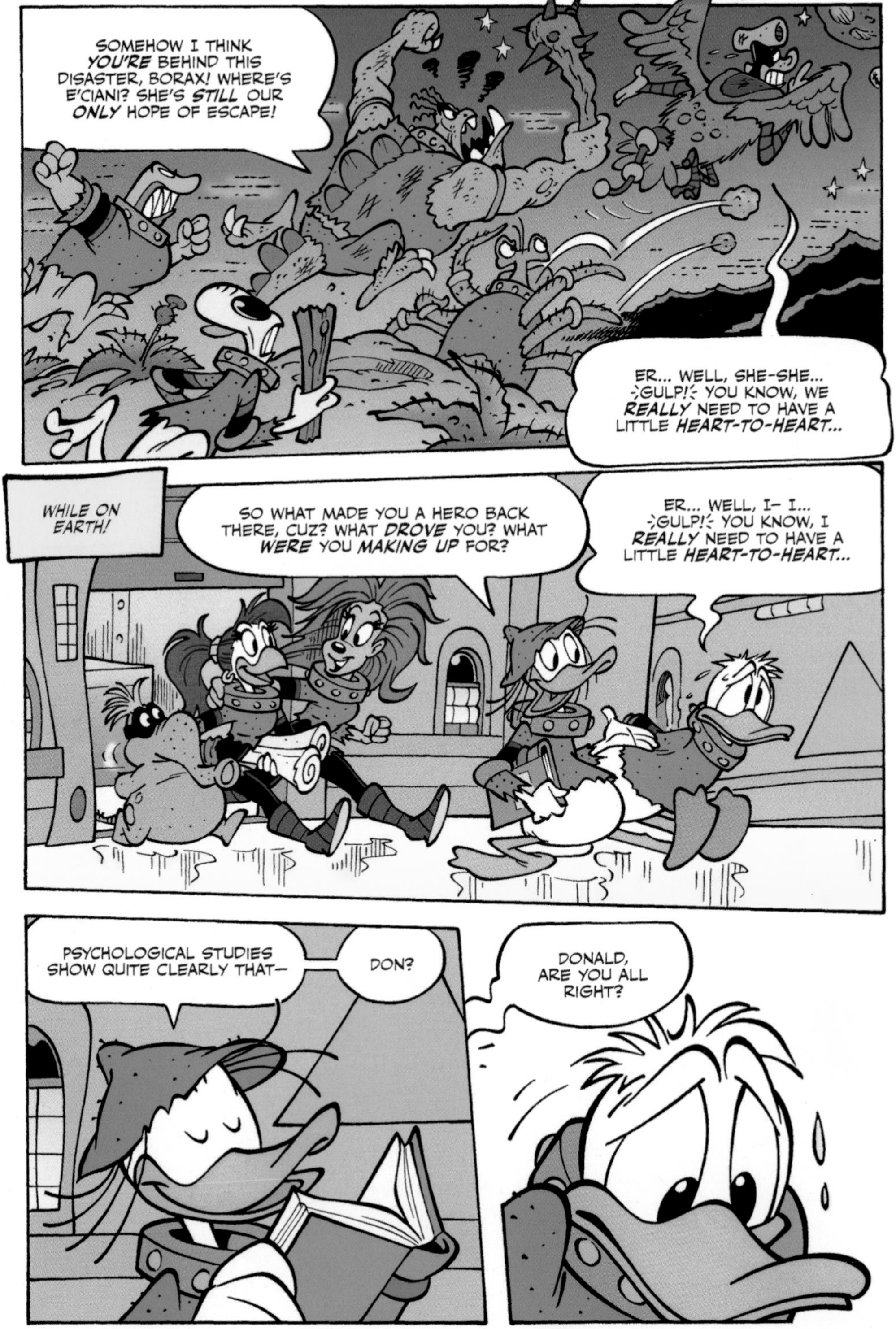
SOMEHOW I THINK YOU'RE BEHIND THIS DISASTER, BORAX! WHERE'S E'CIANI? SHE'S STILL OUR ONLY HOPE OF ESCAPE!
ER... WELL, SHE-SHE... -GULP!- YOU KNOW, WE REALLY NEED TO HAVE A LITTLE HEART-TO-HEART...
WHILE ON EARTH!
SO WHAT MADE YOU A HERO BACK THERE, CUZ? WHAT DROVE YOU? WHAT WERE YOU MAKING UP FOR?
ER... WELL, I- I... -GULP!- YOU KNOW, I REALLY NEED TO HAVE A LITTLE HEART-TO-HEART...
PSYCHOLOGICAL STUDIES SHOW QUITE CLEARLY THAT—
DON?
DONALD, ARE YOU ALL RIGHT?

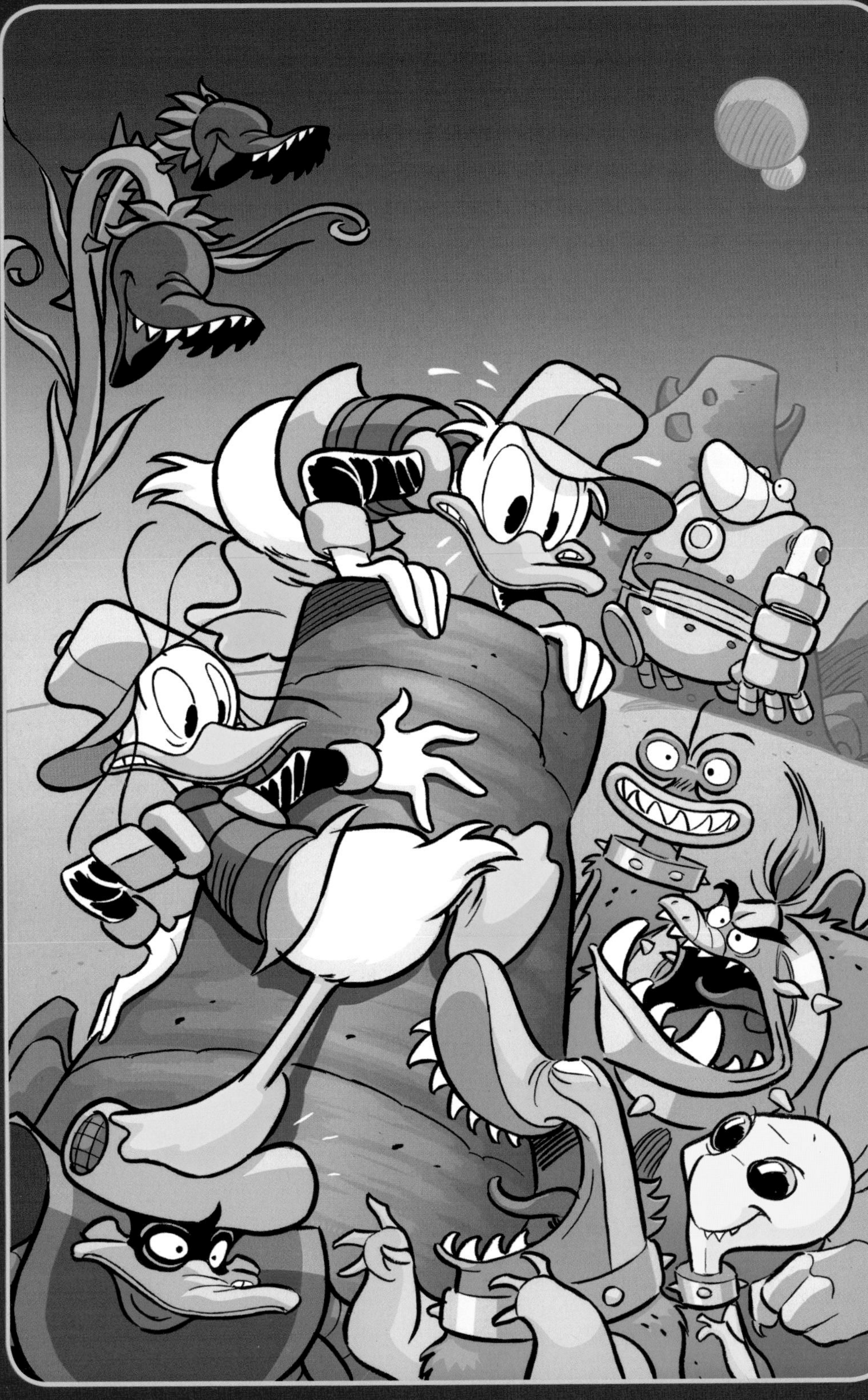

Art by Andrea Freccero, Colors by Ronda Pattison

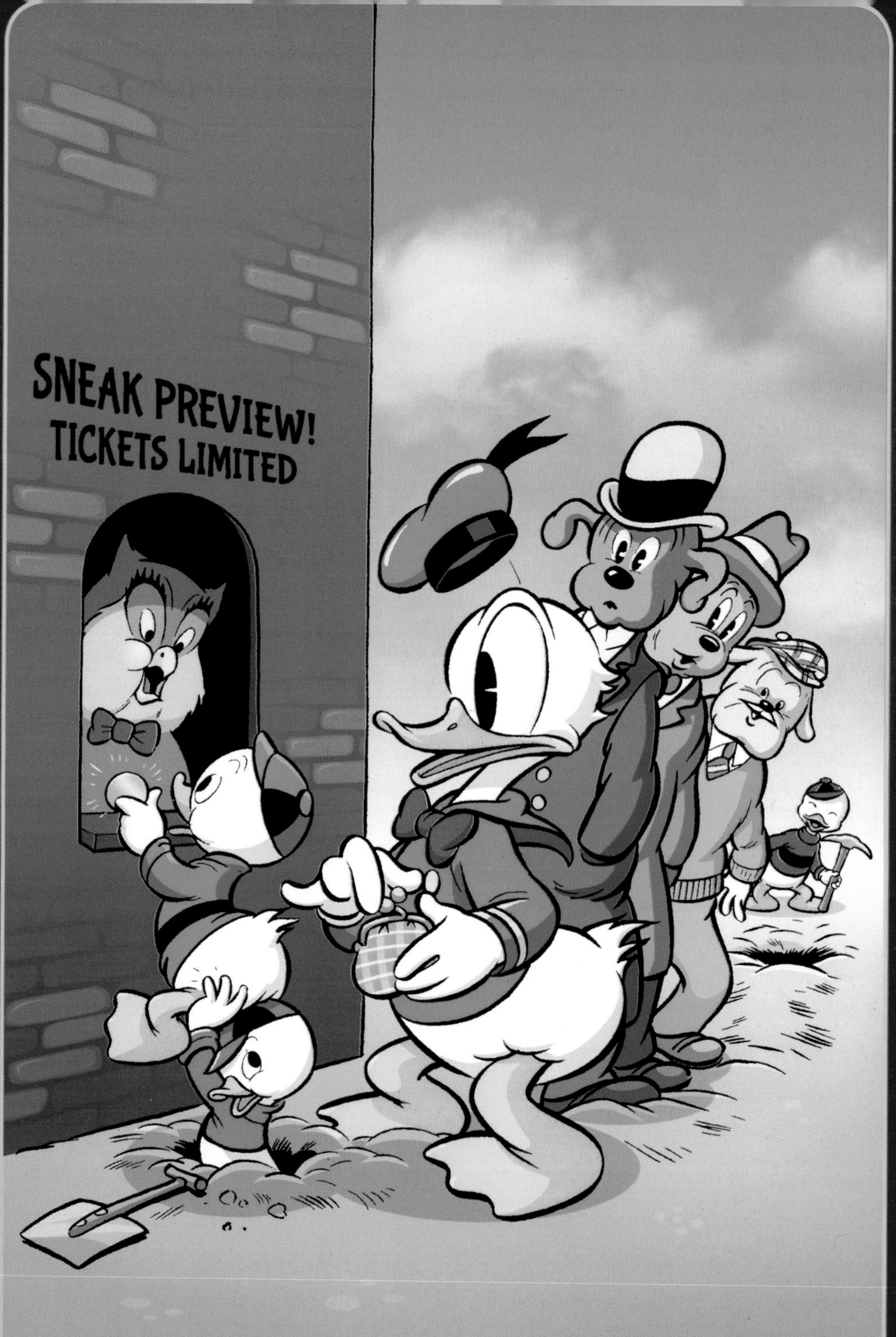
SNEAK PREVIEW!
TICKETS LIMITED

Art by Walt Kelly, Colors by Ronda Pattison

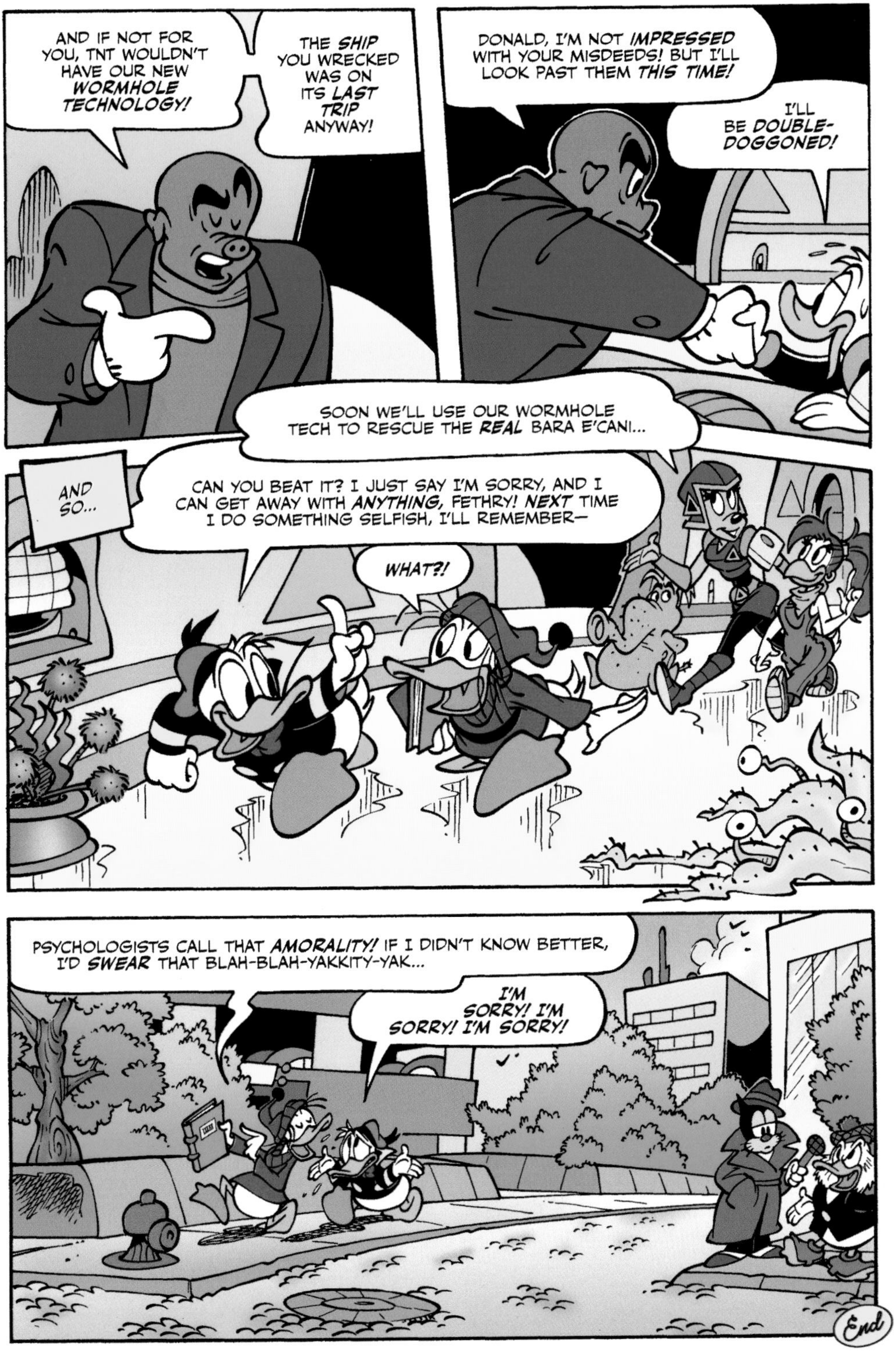
AND IF NOT FOR YOU, TNT WOULDN'T HAVE OUR NEW WORMHOLE TECHNOLOGY!
THE SHIP YOU WRECKED WAS ON ITS LAST TRIP ANYWAY!
DONALD, I'M NOT IMPRESSED WITH YOUR MISDEEDS! BUT I'LL LOOK PAST THEM THIS TIME!
I'LL BE DOUBLE-DOGGONED!
SOON WE'LL USE OUR WORMHOLE TECH TO RESCUE THE REAL BARA E'CANI...
AND SO...
CAN YOU BEAT IT? I JUST SAY I'M SORRY, AND I CAN GET AWAY WITH ANYTHING, FETHRY! NEXT TIME I DO SOMETHING SELFISH, I'LL REMEMBER—
WHAT?!
PSYCHOLOGISTS CALL THAT AMORALITY! IF I DIDN'T KNOW BETTER, I'D SWEAR THAT BLAH-BLAH-YAKKITY-YAK...
I'M SORRY! I'M SORRY! I'M SORRY!
End

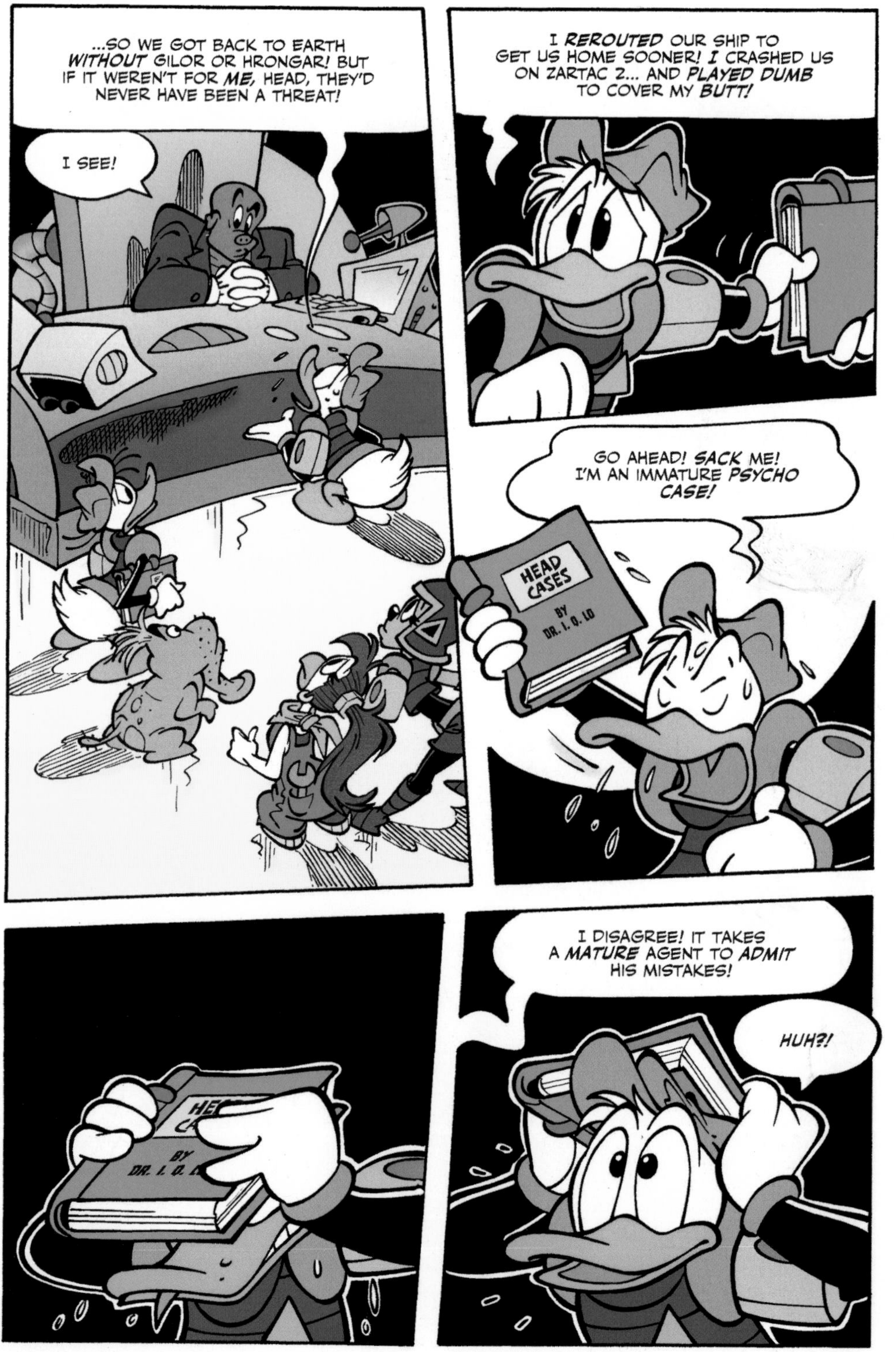
...SO WE GOT BACK TO EARTH WITHOUT GILOR OR HRONGAR! BUT IF IT WEREN'T FOR ME, HEAD, THEY'D NEVER HAVE BEEN A THREAT!
I SEE!
I REROUTED OUR SHIP TO GET US HOME SOONER! I CRASHED US ON ZARTAC 2... AND PLAYED DUMB TO COVER MY BUTT!
GO AHEAD! SACK ME! I'M AN IMMATURE PSYCHO CASE!
HEAD CASES
BY DR. I. Q. LO
I DISAGREE! IT TAKES A MATURE AGENT TO ADMIT HIS MISTAKES!
HUH?!

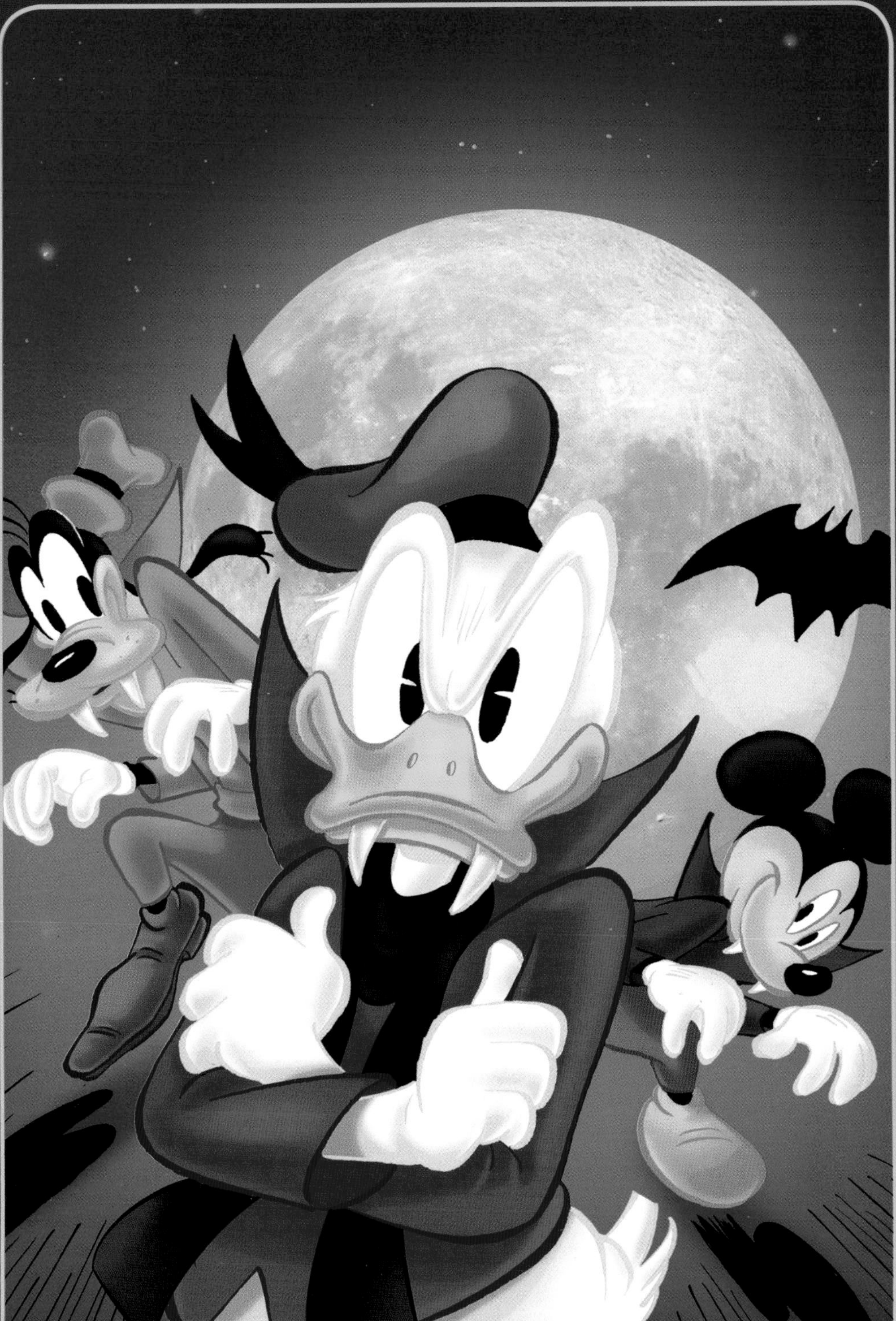

Art by Ulrich Schroeder, Colors by Hachette

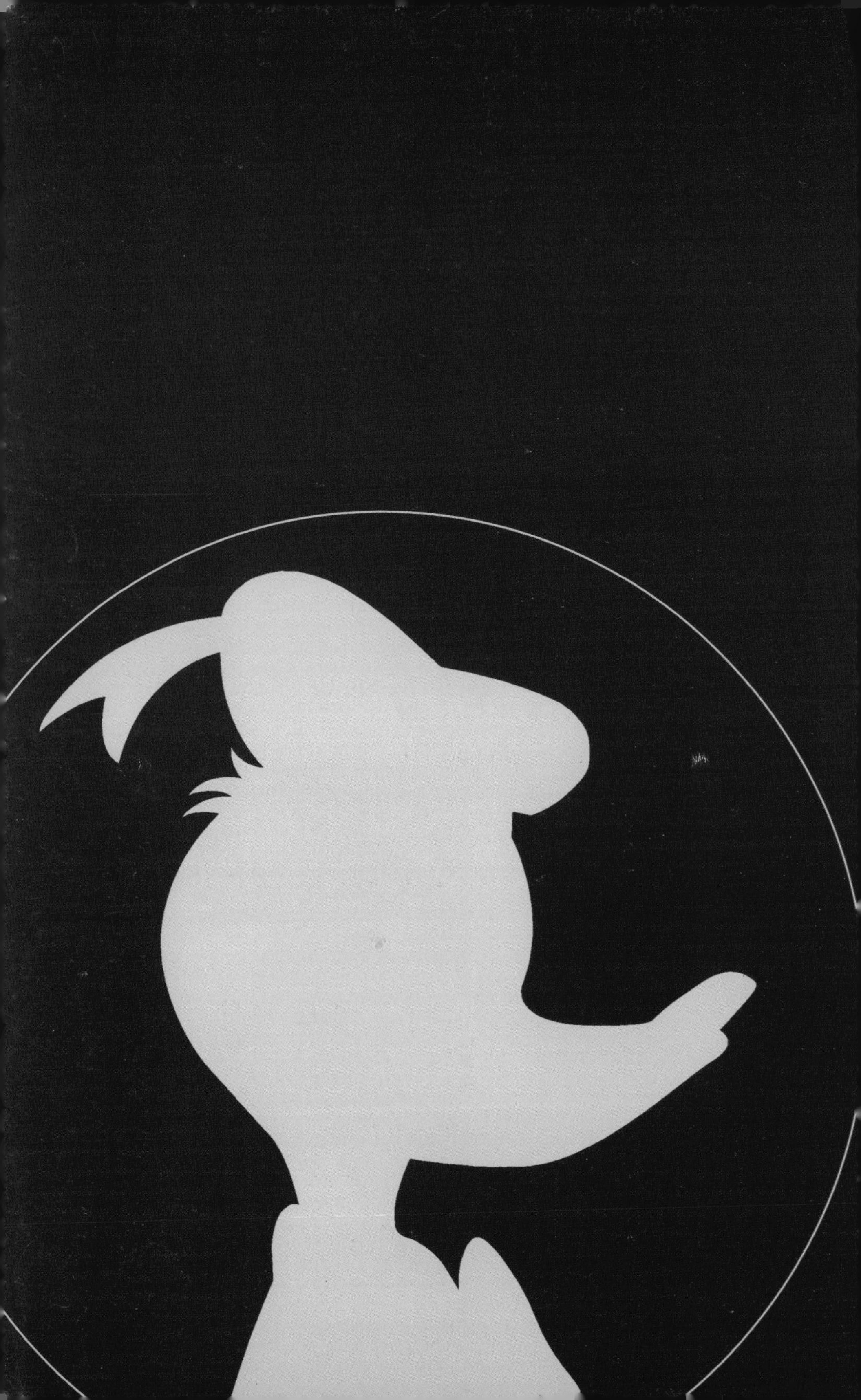